Beyond the Surface

Matt Hebert

ISBN: 1977961029
ISBN 13: 978-1977961020
Library of Congress Control Number: 2017915766
LCCN Imprint Name: Omaha, Nebraska

For my dear and loving wife:

In my staggering, stumbling darkness, the Lord is my guiding light. In my fitful worry and strife, He has calmed my storm and founded me on a rock. Her name is Gabriella.

Part One
New Horizons

Chapter One
Enough

"Yeah, right!" Kreymond laughed, his smooth brown face pulling tightly into a smile. "How the heck you gonna talk to me if you're trekkin' across the world?"

Sembado replied with a sheepish grin but remained silent.

"I get it, man," Kreymond continued, shaking his head. "I mean, I wouldn't do it, but I know why *you* are. You *have* to go. Just like I *have* to stay. Who knows, maybe me and Zet'll catch you on one of these surface drones they got me workin' with."

Sembado crossed his arms and leaned into his friend.

"You're what I'll miss most of all," Sembado said quietly.

"Whatever, Sem," Kreymond laughed. "You lost Mel and your gramps, not your whole damn family."

"I know that," Sembado said. His soft chuckle could not dispel the tears that threatened to spill over his eyelids. They burned worse than he remembered. "But your spirit, Krey. That positive, unbeatable spirit."

"Ah, come on," Kreymond said, pulling Sembado in tightly. "You've got it too, man. You can't lose that."

1

"But I think I am," Sembado replied in a whisper.

A startling jolt brought Sembado's concentration back to the Southern California trail. He shifted his weight yet again. The horse's rump undulated uncomfortably under his as its rider carefully navigated the rough terrain. Sembado held the rider's waist firmly, but craned his neck to the side so the man's long, greasy hair stayed away from his face. He looked to the left to see his companion, Kaluna, struggling with a similar arrangement. Their eyes met and she pursed her lips. She maintained eye contact with Sembado, but he struggled to find meaning in Kaluna's bitter gaze until she too shifted her weight and grimaced. Sembado looked away to his right. The morning sun highlighted the ocean's ripples as its black waves crashed their chorus against the shimmering sand. The rider addressed Sembado as the horse dug in for the ascent up the next great hill.

"So you said the islanders from Catalina dumped you on the beach, huh?" the man asked.

"Yeah," Sembado said quietly.

"Those people aren't right," said the man. "They live a simple life, but only because they have to. As soon as you people turn up with your modern conveniences, they abandon their simplicity for strife and deceit. They are not true children of the natural. That's why they've been stuck on that island for so long. They envy your ways. The *old* ways. They should want for a peaceful and justifiable life. Not one with hurried, anxious advancements. All they care about is improving their position so they can stop collecting food and water on a daily basis."

"Well, we don't want that hurried kind of life either," Sembado said. "But is it so wrong for them to want a break from collecting food and that daily grind?"

The other men jeered bitterly from their mounts. Some laughed and called to their leader.

"Better set'm straight, Cistern," shouted one horseman.

"Sacrifice, man," cheered another, thumping his chest.

"Alright. Alright. That's enough," Cistern said with a smirk. "My men are very passionate about our way of life," he added, addressing Sembado and Kaluna directly. "In time, you will learn the way, the truth, and the life, but for now you must know this: Stewardship is Sacrifice."

The other men shouted and cheered, beating their chests with clenched fists.

"Humans could not have continued to enjoy this world," Cistern continued over the spirited applause, "without augmenting their lifestyles."

Sembado listened on as the horse slowly sidestepped down the next slope. He looked in awe as the slope fell steadily downward before breaking at a great expanse of beach. The wet sand was electrified in orange and white by the sun as it crept over the peaks from the east.

"Do you really think man can outdo that?" Cistern asked as the travel party took in the glorious beachscape.

The beach was spotted with small black stones, each one polished over centuries by the unrelenting waves. The mouth of a small river broke the beach in half, and at the far end of the beach, another hill began. The morning sun highlighted its green and yellow foliage. Shrubs of every size flanked the sandy path that zigzagged up and out of sight. As they moved across the beautiful beach, a new shape came into view at the bottom of the hill. A group of people was gathered at the water's edge.

Cistern whistled in two short bursts and three of his men split off and raced ahead. The rest of the group doubled their pace; Sembado and Kaluna struggled to hold on as their mounts began the new bouncy tempo.

The three interceptors were slowly circling the group of people as the rest of the horsemen arrived. Five men and two women stood around a large net full of fresh, flopping fish. The remainder of the horsemen joined the containment formation as Cistern trotted his and Sembado's horse straight into the group. He stopped just short of trampling the fishers and their catch; the horse's breath was hot and close in their faces. One of the men stepped forward to speak.

"Sir, we didn't…"

"Seems like an awful lot of fish for your village, Linden," Cistern said, cutting the man short. "And I believe you just lost three elders. Isn't that so?"

One of the women made an audible protest. the man next to her grabbed her to silence her while the man called Linden tried to plead.

"Cistern, please!"

Cistern continued as if there was no disturbance.

"That should leave you with what? Forty people at most? And half children?"

Linden remained silent.

"Then I cannot imagine," Cistern continued, "how in the natural twenty adults and twenty children intend to eat two hundred fish in a single day."

Sembado snuck a troubled glance to Kaluna as a stinging silence reigned over the uncomfortable exchange.

"Can anyone else do those numbers?" Cistern asked. "Brant?"

"Five fish per person, Cis," one of the horsemen responded.

"Five?" Cistern responded coyly. "Doesn't that sound like a lot?"

"Sounds like a damn banquet," The man called back.

"Cistern, you know we're having trouble compensating," Linden reasoned. "Our population is young. Most of our children aren't even…"

"Who told you to have so many?" Cistern shot back, losing his playful tone. "You know damn well this region isn't zoned for food preservation. What's so hard about having enough for today? Huh? And we just sanctioned a small plot for your village to help with your problems."

"Only ten tomato plants," one of the women protested. "The children eat them as they're turning red!"

"Then tell the greedy little bastards they've had enough!" Cistern shouted. "And so have I! Now, you will release half of those fish before they stop squirming."

The tense pause was filled by the sound of babbling wavebreak.

"I said now!" Cistern bellowed. The horsemen followed their chief's lead, stepping their horses closer to the net until the fishers complied. They released their entrapping circle on the water's side, only allowing their captives access to the receding tide. The fishers bumbled with their net and soon dozens of fish were jumping in the shallows and swimming into the sea. When about half had escaped, the fishers pulled the net back up.

"Keep going," Cistern commanded.

"But that was half," Linden whined.

Cistern's nostrils flared as he marched his horse forward toward Linden. His rough face, tangled mane, and wild beard gave an animalistic appearance. Linden backed away as the large animal imposed into his space. Sembado held tight as Cistern directed the horse with one final flourish, knocking Linden backwards onto the net of remaining fish which spilled out on to the foamy beach before the other fishers could react. By the time Linden could move and respond, merely fifty fish remained trapped in the tangled weave.

One of the women stepped forward to lash out, but two of her companions grabbed and subdued her. She beat on them instead.

"Your rations are clearly defined," Cistern said bitterly. His followers glared down from their mounts. "They are sufficient. They are enough." Cistern did not wait for a reply, but turned his stead and continued toward the next hill. His horsemen flanked either side. "Make sure to keep an eye on them," he said to the nearest man.

The climb up the next hill was a silent one. Sembado traded views between the colorful, rolling hills to his left and the churning Pacific waves to his right. He wrinkled his nose and craned his head as Cistern's messy hair was tussled in his face by the salty sea breeze. He swatted it away impatiently, revealing the curious pattern of a puffy scar which laid just behind Cistern's right shoulder. The convergence of the curved lines would have appeared organic if not for the stark symmetry.

"Do you mind?" Cistern snapped, gathering his hair and pulling it over his shoulder.

"What's with the scar?" Sembado replied.

"It's not a scar," Cistern replied. "It's a brand. It's the Steward symbol and a mark of honor for me and my riders."

"Oh, something new and refreshing," Kaluna mumbled from her horse.

"What's that?" Cistern called over the cliff's noisy gusts.

Kaluna remained silent as they meandered up the hill. They trailed the coastal bluffs for another hour before they were directed to slow for a break.

"We'll move to the ruins," Cistern commanded. The horsemen veered to the right. Through the trees and overgrown buildings, Sembado saw a strange, blocky mass. It was a humble looking structure, but trimmed of growth and vines while all its neighbors were indiscernible among their brush and shrubs.

"These ruins are over a hundred years old," Cistern announced as they rounded the corner into an open courtyard.

Sembado's stomach rolled and his heart leapt as he took in the full effect of the concrete form. His mouth hung open as the symmetry, order, and simplicity converged along simple lines, humble materials, and a series of angled walls. A small, lowly channel divided the two sides of the space all the way to the cliff beyond. The two forms on either side of the channel stood in complete unison, a real life mirror for the weathered concrete twins that flanked either side of the courtyard.

"These ruins are maintained as a reminder of man's greatest folly," Cistern narrated as the team dismounted their horses. "Control," he added. "We try to control everything."

Sembado's heart climbed higher as he ignored Cistern's lecture and embraced Kaluna. They moved through the courtyard organically, straying away and back to each other as they took in the awe-inspiring setting.

"I understand that you find this environment inspiring and unique," Cistern called to them. "But I must warn you to avoid this temptation. This place was created as a celebration of man and his achievements. A monument to his obsession with finding a cure for everything."

Sembado and Kaluna met at the end of the courtyard which overlooked the ocean below. Cistern and his men had tied off their horses and followed the two revelers to the end of the space. Cistern granted them another moment of peace and tranquility before continuing. Gulls floated overhead on the breeze. Its salty funk rustled the leaves and filled their nostrils.

"Illness and disease are human's only natural predator," Cistern stated quietly. "It took us but a few centuries to defeat, capture, and master all other creatures. Poisonous snakes…giant cats…sharks for all that is natural!" He paused as he regained a measured tone and cadence. "But not disease. Infections. Viruses. Cancer. Some of the smallest creatures on Earth had confused and baffled man up until the last war! But we had made progress. This place? It was named for a man who created a vaccine. It changed the world, and saved thousands of lives a year…" Cistern trailed off. He observed the circling gulls as they moved into rocks below where some animal carcass was being picked over by scavenging crustaceans.

"Did you know that we used to have a list of animal species that were in danger of becoming extinct?" Cistern asked out loud. "And did you know that we had equally long lists of animals we considered invasive species? These were animals that somehow had made it to a foreign place, usually by man's mistakes, and then flourished there because they had no natural predators in that area. Some ship or plane or truck would inadvertently carry the poor bastard thousands of miles and then people would try and kill it off for being in the wrong place. Human beings have spent their entire existence eradicating other species and destroying habitats, all the while eliminating their own predators, defeating diseases, and giving themselves and their young unnatural odds of survival. Doesn't that sound pretty invasive to you?"

Kaluna remained silent, but squeezed Sembado's hand harder. Sembado considered the conflict as Cistern continued.

"Human beings are the only animal on earth that can control other animals, but there is no one to control us. It really only makes sense that we would need to be especially careful to control ourselves and each other," he said to the subdued applause of his men.

Sembado stared into the azure sky; his hand trembled in Kaluna's. Cistern's words were a near echo of the impassioned induction speech his grandfather had given him when he first joined the rebellious *Elephant's Guild.*

It seemed like a lifetime ago...

"What else should a government have control over?" Sembado had asked. He had agreed that he

was afraid of crossing the government, something that he had prayed would never happen, but he knew that the tight control they had on the masses had been for their own good.

"Themselves!" Grandfather had answered. "Themselves, Semmy, don't you understand? They don't have control of themselves." The statement had echoed in Sembado's head as he tried to wrap his mind around the concept. He had voiced his conundrum aloud.

"What would the government need self-control for? It doesn't do anything wrong." Grandfather looked disgusted.

"They've been brainwashin' ya for too long!" he had shouted. Sembado jumped, feeling startled and uneasy. He had never seen his grandfather so animated or angry. Grandfather had taken a minute to gain composure before continuing.

"Don't you know what corruption is, Sembado? That's why we're here, in this complex and under this floor. So long ago, when I was younger than you, the people in control of the world were becoming more and more corrupt. They took advantage of their power and started to scare themselves, so they built these damn inside-out fish tanks to keep a better eye on themselves, not us. Doesn't that make any sense? People in power are still people."

11

Sembado's emotional recollection must have shown on his face, but Cistern mistook it as a reaction to his own thesis.

"Alright, men," Cistern called. "I think the horses need water. Let's tend to the mounts and ourselves."

The horsemen obeyed, and soon Cistern, Sembado, and Kaluna were left alone to look out over the rocky landscape that lead to the sea. There was a peaceful silence between the three of them. Cistern broke it with one final thought.

"Hypocrisy is not welcome in our world," he said quietly, placing one hand on Sembado's shoulder. "A good steward will not abide it." He walked away to leave Sembado and Kaluna alone for the first time since their capture.

The two adventurers stood quietly. Sembado mindlessly put one arm around Kaluna's shoulder, and she pulled in closely as he embraced her. They watched the seagulls tease and fight in their aerial confrontation.

"I like what he has to say," Sembado said suddenly.

"I know you do," Kaluna responded with a sigh.

"You don't?" he asked.

"I don't know," Kaluna replied.

"Everything he says...their entire purpose...sounds just like the Elephants," Sembado reasoned. "Except they are even more fundamental about our inherent flaws." Kaluna remained silent while Sembado continued his logic. "They don't even want men worrying about tomorrow, let alone planning some power-hungry, political empire."

"I get it," Kaluna said. "I already know what you liked about it, but haven't any of their methods bothered you yet?"

"You mean the fish?" he asked, pulling away from her so they could look each other in the eyes. "Of course it seemed harsh, but your people care just as much about conserving, don't they?"

"We teach it at a young age," she responded quickly. "So that we don't have to beat it into people later."

"Well, they're gonna have their hands full with all the clueless floaters comin' from the complex," Sembado said sharply. "They might need to teach some hard lessons."

Kaluna crossed her arms, but did not respond. She sighed deeply, looked off at the tumultuous sea, and leaned into Sembado's chest.

Chapter Two
Hole in the Mountains

The cavalcade rode on; their journey continued along the broken boulevard that traced the coastal bluffs. Views of the water were interrupted by the lush, green surroundings, but the smell of the salty sea persisted. Sunlight trickled through the branches that hung over the trail as the horse hooves clomped on the hard-packed dirt, and soon they were moving along a winding avenue that was flanked by ancient, deteriorated houses.

"Welcome to La Jolla," Cistern exclaimed as they moved their way down the lane. "We have to make one more stop before moving further south."

They rounded one last corner to find a shaded, piney overlook. A group of women stood outside a wooden shack that was nestled between some trees. The women were sipping beverages and talking; they waved and called as the traveling party approached. One of the women stepped forward to Sembado and Cistern's horse while the group dismounted.

"It's been a while, Cis," the woman said. She looked up at Sembado while Cistern climbed off the horse; her curly blonde hair glimmered in the scattered sunlight.

"Yeah," Cistern replied, "We patrolled up to Frisco. Just got back. Found these two up north of Oceanside," Cistern added, indicating Sembado and Kaluna, who were being helped off of their mounts. The blonde woman observed Sembado and Kaluna curiously, paying special attention to Sembado's bionic leg.

"More in from the ocean?" the woman asked.

"Yes, by way of Catalina," Cistern replied.

"Oh," the woman exclaimed, turning to Sembado and Kaluna. "Well, more of your friends have arrived to the south. Down in San Diego proper."

Sembado and Kaluna exchanged an excited glance.

"A ship?" Sembado asked. "Is there a large ship?"

"Ah," the woman responded. "You've got some determined friends."

"Hey, Mim," Cistern interrupted, "Let's wait to talk about that, huh? I'd like to get these two downstairs first."

"Oh. Yeah. Sure thing, Cis," Mim called, but Cistern was already leading Sembado and Kaluna into the timber hovel.

The inside of the shack was humble, but clean. A few more people greeted Cistern, but he gave them hurried replies as he ushered Sembado and Kaluna to a corner of the room where a railing surrounded a hole in the floor. Wooden plank steps led down into a rocky tunnel that turned down and disappeared out of sight. Cistern went first with Sembado and Kaluna following tentatively.

The stairs were almost dark with little ambient light from the shack above; a dim glow could be seen from somewhere ahead. Sembado moved slowly down the steps, gripping the wooden handrails that lined the stairwell. Kaluna gripped the back of his clothes as he shuffled methodically down the steps. Cistern's silhouette was not visible in the darkness, but Sembado could barely see a black mass to accompany the sound of footsteps that could be heard from just below. The steps seemed endless. The challenge was highlighted each time Sembado slipped off the edge of the moist, old planks, but the light from the end of the descent grew stronger with each footfall. Soon the light was bright enough to reveal Cistern's profile as he landed at the bottom and stepped away to the left. Sembado and Kaluna reached the bottom landing as well, and turned to see a wet boardwalk lead into a sun-lit cave. Cistern was greeting and speaking with a man and a woman. The man stood on the rocks below the boardwalk while the woman handed him a torso-sized metal tube. It was decorated to loosely resemble a fish. To the right, the cave's mouth opened to the ocean; the churning tide swelled inside the cave, licking at the feet of the man who stood below. He quickly dumped the metal tube in the swell before it retreated back out into the world. Cistern introduced Sembado and Kaluna as they stepped out onto the boardwalk.

"Tilo and Kena, these are Sembado and Kaluna. They come from below the surface," Cistern said to the middle-aged couple. Tilo and Kena regarded Sembado and Kaluna politely, but were too enveloped with the task at hand.

16

Kena lifted another mechanical fish down to Tilo while Cistern continued his idle monologue.

"Those are drones if you are wondering. They keep track of you lot coming in from the underwater villages. Not many people are privy to this operation, but I know you two are doers. Leaders. I have seen no other pair wander in from the ocean alone, even if by way of Catalina. Just to struggle through the wilderness alone? I can tell you two are different."

Sembado and Kaluna exchanged looks, but said nothing. While Cistern's words were respectful and benevolent, the tone of his voice hinted at something harsher.

"Now you will either take advantage of your passion, make something of this world you've been gifted, and succeed, or your spirit will defy me, defy nature, and you will perish. The choice is yours."

Sembado felt Kaluna's eyes on him, but his were fixed on Cistern's feet where the rocky ledge sat wet with puddles from the tide. The silence grew deafening in his ears as Kena and Tilo suspended their task in order to witness the outcome of Cistern's ultimatum.

"Please know that I would be honored to have you at my disposal," Cistern added. "But if you prove to be a challenger…a spoiler…I will not hesitate to destroy y…"

"Look!" Sembado snapped, interrupting Cistern, to everyone's dismay. "I get it. We get it."

While Tilo and Kena seemed concerned with Cistern's potential reaction to Sembado's insolence, Cistern himself appeared unfazed as Sembado continued his objection.

"There were people like you all over where we came from, but I get that unlike them, you have a real pursuit…a passion that isn't just power itself. I need you to understand that we're okay with that. We want what you want." Sembado paused as he chose his words carefully. "So please stop trying to warn us, and scare us, and show us how much you mean business. Like I said, we get it. You care about your way of life. Give us a chance to do the same."

Kena and Tilo appeared anxious, but Kaluna looked satisfied for the first time in days. Cistern's eyes were locked with Sembado's. They showed neither menace nor defense, but were emboldened by the passion and determination with which Sembado spoke.

"I am pleased with the conviction in your voice," Cistern said with approval. "Mereth will be pleased too."

Kena and Tilo hurried back to work as Cistern led Sembado and Kaluna back up the stairs.

Bright sunlight poured through the doorway and into their eyes as they crested the top of the stairs. The silhouette of a figure appeared in the doorway.

"He's in there with some newbies," Mim could be heard saying.

A man walked through the door; he was breathless and pale.

"Cistern," the man got out between breathes. "They've arrived to the south."

"Yes, we know," Cistern replied dismissively. "Is that all you've come to say?"

The man shook his head in response; he was bent over with his hands on his knees.

"No...," he gasped. "There are many...many more than we thought."

"Mim, what is he talking about?" Cistern called to the old woman outside. "You didn't say anything about this!"

"Didn't know, deary," Mim called back. "Thought it was just an old boat."

Cistern helped the man to stand and collect himself. The man took several more deep breaths before he was settled.

"Alright, Brody," Cistern said in strained reservation. "Tell me what you've seen. How many are there?"

Brody avoided eye contact with Cistern, choosing instead to look anxiously at Sembado. There was fear in his eyes.

"Brody!" Cistern barked, grabbing the man by the collar. Kaluna grabbed Sembado's hand and squeezed.

"Thousands," Brody said. Kaluna's grip tightened.

Cistern let go of Brody's collar with a jerk, and the young man fell backward against the wall. He caught himself as he slid toward the floor, but was stuck in an awkward position. He looked up fearfully as Cistern towered over him, and cringed when he extended a large, hairy hand.

"Oh, stop sniveling and stand up," Cistern said firmly, pulling Brody to his feet. "We need to get down there and help Mereth sort this out."

With a flurry of action, and continuous input from Mim, it took Cistern and Brody only a few minutes to round up four fresh horses and give Sembado and Kaluna a minimal introduction to riding.

"We'll keep it as slow as possible for you," Cistern called from ahead, "but try and stay as close as you can."

Cistern and Brody led the way while Sembado and Kaluna trotted behind carefully. The horse Sembado had been given was a female named Shilah. Her brown coat and golden mane glistened like molasses and honey in the sunlight. The heaving movement of the horse was more comfortable when Sembado rode alone. The team slowed to a saunter as the horses navigated a steep cut in the slope ahead. Kaluna moved her horse alongside Sembado's, and they exchanged a look.

"I don't feel good about this," Kaluna whispered.

"Oh, stop," Sembado responded. "*The Beluga* is down there, and we're on our way."

"Sembado," Kaluna hissed, but he moved ahead with the others.

"So what's the big deal with these new people anyway?" Sembado called to Cistern. "Too many to keep under your thumb?"

"It's not about control, Sembado," Cistern stated sternly. "I told you that. But that's a lot of mouths that we haven't planned for. That's a really good way to make people panic, you know."

"What will you do with them then?" Kaluna called from the back.

"There's only one thing to do," Cistern replied. "They'll have to move out into the wild and find room for a village of their own."

"Yeah," Sembado laughed, "I don't think you realize how helpless most of those people are."

"You mean wandering through the wildness like you?" Cistern teased.

"Well, yeah," Sembado confessed. "I mean…Kaluna's people now how to handle themselves, but they're probably one in a hundred in this coming mass."

"That's fine," Cistern said resolutely. "We will deal with it when we must. Until then, let's just work on getting down to that boat there."

Sembado looked to the distance and saw it. *The Beluga* sat grounded in the sand; she leaned hard to one side. A countless number of smaller vessels floated all about.

"Then let's get a move on," Kaluna called as she galloped her horse past the others.

Chapter Three
Not Everyone Made It

Sembado could do nothing to keep Shilah restrained. The lively animal was eager to match pace with her brothers as Kaluna took her mount from a quickened jog to a full, hard gallop. Cistern and Brody called and chirped at their own horses to keep the spirits high as the group turned down the final descent to the old San Diego boulevards below. Sembado was last to clear a break in the trees. His mouth fell open as the enormity of the new arrival took hold of his entire field of vision.

An evacuation of *The Beluga* was still underway. The old cruise liner sat high out of the water. Its docking bay, which normally sat at the water line, was now a full ten feet in the air; ropes and ladders had been fashioned to the side. Scores of rescuers waded in and out the shallows; they carried away the frail survivors, small children, and salvaged materials. Sembado cringed at the sight of dozens of dead bodies which bobbed listlessly in the swells. Others had been collected and laid out away from everything else, arranged in neat rows. Large funeral fires were already being stoked nearby.

All around *The Beluga,* the scene was the same. Hundreds of small surface crafts and submarines littered the beach; more had anchored in the water, their passengers opting to swim ashore. A line of new arrivers could be seen stretching out into the waves. It seemed to disappear to the horizon.

Sembado and Shilah continued to fall behind the others; Kaluna was now streaking down the main road that lined the beach, and even Cistern struggled to keep up. The other two horsemen broke off from their pursuit and cut down a sand slope on the right. Sembado watched them land in a flurry of sand, each dismounting their steeds to assist in the beachhead efforts. Sembado looked back to Kaluna where she had just turned right herself, continuing to drive her horse hard across the beach and out into the shallow waters that surrounded *The Beluga.* He quickened Shilah's pace as best he could, urging the horse to close the gap. Soon they were racing across the sand; disoriented survivors toppled out of Sembado's way. Locals could be heard offering what food and provisions they had. Sembado slowed the horse to a proud march as she clopped through the salty foam and surf. Sembado climbed off Shilah carefully, but his clumsy splash-down caused her to toss her head and move out of the water. A local called her over by name, took custody of her, and led her away.

Sembado suddenly realized how overwhelmed he felt, being surrounded by hundreds of people for the first time in weeks. Feelings of claustrophobia and anxiety washed over him with the lapping waves. The tall, broad side of *The Beluga* towered over him, imposing its steely will. Another person fled out of the water, accidentally pushing Sembado as they passed. The constantly shifting sands underfoot offered little stability, and Sembado nearly lost his balance. As another small group went by, Sembado caught a glimpse of Kaluna. Still high on her horse, she used her improved vantage to help call and guide people out of the deeper water. Half a dozen survivors held on to her and her horse as she moved them up and out of the water. Despite her effort and progress in helping with the masses, Kaluna's eyes never stopped darting around. She looked this way and that, all around the crowded masses. Sembado stood where the water was at his waist, helped receive Kaluna's rescues, and directed them up the beach. When she was close again, he chanced a quick word.

"Do you see him?" Sembado asked.

Kaluna didn't answer, but turned to make another pass. He watched her carefully guide her horse back and forth in the deep water. She came back with another group of draggled survivors.

"It's not like him to lay idle somewhere," she said. "He would be out here, doing this work."

Another group pushed past Sembado and Kaluna, splashing her and her horse. The horse protested and jerked, nearly bucking Kaluna. Sembado backed away as the horse jumped up on its hind quarters. The front legs came out of the water, thrashing wildly in Sembado's face, while Kaluna was tossed backward. The horse then hopped forward on its front legs, its rear hooves splashing out of the water. Kaluna was jostled violently off the back end, turning end over end as she splashed down in the water. As soon as he was free of his rider, the horse took off out of the surf and galloped away. Sembado hurried to where Kaluna had disappeared in the water just as she emerged again. Her hair was stuck over her face and she was hacking up sand and salt water. Sembado helped her to her feet as she pushed her hair out of her eyes.

"Are you alright?" Sembado asked, picking a piece of seaweed out of Kaluna's hair.

"Yea, I'm fine," Kaluna coughed, spitting out more sand.

"She'd be a lot betta' wit'out dat sand in her teeth!" a voice called from above.

Sembado and Kaluna looked up to see Kaluna's uncle Mahana peering down from the deck of *The Beluga*. A woman at his side helped support him; he looked uncharacteristically slim. Despite appearing winded and tired, he wore his signature grin and chuckled at the perplexed looks on Sembado and Kaluna's faces.

Kaluna immediately threw herself up one of the rope ladders that led to the docking berth. Sembado scurried up behind her. They quickly moved their way through the system of catwalks that led up into the belly of *The Beluga*.

Sembado helped Kaluna up onto the metal staircase that led to the main deck. With the ship leaning to one side, the trek up the stairs was awkward and difficult. A few straggling survivors passed them on their way. The smells inside the ship were sickening. A bloated body lay abandoned on one of the stair landings.

"This way," Kaluna said, breathing into the crook of her arm. "I see daylight up there."

They pushed open a cracked door to find themselves on the weather beaten sundeck.

"There they are," Mahana's companion shouted. She had Mahana propped up under a shaded awning. Kaluna approached her uncle slowly. His skin hung loosely on his face and neck, but the warm light still sparkled in his large, brown eyes. Sembado stood back as Kaluna met her uncle's attempt at a warm embrace. He tried giving her a big squeeze, but he seemed too exhausted. Kaluna hugged him generously all the same, but that seemed to wind him too.

"Take it easy, Manny," the woman at his side said. "You need some water, food, and rest."

Mahana chuckled as Kaluna released him from her hold. He closed his eyes as he caught his breath.

"Kaluna," he said with his eyes still closed. "Dis is Jain. She's a very good friend, now. And Jain, dis is my b'loved niece, Kaluna."

Mahana peeked open one eye and fixed it on Sembado. He closed it again with a soft chuckle.

"And dis young man is dee one an' only…"

"Sembado Grey," Jain said, extending a firm handshake to Sembado. "Yes, quite a reputation."

Sembado returned the handshake with a smirk. The idea that he had any kind of reputation seemed quite ridiculous. Their greeting was interrupted by another of Mahana's cough attacks.

"We need to get him off this blasted boat," Jain said. "The whole trip here, he kept trying to be some damn hero. He refused to eat or drink anything while the others were still hungry."

While Kaluna and Jain continued to poke and prod Mahana, Sembado looked around the deck to find any available materials with which to fashion a wheelchair. He walked up the deck, the sun beating down on his already burnt neck. He kicked around random items. Shifting a pile of overturned chaises revealed a concessionaire's cart with two big wheels on one end. Sembado used his bionic leg to break off the top two shelves of the cart so that only the base frame and wheel remained. He brought the wheeled assembly back to the others. With a concerted effort, they lifted Mahana and his reclining deck chair so that the wheeled platform could be wedged underneath the back legs. The task was humbling as Mahana, even with his considerable loss of mass, still measured at least two-hundred fifty pounds. Sembado realized with frustration that despite his powered prosthetic's incredible ability, it was essentially rendered lame due to his inadequate upper body strength. Finally, with the wheels firmly in place, Sembado demonstrated that with weight applied to the back side, he could roll Mahana forward with little effort. At Jain's behest, they wasted little time moving Mahana into the interior core of the ship where they encountered their first staircase. With the women at Mahana's feet, Sembado guided the improvised wheelchair down each step. Again, Sembado's leg's potential was stunted by the awkward shuffling and uncomfortable posture that was required to shimmy Mahana down the narrow steel steps. The women struggled too as their light frames combined with their malnourished fatigue to toil under Mahana's girth.

The next landing featured the foul corpse. Jain nearly dropped her share of the load; she wretched for a whole flight and a half. With all of their hands occupied with the task at hand, there was no salvation of a sleeve or rag to be held over the face. The smell was oppressive, and the heating of the ship by the bright sun had done nothing to help, but the ghastly odor was just the motivation they needed. Their pace doubled in speed until they came to the cavernous docking bay. After the dark passages and shadowy stairwells above, the sunlight that glared in from the large opening in the side of the ship was blinding. The docking catwalks that would have led around the various docked vessels now hung slack and crooked. Sembado relieved the women of their task as he could use his powered leg to navigate Mahana through the tilted mess. He pushed the wheeled chair to the edge of the opening and stopped. Kaluna and Jain joined him in looking over the ledge to the water below.

"We certainly won't be able to carry him down those flimsy rope ladders," said Jain. She looked sallow from the last hour's efforts.

"It's not the ladder I'm worried about," Sembado quipped. "It's my back."

"Maybe we could tie the ropes around him and lower him down?" Jain suggested.

"Are you serious?" Kaluna protested. "That would destroy either our hands, his body, or both."

"Well, I don't know," Jain responded. "We need to get him off this horrid ship and its right there!"

"You could always jus' trow da old fish ova' board," Mahana said suddenly. The others turned just in time to see Mahana teetering over the precipice before falling head first into the foaming surf below.

"Manny, no!" Jain cried.

Kaluna jumped in after him. Sembado fought back a grin at the old Hawaiian's practicality. He assisted the distraught Jain down the clumsy, swinging rope ladder so that she could slap Mahana about the head just as Kaluna stood him up in the swirling shallows.

Jain's assault turned to a loving embrace just as Cistern and a few others arrived to help. They moved Mahana onto a more conventional gurney. Cistern whistled to a nearby driver and her team of horses. The woman's four horses pulled a large covered wagon which was already loaded with several infirmed. Mahana was gingerly lifted into place.

"We can only take one extra," the driver called from up front.

Kaluna and Jain exchanged a tense look.

"Oh, please," Jain said. "I need to be with him."

Kaluna rolled her eyes and gasped.

"Well, make up your mind," Cistern said. "We need to get these people to the bay!"

***

Sembado held Kaluna close as they watched the covered wagon quickly disappear into a thick palm grove to the south. She slowly pulled away, looking up and down the beach.

"What are you doing?" Sembado asked.

"Well, I'm not standing around waiting to see what happens to my uncle," Kaluna replied. "Help me find a horse so we can track them down."

They trekked up the beach, moving toward the tree line at the edge of the sand, opposite the water. There, at one of the countless palm trees, they found Shilah tied to a tree.

"I guess she just can't get rid of me," Sembado joked, petting the horse's neck and mane.

"As long as she's rested enough to be useful," Kaluna responded, ever focused.

She climbed up on the horse, commanding Sembado to unhitch it from the rough husk of the palm trunk. Sembado let the lead hang; Kaluna used her heels and verbal commands to move Shilah around in a circle before directing her to the south. Sembado measured his pace behind Kaluna and Shilah for a few moments, and then sprung off his bionic leg. He used his hands to break his landing as he plopped down on Shilah's back, just behind Kaluna. The nearby rescuers and survivors stared in awe at the incredible feat. Sembado's landing spooked Shilah just enough to get her to pick up her pace. Kaluna doubled that pace until they were moving at a slow gallop toward the copse of palms into which the covered wagon had disappeared.

The fallen sun glared various shades of orange and red and purple as they moved into the shadows of the tattered fronds. Kaluna slowed Shilah to a saunter as they crossed under the thick canopy. A local walked along the path and lit a series of torches.

"The sick?" Kaluna asked the man. "Where would they take the sick or injured?"

"Oooh, I'd head up to the main lodge on the bay," the man replied, pointing to the south and east. "If you've just arrived from the water, then you'll have to answer to Mereth first."

"The main lodge?" Kaluna repeated.

"Yeah, just follow this path through the trees. You'll see it all lit up. Can't miss it."

Kaluna and Sembado made sure to each thank the torchman while they moved on into the broken twilight that trickled through the bent and broken trunks. As the colorful dimness faded softly to the west, a host of fiery pinpricks flickered through from beyond the brush to the east. Breaks in the bushes revealed a vision of what was to come: layers of light, depths into the distance, and a towering pinnacle. Kaluna guided Shilah down the trail to the clearing ahead. The trees broke to reveal a calm body of water with a large, multi-tiered lodge nestled on the near shore. The roofline of the large timber structure was backlit by a million celestial bodies that shimmered boldly in the ever-growing darkness. The building rose in three levels, checkered with windows, and glowed with the light of a hundred candles. It reminded Sembado of a dark and mysterious birthday cake. The top two levels had full-length balconies with railings fashioned of branches and small planks. People could be seen milling about and socializing on the balconies; more were visible through the windows. Large doors standing at the front of the lodge were opened, and more golden firelight briefly spilled out onto the sandy landscape. For that moment, the light from inside coupled with the torches that lined the trail and several smoky bonfires to illuminate a small village of tents, lean-tos, and other humble shelters.

"Looks pretty crowded," Sembado said.

"Yeah, well, Mahana's in there somewhere," Kaluna responded, pointing to where the covered wagon and its team of horses were parked alongside the expansive building. She snapped Shilah's reins and they moved along the trail, drawing ever nearer to the lodge. The closer they got, the higher the main peak of the roof seemed to climb into the night sky. As Shilah shuffled past the tents and lean-tos, Kaluna and Sembado saw several people huddled around each bonfire. Their ragged fatigue told a story of suffering and survival. To his right, Sembado saw some intact garments that were garish and out of place in the humble surroundings. The clothing evoked such powerful and vivid memories of the underwater complex that Sembado nearly lost his breath. He caught himself making a pathetic kind of whimper; involuntary, stinging tears welled in his eyes without notice.

"These are my people," he muttered under his breath.

"Huh?" Kaluna asked.

"Nothing," said Sembado. "It's just…some of this clothing looks so familiar." He looked down at his own attire. He still wore the piecemeal coverings that had been forced on him by the aggressors of Catalina. It was a collection of crude materials and natural husks bound together with jute twine and strips of leather. The shorts stopped above the knee while he was perched on Shilah's back. His exposed skin was cracked and sunburned, but it appeared as a rich brown in the passing fire light. The escapees from the complex looked up at Sembado with fear and reverence. With his bionic leg hidden on Shilah's left flank, Sembado looked completely wild and native to them. Kaluna's stony gaze and their bareback riding style did little to dissuade the onlookers' wonderment. The children whispered questions and pointed, but were quickly hushed. Sembado rolled his eyes and nearly chuckled thinking back to Jain's comment about his reputation.

Of course...these people have no idea who I am. They wouldn't look so impressed if they did.

Kaluna brought Shilah to a quick halt at an open hitching post. Sembado climbed down first, helping Kaluna land soundly on her feet. Sembado tied off the reins and hurried up the steps just as Kaluna threw open the door and marched inside.

Chapter Four
The Matron Of Mission Bay

Sembado ducked inside the lodge, pulling the heavy doors shut behind him. The foyer had a high ceiling and was flanked on three sides by overlooks from the lofts above. A big, old, broken wagon wheel was suspended from the high ceiling by ropes and chains. It had piles of melted candles burning on it; they had individual wicks, but the generations of melted candles had formed one continuous ring of wax around the circumference of the cracked, wooden wheel. The overlooking balconies above, much like the rest of the space, were crowded with people. There were a hundred conversations to hear, each a slightly unique iteration of the next: the survivors of the complex were many, hungry, and weak.

Sembado moved through the crowded foyer to the archway of the next room. While he had grown nearly unaccustomed and uncomfortable in these dense crowds, the congestion was eerily reminiscent of his old neighborhood retail district, the Civillion. He teetered on the step down of the next room, a low-lying, timber-hewn den. Its floor was made of flagstone and sat nearly a foot lower than that of the foyer. A large stone fireplace

35

crackled on one end. The rest of the room was nearly packed with mats, cushions, and other make-shift cots. Some were tented with fine mesh. Sembado scanned the temporary infirmary. Every bed was full; an extra body could be seen fretting over almost each and every patient. Sembado's eyes finally fell on a nearby corner where Mahana was stretched out on a lumpy mattress. Kaluna sat at his feet. Cistern sat at his side with Jain and another woman.

Immense amounts of body heat emanated from the congested room. The fireplace aggravated the situation. Sembado squeezed past a few people, taking care not to bump or upset the multiple bags of fluid that hung above many of the infirmed. His patience waned with his dexterity as moving through the close quarters became increasingly more precarious. He felt as if his leg were humming in response to his frustration. It was all he could do to maintain his inner peace as he finally found a seat next to Kaluna at her uncle's feet. He sat down silently while the others continued their quiet discussion

"I a'ready to'd ya," Mahana said between labored breaths. "I was on'y leadin' da pack whi'e we was adrift. I don't have any intres' in leadin' anymo'e. I'm too o'd and too ti'ed to worry 'bout it. Me and Jain he'e jus' want to live a quiet and peaceful life now."

"Well, we appreciate your willingness to compromise and submit," said the woman next to Cistern. "We've had some challenges with the people coming from your underwater home, but it hasn't been getting them to submit. On the contrary, the challenge is motivating them to work for us, our cause, or even themselves."

"They've come from a very different cultural background," said Jain. "They are used to complying with authority and enjoying frivolous distractions."

"Ugh," Cistern groaned. "That sounds like a shameful path to walk."

"Calm down, Cis," said the woman. "We've talked about this. We need to be supportive and firm for the weak."

"Can't be too supportive, Mereth," Cistern responded. "We might hurt them."

"Oh, don't be ridiculous," the woman named Mereth said. "Go on and get some rest. We don't need you here making everyone else uncomfortable."

Cistern shot up, huffing like a pouting child. Mereth pursed her lips as she watched him shuffle through the crowded ward. Sembado watched her eyes follow Cistern as he made his way out into the foyer and then to a room beyond. Her eyelids were wrinkled, breaking above her light brown irises like slacks that are too long. The crow's feet at the ends of the lashes were jagged and dramatic. Decades of exposure and the low, glowing firelight gave her sunkissed skin the near appearance of chocolate.

"You'll have to forgive Cistern," Mereth said. "He is very proud of our lifestyle, but he doesn't know how else to show it except with...pride!"

"So our people," Jain said with interest and concern. "How can we help you help them?"

"An interesting question," Mereth replied. "That depends on how you think they need help."

"Well, obviously they need food," said Jain. "And water too. I think they could use a…"

"I know what people need to survive," Mereth said, cutting Jain off with a congenial touch to her hand. "I don't mean to be rude here, but we all need those things. The problem I see before us, and correct me if I'm wrong, is that your people don't know how to find or make any food for themselves."

The lack of objection prompted Mereth to continue.

"Now, we already have a solution for that," Mereth added, lowering her voice to a whisper. "All new citizens coming in from the water, including all of you, will be put through a series of educational courses to train you to appreciate our system of purposeful living, and how to achieve those techniques for yourself. But I must be frank, it is not the education classes that have me worried. The courses are neither difficult nor complicated. What concerns me is potential resistance we may face from some of your people. As I understand it, you four were all key players in the destiny of these people. You are leaders, but you are also open minded. You know what you must do here to be successful. It is quite simple: you must comply."

Mereth paused for a moment in what Sembado guessed was an attempt to judge their reactions to her last statement. He and Kaluna had already been relentlessly subjected to this manifesto in their travels with Cistern.

This way of life was simple and peaceful, but it was also mandatory. He watched Mahana and Jain for a reaction, some facial mannerism that communicated doubt or misgivings, but they both just nodded in agreement with Mereth. Satisfied, Mereth continued her monologue.

"That is all we ask. That we not have to bother with needless mutiny or resistance. We have devised a simple life with simple rules. Do you think that is too difficult of a reality for your kind to cope with?"

Again, the group was silent. Mahana dropped his head on his pillow. Kaluna looked away. Sembado made eye contact with Jain, but was too unfamiliar with her to decipher the wetness in her eyes. Seeing that no one else was going to volunteer their input, Jain spoke up in a less confident tone than before.

"Our people have only just escaped a very domineering authority in the form of governmental autocrats," said Jain, measuring her statement as Mereth, Kaluna, and Sembado carefully listened to her word choice. "But the vast majority of these people did not play a hand in an insurrection or rebellion. They were simply caught in the crossfire, escaped, and are trying to deal with this inconceivable thing called struggle for the very first time. I don't think they will cause you trouble. Most of them have already accepted this new reality that is devoid of lights and screens and buttons."

Sembado thought on Jain's words. He agreed that her description accurately portrayed the vast majority of survivors from the complex, but he worried about any rebellious personalities to whom she might be exposing to unnecessary risk.

"Um…yeah, I don't agree with that one hundred percent," Sembado said, drawing a smug smirk from Kaluna, a worried stare from Jain, and a calculating gaze from Mereth. "I think there are many more people who played an active role in the overthrowing of our government. I mean, Mahana and Kaluna's entire people had invested their very existence in the rebellion and moving the escapees to hope and freedom. Many more from the complex have some pretty clear and passionate doubts about rules and leaders, and would not be overly eager to trade one set of rules for another. I'm willing to deal with this prospective way of life because I want it. What's the alternative for someone who isn't so keen on it? What, they trade their newfound political freedom with confined space and immobility for wide open spaces and a way of life that's dictated to them? Don't get me wrong, I will try and help you convince them of the benefits here and why this trade-off is our best option, but I just want you to realize how unappealing Cistern's delivery, for example, is going to come across to an entire culture of people who have just rid themselves of an indoctrinated lifestyle."

Mahana's eyes were open wide and Jain looked more flustered than ever, but it was not until Sembado saw the change in Kaluna's troubled expression that he realized he may have spoken too much.

"I mean, I'm not saying you should anticipate a lot of resistance," he added to Mereth, who looked neither upset nor amused. "I...I just get why this lifestyle is so important. Why it needs to be sustainable. And I think more people will too. But they will want to be given a chance to understand and choose. Even if they never had a choice in the first place, they will at least feel like a more integral part of your grand solution here."

Sembado's drawn out reply had become a little too loud, and Mereth appeared concerned with how troubling their conversation may come across to those recovering around them.

"I appreciate your concerns and perspectives, Sembado," she said in harsh whisper, "but I hardly need the help in finding the right tact in telling people exactly how I want them to live their life. I have been doing this for a very long time. And we've dealt with some pretty terrible disasters. Now, we knew you people would arrive eventually and we've planned for that too. For what it's worth, I will take your insights into consideration, but must ask that we continue this conversation at a later time."

Without allowing Sembado to respond, Mereth got up slowly, using the bed frame for support, and worked her way out of the room with methodical confidence.

Sembado watched her go; she was taller than she seemed sitting down, nearly his height, but stooped from her age.

"Now, what the hell'd you have to do that for," Jain snapped.

Sembado looked around in dismay.

"What?" he said defensively. "I don't think she…"

"Oh, cut it out, Sembado," Kaluna said, punching his shoulder hard. "Jain's right. It was going to be hard enough for these escapees to physically prove themselves to Cistern and the rest of these fanatics. Now they're *all* going to be working uphill on this ideology front, and some of them don't even see things the way you described them."

"Well, yeah, but we can talk more about it. We'll work it out," Sembado replied. "She is much more reasonable than Cistern, you know."

"Ugh, just stop," Kaluna said. "The only thing I'm agreeing with her on is that that is enough for tonight. We both need some sleep. Now come on."

Kaluna bid Mahana and Jain goodnight, but deprived Sembado of the opportunity as she dragged him away by the arm before he could say another word.

Chapter Five
House Rules

Sembado woke in the crowded room that kept him through the night. He had slept sitting upright in the corner with Kaluna curled up at his side, but he could no longer feel the pressure of her body against his hip. He had not yet opened his eyes, but merely adjusted the weight of his head and the tension with which he crossed his arms with the hope that it would facilitate another half hour of rest. But before he could doze off, his senses were made profoundly aware of how many more people had elected to sleep in the same tight quarters as him. Sembado shut his eyes tighter, trying to ignore the sweet funk that was produced by dozens of sleeping bodies being confined for hours without any fresh airflow. The earthly aroma was nearly outdone by the sound. The chorus of raspy breathing reached concurrent highs and then waned again. The snoring, grunting, and farting made Sembado long for the muffled silence and intimacy he and Kaluna shared in their voyage across the sea. The longing he felt for her comfort and company finally tore open his eyes as he made sure she had not just sleepily shifted out of reach; she was nowhere to be seen. Not in this crowded room at least. The pale morning light that crept through the shuttered windows offered only a modest intensity. He had to step high and slow to avoid the many fingers and faces that lay closely packed upon the creaking floor. The awkward, high-kneed dance would have been precarious in the best of circumstances; his sleepy haze made keeping his balance nearly impossible. Sembado slowly made it all the way to the door while managing to only kick one unfortunate man right in the back of the head. Sembado offered the most sincere apology he could manage, but the man appeared blissfully unaware that he had even been wronged in the first place.

The hallway beyond offered a reprieve for Sembado's senses and posture. He stood up straight and stretched as the smell of smoke and food wafted from the floor below. He worked his way down the hall to where the interior balcony overlooked the lodge's entrance. Sembado joined the slow stream of people who were shuffling down the stairs. Some of them walked to the large hall that sat adjacent to the comfort room Sembado and Kaluna had visited the night before, but Sembado opted for some fresh air, quietly opening the large doors that led outside.

The morning sun casted long shadows to the right as Sembado took in the chilly sandscape that lay in front of the towering lodge. The camp folk stirred more earnestly than those inside, most were already poking and prodding their fires back to life. At the foot of the lodge's front steps, Kaluna sat huddled under a blanket. She held a mug of something hot which billowed steam in the dewy morning air.

Sembado quietly sat down in front of her so as to not block the steps any more than she already was. She set her mug down briefly so that she could flap and fan the blanket around Sembado's shoulders, spreading her knees slightly so that he could lean back into the warmth of her embrace. He felt both physical and emotional comfort as she held the back of her hands on his neck, the warm mug they gripped emanated a steady heat on his matted, ginger hair. The mug's aromatic cloud of vapor filled his nose with the bold smell of coffee.

"I'm sorry for being so dismissive last night," Kaluna said. She turned her head and gently pressed her cheek against the back of his head; she rested it there while she waited for his response. Sembado carefully let the weight of his head push back against Kaluna. He let her apology sink in as he thought on how her words had made him feel the night before. She slowly pulled away to take a sip from her mug, letting his head fall backward slightly.

"I'm not mad at you," Sembado said quietly. "And I'm not hurt by what you said." He paused as he searched for his own words. The haziness of the promenade in front of them had given way to a clear morning as the dozen or so smoky bonfires had been reined in with fresh, dry wood. Sembado took another deep breath.

"But I do feel stupid for being so forthcoming and honest with Mereth. I know we need to find some kind of compromise with these people, but I feel like I've already stuck a lot of good people in an uphill struggle in earning their trust now. You were totally right last night. If anything, I wish you would have gotten me to shut up sooner. The kind of balance we need to strike with Mereth and Cistern's way of life is only going to come in months of slow and steady reasoning, not in one decisive conversation."

Kaluna finished her coffee and set the mug to one side. Sembado took the opportunity to lean his head and torso back against her chest. She leaned into him, wrapping her arms loosely below his chin.

"That's the kind of long-term vision my grandfather had," Sembado said wryly. "The kind that Mahana has. I don't. How do you even start...?"

"Oh, Sembado," Kaluna said, squeezing his chest. "You're talking about years of experience, mistakes, and success. You can't learn that. It's just age and wisdom."

"Great," Sembado huffed.

"Oh, stop," she responded. "Let's get you something to eat."

Sembado complied, slumping out of her grasp and standing up. He helped her untangle herself from the blanket and stand as well. They shuffled inside where a line for breakfast had formed outside the main gathering hall. Inside the hall, a pile of clean rags was being dispensed to the hungry as they slowly passed through the line. They held the rags loose, creating miniature hammocks which were filled with raw fruits and vegetables and small pieces of sun-dried fish.

Kaluna took one large orange and a piece of fish. Sembado received two pieces of fish, a small bunch of grapes, and a nectarine. They were prodded through the end of the serving assembly where the line of people was starting to accumulate in a misguided mass. A shouting match broke out when one man's breakfast knapsack was knocked from his hands. The directionless crowd continued to swell; those who had just received provisions had not been given a clear or direct path out of the great hall which dead-ended on the far side. As the throng of harried breakfast-goers found their way to the dead end they began to back up more. The tenuous energy in the air threatened to break into panic at any moment. Kaluna held tightly to her morsels and quickly cut back through the crowd, leading Sembado back from whence they came. A few others tried to follow their lead, but the extra bodies caused additional restlessness with those just arriving. Sembado struggled to slip through the crowd as gracefully as Kaluna. He turned his shoulders this way and that as he pushed through, leaving a stream of apologies in his wake. They were able to push out into the foyer just as more people rushed down the stairs. One of the women stopped and looked over Sembado and Kaluna's food.

"Are they really running short of food in there?" she asked desperately.

"Well, he shouldn't get two pieces of fish!" someone shouted.

"Yeah man, you gotta share what's left!" another called.

Suddenly, the front door blew open. The bright morning light silhouetted Cistern who was flanked by several of his men. He looked around wildly, observing the full blown chaos that now consumed the great hall and the horde that was preparing to accost Sembado and Kaluna. He slowly but confidently grabbed Kaluna and then Sembado, and moved them behind him and his men and then out the large front doors.

Sembado and Kaluna were safely outside before they heard Cistern erupt in a verbal onslaught. He angrily chastised anyone within earshot for their greed and stupidity. The remainder of his rant was lost as he and his men pushed deeper into the great hall.

"Cover that food," Kaluna instructed as she quickened her pace. Sembado followed her down the front steps, but they turned sharply before they reached the tent village. They moved around the side of the lodge and into some flowery bushes behind the large building. The spot that Kaluna chose was hidden by the initial front of foliage, but also lay under a break in the canopy above so that late morning sunlight poured in from on high. They sat and quietly ate. The fruit and fish were the most substantial meal Sembado had eaten since the Catalina islanders had dumped him off his submarine and into the tide just over a week before. His sated belly and the warming sun combined to make his eyelids relaxed and heavy. With Kaluna's consent, he curled up in some loose under-growth and fell right back to sleep.

A couple hours later, Sembado woke up to Kaluna laying large leaves over his head.

"Wha...what?" he said sleepily.

"Well, I didn't want to see your pale tailfin get burned for the umpteenth time," she snapped. He rolled over into the shade and propped himself up on his side; his legs were tucked up tight and his arms were folded under his head.

"Looks like noon," Sembado said, peering up at the looming, bright light overhead.

"Probably close," Kaluna replied. "I think they're finally figuring out some system of order," she added, pointing through the branches to where some of the survivors had formed a line that wrapped around the backside of the lodge.

"Didn't make any sense to have that food line inside anyways," Sembado said, shaking his head. "This weather is more than agreeable and there isn't even close to enough room in there."

"Yeah, but I think you're forgetting that they never have this many directionless idiots running around," said Kaluna.

"Yeah, that's true," Sembado conceded. "Hey, you haven't talked to Mahana yet today, have you?"

"No. I was waiting for the crowd control to kick in," Kaluna responded.

"Well, they seem to be following some kind of process now," Sembado said, pointing to the line that wrapped around the lodge.

"Yeah," Kaluna replied. "But I was also waiting for you to wake up from your beauty sleep."

Sembado pursed his lips and rolled his eyes as he clamored up onto one knee.

"Well, I'm ready to go now," he sassed. "I couldn't possibly get any prettier."

Kaluna smirked, shook her head, and climbed to her feet. She walked toward the lodge with her usual, purposeful gait. The survivors that waited in line regarded her confidence with reverence. Sembado followed after, finding amusement in the peoples' expressions.

Rounding the corner to the front of the building, Sembado saw that the food line had in fact been moved outside. Cistern stood by while his men patrolled the queue with their authoritative presence. Sembado's heart felt a comforting tranquility as he observed the subdued order and control with which the line was being managed. It was a stark contrast to the crushing anxiety that could be felt in the morning's disarray. He followed Kaluna inside where they walked to the crowded hearth room that bedded the weak. The room was significantly less congested than before with far fewer visitors packed around the beds. In fact, as Sembado looked around, he noticed how many of the ragged mattresses themselves were no longer occupied. He and Kaluna quickly moved to Mahana's bed. Mahana was propped up with some pillows behind his lower back; he was reading through a small stack of documents. Jain was curled up sleeping on a nearby bed.

Kaluna greeted her uncle with a long, firm embrace. Mahana's face showed over Kaluna's shoulder as they hugged; he was uncharacteristically gaunt but his eyes were squeezed tight as he beamed with pure comfort. Even with Mahana's reduced girth, Kaluna still lay across him like a child.

"Mmm, aloha, ohana keiki," Mahana said. He rubbed her back with his great brown hand before they let go, and she sat down by his side. Sembado greeted Mahana with a much briefer hug and sat down on the adjacent bed.

"This place seems to have cleared out quite a bit just overnight," Sembado said.

"Mos' were jus' here for a lil' sun exposur'," Mahana commented as he straightened the papers on his lap.

"What are all those?" Kaluna asked, thumbing through the first few pages.

"Oh, jus' the plans Mereth has for us wata' folk," Mahana replied, setting the papers onto a small side table. "You really got 'er wo'ked up las' night," Mahana said to Sembado with a chuckle. "She wan's me to sign some o' dese pledges dat I won't go leadin' no subve'sive mo'ements. She wants me to give up any autho'ity as a leada', an' rebuke my somethin' rutha'."

Sembado hung his head and ran his hands through his fiery hair. The sting of the previous night's dismissal from Kaluna reemerged in his gut.

"Oh, calm down dere, 'ula'ula," Mahana laughed. "Ain't nobody blamin' you for nothin'. Dis trip was my last 'oorah, ya know? Ya ole Hyron had his last adventure just in da nick o' time. Dis one nearly kill'd me. I don' wanna cause any mo prob'ems for dese folk den dey wan'."

Mahana took Kaluna's hand in his. Her small tan fist was enveloped by his large fleshy palm.

"Ya'll hea'd what I had ta say las' night. Dey know how I feel 'bout it. I t'ought I was bein' pretty clea', but dat Ciste'n set t'ings off in da confrontational direction and y'all started arguin'. I ain't signin' nothin' I wasn' gonna agree to anyway. Trus' dat. But I gotta level wit ya, Semmy. My lil' Luna's right bout not t'rowin' dese utha floatas unda da boat. Ya gotta lea'n to sta't playin' ya ca'ds closa to ya ches'."

"I know it," Sembado replied earnestly. "I was just saying that to Kaluna this morning."

Kaluna nodded her head in agreement.

"Look, ya two," Mahana said lightly. "Something else ya gotta unda'stand is dese a'e new peop'e wit new ru'es. At some poin', ya gotta stop wo'ying bout da uttas and make su'e yuh two got eachutta's backs, huh? Dere gonna be a whole lotta *crazy* t'ings ya'll encounta out dere. I know ya wo'ying bout leadin' da pack and bein' good leade's, but I'ma tell ya from sperience, at some poin' ya gotta watch out fo' yaself firs'. It ain't mean or pers'nal, just life. Ain't no point rescuin' ya neighbor's house from fi'a when ya own is jus' sta'tin' to smoke, huh?"

Sembado and Kaluna nodded to show their respect and understanding to the wise words. They sat and quietly chatted for some time. Mahana exchanged anecdotal stories of his voyage with Sembado and Kaluna for stories of theirs. He acknowledged that their story of discovery, betrayal, and survival was far more compelling than his own. *The Beluga*, it turned out, had become an unintended triage when a rash of stomach illness and diarrhea spread through the slow floating convoy. Mahana had to break to catch his breath from laughter when his colorful story about his own gastronomical ailments turned Sembado's face nearly the same color as his hair. The commotion was enough to stir Jain from her much needed rest.

"Oh, Manny, please," she said, rolling over to stuff a pillow on her head.

The raucous laughter also drew the attention of one of the sick ward's keepers. The young man walked over with an air of inflated purpose.

"I believe you are the two whose attendance Mereth has specifically requested," he said to Sembado and Kaluna in a very dry tone. "An announcement is to be made on the front veranda momentarily. Please go there now."

He turned and walked away; his wavy blonde hair swished about his shoulders.

Mahana made a curious and thoughtful face.

"Betta' get goin'," he said quietly. His voice was nearly hoarse from his much needed laughter.

Chapter Six
The Hand that Feeds

Sembado and Kaluna stood at the top of the lodge's front steps and looked out over the gathered mass. Hundreds of people sat packed on the sand; they looked off to the south. A group of large boulders served as a stage. Upon them, Mereth, Cistern, and a few other people stood. The moody blonde messenger was among them. Sembado and Kaluna took a seat on the steps as Cistern called for order. A hush fell over the murmuring crowd. Cistern stepped aside so that Mereth could assume the most prominent position on the rock outcrop. The air was still but energized as the gathering waited for their news.

"Thank you for your peace and patience," Mereth called over the crowd.

Sembado was struck by the power and clarity of her voice.

"This is not any of our preferred format," Mereth continued. "But it is important that we transition out of this recovery mode as quickly as possible. We will soon be hosting courses for you all in an effort to give you the tools and knowledge you need to leave this place and venture out on your own."

An energetic whisper raced across Mereth's audience. A brief bark from Cistern re-collected their attention.

"Those deemed the healthiest among you will be made a priority," Mereth said. "This will allow the weak and infirmed a longer recuperation period. It is mandatory for you to move on and found your own villages. This place is not allocated the resources needed to support this population. Additionally, more of your kind are expected to arrive and we are already at a hazardous population density. As soon as classes are prepared, those identified as eligible will be notified. Once again, we appreciate your patience and sacrifice."

She waited and looked out over the crowd; the pregnant pause was just long enough to cause uncomfortable stirring among the masses.

"Stewardship is sacrifice," she stated, eliciting loud cheers and chest thumping from Cistern and the others. "That is all."

The members of the seated crowd slowly stood and shuffled off in various directions. A few trailed back into the lodge. Sembado and Kaluna stood up and stepped down the stairs to avoid being in the way. They waited under the shade of a tree while the crowd slowly dispersed. Sembado couldn't help but notice how the sand and sparse grass that made up the assembly place had been beaten and trampled by the thousands of footprints left behind.

"Typical, isn't it?" Cistern said as he approached Sembado and Kaluna. "Look at the damage even a simple gathering can cause."

"Wouldn't a herd of wild animals have done the same thing?" Kaluna asked, genuinely curious.

"But we are not a herd of wild animals," Cistern responded sharply. "We should not need to gather like this. Every day we spend not sending these people off on their own is another day that this microclimate and local ecology has to suffer their impacts."

"I think the environment will recover just fine once you get these people spread out a little bit," said Sembado.

"Oh, do you, Sembado?" Cistern snapped back. "That's the exact attitude that billions of people took to push this planet to the brink of destruction. So don't tell me you're not worried. You don't have the slightest idea what you're talking about."

The volume of Cistern's voice and his physical posturing started to draw people's attention. Some of his men came and stood by his side; they scowled at Sembado as Cistern continued his verbal assault. His eyes flared behind his rough hair and beard.

"I'm not gonna cut you the same slack Mereth wants to," Cistern spat. "Okay? We've got standards, man."

"Now, *you* don't know what you're talking about," Kaluna objected. "She ripped into him last night as bad as you are."

Cistern ignored Kaluna and pointed his finger angrily at Sembado's chest.

"You and your fancy leg and little miss here better fall in line or you can swim your pampered asses back out to sea! Comply?"

He did not wait for a response, but turned instead and walked away. His men took turns glaring before each broke off and followed Cistern away, pushing through the ring of gawkers that had gathered around them.

As the circle of onlookers broke away, Mereth pushed her way through the crowd. She approached Sembado and Kaluna with a look of exasperation and concern.

"I did not tell him to say those things," Mereth declared, grabbing Sembado by the wrist and leading him and Kaluna around the side of the lodge. Mereth looked around to confirm that the shady corner offered adequate privacy. Satisfied, she continued her appeal in a harsh whisper.

"Cistern's outburst had nothing to do with our disagreement last night. I promise! I will continue to work with you two and Mahana and Jain to find the solution that best fits your people. That's my commitment."

She paused to look around again.

"Cistern has become a problem for me," she whispered even more quietly. "I used to regard him as a key asset and dedicated follower, but his principles are unyielding and he does not understand compromise. All he knows is stewardship. That's it. He will not abide any other way."

"But you've said the exact same thing," Kaluna protested quietly.

"Yes!" Mereth responded. "And I will hold fast in my dedication to this lifestyle as well. But I also know the value in winning people over. In playing the long game. The bigger picture. Cistern is here and now. Always. You understand compromise. I know you do. I know your uncle does. I need to harness that."

"So what are you saying?" Kaluna asked impatiently. "Last night you ripped into Sembado for saying exactly what you are."

Sembado crossed his arms in defiant agreement.

"That was my emotional response," Mereth replied. "I'm not going to say that's not how I feel, but we have *got* to find a way through this together and I understand that."

She paused, sighed, and looked down at her feet.

"Cistern's another story," she said, shaking her head.

Sembado and Kaluna took the opportunity to exchange glances. Sembado looked back and forth between the top of Mereth's bowed head and Kaluna's insightful gaze.

"What's going on?" Sembado asked. "What has happened that he has you worried like this? Our entire journey here he deferred every decision to you, no matter what. Now you think he's just going to start going rogue?"

"It's not about listening to me," Mereth said as she looked up with moist eyes. Her sun-beaten, wrinkled face directed the tears in a wild, wavy path. "You do not know who I am. You have no idea what I do for my people."

Sembado felt Kaluna's hand creep into his ever so slowly.

"The people you saw on your journey here with Cistern," Mereth continued. "The ones who were fishing. That is how people live now. Cistern and his men, riding patrols around the countryside to keep the villagers in check. That is also an option. But this," she said, indicating the lodge. "This is unique. This is not normal. This," she sniffled and wiped more tears out of her eyes. "This is a palace. I stay here and I dictate life to the others. I alone make these rules. This role was passed onto me from my mother."

Kaluna squeezed Sembado's fingers lightly.

"So I have done my duty to guide these people firmly. To give them something to believe in that is greater than themselves. Something to live for, but more importantly, something worth dying for."

Mereth leaned against the exterior wall of the lodge and sighed.

"I've known Cistern since he was born," she said with a heavy sigh. "I named him. A cistern is a type of well that collects rain water to be used for later. He was destined to be what he is. And when his mother passed away from illness, I raised him as my own. Caring for this lifestyle and seeing it continue are in his blood and bones. So seeing me suggesting compromise with you people is not just foreign to him, it's a sacrilegious betrayal."

Mereth placed one hand on her forehead and massaged the leathery skin. It moved fluidly under her old, boney fingers.

"What I'm trying to explain is very complicated," she added without looking up. "You couldn't understand having your elders teach you a truth and path your whole life just to have it pulled out from under you. To be told that everything you knew could be compromised and changed."

Sembado openly laughed before he could catch himself. Mereth looked up, her eyes wide with surprise.

"You think that's funny?" she asked. Her tone was one of genuine surprise.

Kaluna leaned her head against Sembado's shoulder and closed her eyes. Mereth looked back and forth expectantly between Sembado and Kaluna. Sembado's heart and mind raced with all of the passionate ironies that were emotionally knotted inside him. He struggled to pick just one.

"Do you realize that you are describing my entire childhood?" Sembado asked. He did not wait for a response. "And that all I have known for the last year and a half is the fallout of these kinds of dictated lifestyles finally blowing up in their masters' faces? 'Cause, guess what, everyone gets sucked in. The only thing you've got going for you in this case is that your intentions are actually noble. Where we came from, this environment being first pursuit was just manipulated into a power-hungry system of consumer control. So tell your boy Cistern to get over himself. I've known more disappointment, betrayal, and deceit from my leaders than he could shake a leafy green stick at."

Mereth stood with her mouth agape. Kaluna smiled a satisfied smirk as Sembado pulled her away to the front of the lodge.

"And one more thing," Sembado said to Mereth. She did not turn around so he spoke to the back of her head. "Put us in the first round of those classes so that we can get the hell out of here!"

Chapter Seven
Learning Opportunities

The next few days passed rather quietly. Sembado and Kaluna made regular visits to see Mahana who was walking again, but still required ample rest. In an attempt to find peace for Mereth's more zealous followers, Sembado and Kaluna found several dozen of the rescued who were willing to be split off ahead of the survival classes to join nearby, existing villages. The others were put into gathering parties to pick local fruits and berries, easing the burden on the food lines at the lodge. With Cistern's departure on another northerly patrol campaign, the remaining tension in and around the lodge had all but subsided. Sembado and Kaluna also helped pitch a positive spin on the impending classes. With all of the progress combined, the camps surrounding the lodge were nearly buzzing with faith and optimism. Much to Sembado's chagrin, the nickname "Port Hope" had even begun floating around the haggard survivors' campfires. Every time he heard it, he rolled his eyes.

Finally, the day of the first village leaders' class arrived. Sembado and Kaluna gathered in the large hall of the lodge with a dozen other men and women. Mereth stood at the front of the hall with a few assistants.

"Alright," Mereth said, quieting the excited chatter from the audience. "You all have been chosen for your leadership qualities which will be absolutely necessary for your survival as well as every man, woman, and child in your future villages. Each of you will be partnered with a few dozen villagers to follow your guidance and leadership. They will all be taking basic classes to help support their roles, but yours is a vital one. You will be taught the rules of our lifestyle and how they apply to the way you move your people, settle your people, shelter and feed your people. In this room, we will teach you to be shepherds of shepherds."

Mereth introduced her assistants before leaving the class to tend to another. Sembado, Kaluna, and their classmates spent the remainder of the morning listening to the assistants describe the strict 100 person limit of each village, and how the territory of each village must be able to accommodate ten acres of land for each villager to control their biological footprint. A presentation board was used to describe these numbers graphically; a map showed how these villages and their respective territories were already occupying vast swaths of the surrounding foothills. According to the instructors, Sembado and Kaluna's class of village leaders would be tasked with moving their followers great distances to the east where new territory was being approved for settlement.

After several hours of instruction, the assistants took a break from the rules of governance to allow the class to eat. While they broke bread, the instructors used the time to become more familiar with the students. The class was comprised entirely of pairs; each village would have a male and female leader. Sembado and Kaluna soon learned that they were the only pair that was not already in a long-term, romantic relationship.

"It is not a requirement," one of the instructors commented. "It is simply a common side effect. Like any other male and female relationship, we neither encourage nor discourage our leaders to be romantically or sexually involved. While mating of males and females will be required to maintain your village population, you will find that some of your adult villagers' homosexual relation-ships are quite practical in avoiding overpopulation. The 100 villager limit *is* obligatory and has had to be strictly enforced in the past."

A hush fell over the room while many of the students avoided eye contact, choosing instead to focus on their modest lunches.

"Please understand that this entire system can only succeed if we minimize the exceptions to these rules. Heterosexual couples are responsible for their own pregnancy prevention and mitigation. There have been some very rare instances where a new mother and her baby are allowed to transfer to a neighboring village that is in need of members, but you must instill the rarity of this circumstance in your followers. These are rare exceptions, not open options."

The response from the class was beyond subdued. The sheepish look on the instructor's face indicated that he was aware of the morose impact his advice was having.

"Okay, maybe we should take a real break," he said. "Let's take a half hour to stretch our legs. Feel free to get outside for some sunshine and fresh air, but please be back in here in thirty minutes."

The class could not have been more hasty in departing the room. Sembado and Kaluna waited for the others to hurry out before getting up. They slowly shuffled into the foyer; they stretched their stiff limbs and yawned. Bright daylight poured in through the big front doors which were propped wide open. Sembado and Kaluna's classmates were gathered near the bottom of the front porch steps; they whispered at each other anxiously.

"Well, you don't have children, Rilah!" Sembado heard one of the women hiss at another. "Of course it doesn't turn your stomach like it does mine!"

Sembado and Kaluna stood on the top step and observed the group as they bickered back and forth. The arguing continued to become more personal as it went on. Sembado descended the steps slowly, one at a time, until he stood right next to the group. They regarded his presence indifferently. The women stopped arguing and their tight knit circle parted on Sembado's side. They stood in silence and stared at him; some wore expectant gazes, others glared bitterly. They regarded his bionic leg with suspicion.

"Bickering will not make this better," Sembado said flatly. One of the women that was arguing crossed her arms. The woman named Rilah uncrossed hers and dropped them at her sides.

"We have been through this before," Sembado continued, "only you didn't know it. This is the same as living your life in the Complex. There are rules that you must follow. I admit, they are different...very different, compared to the ones we had in the Complex, but they're just rules. But arguing amongst yourselves will not help you, and it will not help any children you may have."

The mother that had crossed her arms now dropped them by her sides as well.

"This transition will be hardest on us," Sembado added. "Just as going down into the Complex was hardest on my grandfather's generation. This is just a new transition, but, by the time our kids are old, this new way of life will be all they've ever known. So make it easier on yourselves and stick together because no matter what happens, cohesion can only help."

The group of classmates' perception of Sembado appeared to transform from indifference to respect. He turned to climb the steps and found that Mereth and another instructor were standing right behind Kaluna. They regarded Sembado with reverence. Sembado walked past them and back inside. Kaluna followed quietly behind.

"Overdo it much?" Kaluna said quietly as they found their way back to their seats.

"What?" Sembado asked. "I didn't know they were standing behind me. You don't think I don't really feel that way?"

"Yeah, I guess," Kaluna replied. "Now you've probably got some golden mark in their weird journal of outsiders."

"Only if I'm lucky," Sembado laughed.

The instructors filed back in after several minutes, the classmates trickled in shortly after.

A second instructor took over for the afternoon session, but she was even more serious than the first.

"You will do well to remember that the world out there, while useful and supportive, is not going to go easy on you. You will face challenge after challenge. To that point, we will be continuing the difficult subject of population control with a discussion on geriatrics."

The class sat in stony silence while the young woman continued her lesson.

"You will find that your older villagers are by far your most experienced and wise. It is important to sustain their knowledge and experience just as you would any other resource. Practically speaking, many of them will become less and less useful at a very quick rate. Make sure that you are able to harness every useful life lesson you can before they are allowed to pass."

As the instructor was looking around, she made eye contact with Kaluna who wore a displeased expression.

"Do you have a question?" the instructor asked.

Everyone looked around at Kaluna.

"Uh, yeah," Kaluna said. "What do you mean 'allowed to pass'? How do you *allow* someone to pass? I mean, it's kind of an unstoppable process. Using technology to keep someone alive doesn't seem like your guys' style."

"You misunderstand me," the instructor said sharply. "We strongly suggest a maximum age of sixty-five years old."

The only sound in the room was the cracking of Kaluna's knuckles under her table. Sembado tried to reach for one of her clenched fists, but she pulled away and shuffled her chair to the side. Her stony, bitter silence distracted Sembado for the remainder of the afternoon.

"Now, here on these charts, you will see the ideal age and gender distribution to achieve your village's purpose," the instructor said, making a point to avoid Kaluna's steely glare. "Self-sustenance and stewardship of the local environment are your main objectives. Remember, this is a living world in which we get to play an important part, but it is only one part: a steward. Being a steward is a beautiful thing. It is the purest form of leadership that centuries of democracy could not achieve. A steward is a leader who is burdened by all of the responsibility, but has no personal gain at stake. A steward never thinks of him or herself, except when their survival and sustenance will have a direct and positive impact on their environment. In this way, it is actually quite important to keep yourself and your people well fed, healthy, and alert. Not for the primary reason of seeking satisfaction and comfort, but for the secondary purpose: your ability to ward over your territory has a direct relationship with the success of your territory. If you as a leader become ill and cannot guide your village, then they may make an errored judgement on when and where to control a naturally occurring wildfire. It is our jobs to help the world live as it was intended, but not to play puppet master. We are the puppets. We are the servants. We are the slaves. This world must be maintained. Our role is simply to be the hands through which the good works are done. Now, as we close for the day, I will have you repeat three of our guiding statements. Think on them, remember them, and teach them to your followers. Now, repeat after me: Stewardship is sacrifice."

The class obliged the request, but in a less than energetic tone.

"*Stewardship is sacrifice,*" they droned.

"Life should be simple, not easy," the instructor said sternly. "With more feeling!"

"*Life should be simple, not easy,*" the class repeated loudly.

"The work is through us, not of us," the instructor stated with a clear, determined voice.

"*The work is through us, not of us,*" the class said in a clear and unison voice.

"Good," the instructor concluded. "We will meet here again in two days. Now go and make stewards of men."

Sembado sat quietly as the class shuffled out. To his surprise, some of his classmates were actually challenging each other to repeat the three phrases correctly. Sembado bent over to whisper to Kaluna.

"That didn't take long," he said sarcastically.

Kaluna did not respond, but got up abruptly and quickly walked out of the hall. Sembado stayed seated as he watched her go. He remained seated, even as the rest of the class vacated the hall.

The instructor approached Sembado slowly, taking a seat by his side. Their chairs were adjacent, but faced different directions. Sembado looked on dryly and avoided eye contact with the young woman. If he hadn't, he would have seen how the afternoon sun that crept through a skylight highlighted her features. Her straw colored hair lay starkly against her beautifully tan skin. More contrasting still were her soft blue eyes which looked like periwinkle blossoms back-dropped by bare soil. Sembado stared away at the source of the sunlight. The roof had a hatched window which had been propped open to reveal the cloudy, azure ceiling beyond.

"Your friend is quite stubborn," the instructor stated. "But she does have more will and purpose than the rest of you combined."

"I know it," Sembado said flatly. "She is not one to abandon her principles."

"That is a noble quality," the young woman responded. "As long as we keep our convictions grounded and true."

Sembado looked her in the eye with a puzzled look.

"What do you mean by that?" he asked.

"Well," the young woman said, "it is important to have convictions and principles and fight for what you believe in."

She paused while she considered her words.

"But just because you believe something is the truth does not make it the truth, and therefore does not justify your actions as righteous."

"Then how do you know whether what you believe is true or not?" Sembado asked.

"There should be no doubt," the young woman responded. "There should be only facts and evidence. For example, we know for a fact that if humans are allowed to reproduce and advance in technology without limits, we will destroy the world. We had done a successful job of that and it showed. But now we know how to manage our populations, resources, and environments. I can believe in all of that with a clean conscience because I know they are supported by scientific facts. I don't even really need to believe it. Believing in something implies faith. This is not faith. This is trust and understanding and structure. It is what it is. These laws are as undeniable as the sunrise."

"Then what do you think Kaluna puts her faith in?" Sembado asked, genuinely curious for the instructor's analysis.

"Freedom," the instructor responded. "Choice and liberty."

"Well, what's wrong with wanting freedom?" Sembado asked. "Is wanting to be the master of your own destiny really that despicable?"

"What do you need freedom from?" the instructor asked. "I know you and your people had to fight to be free from your authority's grip, but why do you still struggle for independence? This place is as free as you could ever imagine."

"No it isn't," Sembado said while shaking his head. An incredulous smirk spread across his face. "You have given us absolutely no choice or say in our lifestyle or even existence. Kaluna sees this place and your rules as just another form of control. She sees you as the new authority. And frankly, so do I."

"But it's *not* about us," the young woman responded, pushing her blonde hair out of her eyes. Her own incredulous look spread across her face. "We are not the authority. The planet is. Our lifestyle is. We are simply here to help teach and guide what will become your own doctrine. You will be your own authority. Did you not hear our litany? The work is through us, *not* of us. I believe that. We all do. These aren't our rules. They are *the* rules. We are all subject to the same standards, sacrifice, and sometimes suffer for it. But that is the system. That is how this works and stays working. You and your friend Kaluna need to understand that because otherwise, this whole resisting for resistance sake thing is going to get you burned...very badly. If you'd stop worrying about being free to make choices and just appreciate the simplicity of not having choices, you would be a lot better off."

Sembado turned his gaze back up to the rooftop hatches. Fluffy white puffs intermittently cut the sunlight in half. The lighting of the room pulsed with shadow as another wave of clouds drifted by.

"So what?" Sembado said, continuing to look upward. "Does that mean that Kaluna and I are no good for you guys? Because we question things too much?"

"Oh, don't be ridiculous," the instructor said. "We have these rules and we all follow them, but that doesn't mean we don't have personalities. I've talked with Mereth about you two. She isn't concerned about a little attitude adjustment. That's the kind of thing Cistern would get bent out of shape for. She is cautious with you two because she knows you are capable of leading a movement."

Sembado closed his eyes. His head bobbed and swayed uncomfortably. His thoughts were captured by the memories of sitting in the office of the underwater complex's security czar. The man, named Fabian, had connected Sembado's lineage to his troublesome, rebellious grandfather, and the legacy to which Sembado was rather unfamiliar with. The memories burned bright and hot in his mind as the instructor sat and identified he and Kaluna as being "masterminds". He rolled his eyes open and stared firmly into the young woman's large blue eyes.

"We want to live this simple life," Sembado declared. "We have neither the interest nor energy to start any of *movement*. We're just a couple of obstinate young people, okay?"

"Okay," the instructor replied. "That'll do."

Chapter Eight
Puerto Esperanza

Over the next few weeks, hundreds of new survivors reached the shore, were processed through the informational classes, and sent out to form new villages. Mahana was released from medical care and he and Jain joined Sembado and Kaluna on the team that helped the newcomers adjust to the culture shock and environmental transition. Their roles soon garnered respect from all parties.

One late September evening found Sembado eating an ample meal at a large table with Kaluna, Mahana, Jain, and Mereth, and a few of the other native stewards. Cistern They had just been seated when Mereth raised her small drinking bowl in a toast.

"I would just like to take a moment and acknowledge the work you newbies have done here."

The others raised their drinking bowls as Mereth continued.

"You have been thrust into quite foreign circumstances here and yet, in just a few months, you have helped us process and rotate thousands of your people. Reporting and first-hand accounts from the newest arrivers would have us believe that the migration is on a downward fall. You have had an incredible impact on an influx whose magnitude we couldn't have dreamed of."

Her followers took turns repeating the praises while Sembado and the others accepted the compliments awkwardly.

"I would have to agree," Jain said. "The numbers appear to have fallen off sharply."

"All da curio's an' un'appy tanka's done shoved off," Mahana chuckled.

"There were a lot that wanted to stay," Sembado agreed with a nod.

"Well, that brings us to my next point," said Mereth. "We do have plans for all of you outside of Mission Bay."

The length and severity of the silence around the table was directly proportionate to the lack of tack with which the old woman made her announcement. Regardless, she powered on with her usual candor.

"Sembado and Kaluna are very passionate and talented," Mereth declared to the table, "and I don't want that to go to waste."

Sembado looked across the table to Kaluna and then to Mahana. Even the jolly old islander looked uneasy. Mereth wasted no time addressing their overt misgivings.

"You have already agreed to lead a group of followers on a pioneering expedition," Mereth scoffed. "Why do you all look so uneasy? I'm not asking you for anything obscene!"

To Sembado's relief, Mahana postured to field the question. Despite their cultural differences, Mereth had become quite comfortable with Mahana's input and dialogue.

"I respec' deeze youngin' as much as you, Mer," Mahana said, looking down at his great brown hands which he rubbed together with uncharacteristic anxiety. "Trus' me when I say I've seen da incredaba' tings dey ah capaba' of. But dey ah still jus' youngin's and what you' askin' of dem is 'uge. Dis is a long jou'ney. An' afta' dat, a bran' new way o' life. Eita' one o' dose tings wou'd break a lessa' man o' woman by i'sef and you ah askin' em to do bot', one afta' da utta. Ya know whatta mean?"

Sembado's stomach grew hot. The silence around the table seemed to consume any ambient noise like some kind of auditory black hole. He tried to steal a glance at Mahana's face and then Mereth's, but he was overwhelmed with the urge to look at his own lap. The awkward energy came to a head when Mereth cleared her throat with a shrill gurgle before responding to Mahana.

"You know, Mahana?" she began, pausing to release a dramatic sigh. "It almost annoys me how undeniable your input always seems to be."

The tension around the table eased as Mahana relaxed his posture and Mereth continued with a more amicable address.

"Let me start over by addressing what is probably an obvious criticism of yours," Mereth said in a warm in measured tone. "I have absolutely no idea what it's like or what it will be like to go through this transition."

The tension returned to the table, but only for Mereth's native followers.

"Neither do any of my people," Mereth continued, ignoring the nervous fidgeting from her faction. "We were born into this. Now, I will not claim that this life is easy. And that it doesn't take a novice to realize it. I've heard of your modern conveniences. We aren't ignorant to the way the world was. There are a million easier ways to do what we struggle to do every year. Every *season*. But that's where the real grit and determination comes: Knowing that there is an easy way out, but taking the hard road despite all of that. And you're right, Mahana. That's the long game. The lifestyle. The day in and day out of our existence. I know what it's like. I do. But then there's the journey. Getting there. I haven't ever done that. I'll admit it. I don't even travel or patrol like Cistern. I've been within 20 miles of this same spot my entire life. Even before this life, this was revered as the easiest place to live in the world. And it still is. We don't have to ration. We don't have to preserve. We don't have to worry. But Sembado and Kaluna will. Where they're going, it gets cold. Where they're going, food runs out. Where they're going, people freeze and starve to death."

A fresh silence laid its claim over the table. Even candid old Mereth looked to her twiddling thumbs with a somber pause.

"People do die," she added quietly. "People *will* die, but I do not believe Sembado or Kaluna will. They are too determined for that."

"I've known a lot of determined people who have died," Kaluna replied defiantly.

Mereth smiled; her eyes twinkled.

"That is exactly the kind of attitude I'm talking about," she laughed. Mahana added his own soft chuckle despite Kaluna's humorless glare.

"Well, we already agreed we would go," Sembado interjected. "So now it's just a matter of when."

Mahana and Mereth exchanged a knowing look and nodded in agreement.

"It'll have to be after winter, right?" Sembado asked.

"No," Kaluna replied. "We can't wait that long. But if we stay this far south and just work on moving east to begin with, then we might be able to just avoid this first cold season."

"We should become familiar with the others that will be coming with us," Sembado suggested. "We'll need to coordinate resources."

"I don't want to interrupt your flow," said Mereth, "because this is exactly the kind of initiative I admire of you two, but you should know that your resources and followers will be predetermined. Our way has been strained to near failure, and we do not have the luxury of allowing village leaders to hand pick their villagers and supplies. Now, I trust that you understand why we cannot make an exception for you, right?"

Sembado looked from Mereth to Kaluna to Mahana and back.

"Then what's next?" Sembado asked dryly.

"You will leave as planned," Mereth replied. "Of course, heading east is only the big picture. You will pass the first mountains before the desert and find a little hut. There, you will receive the information you need to continue."

"That sounds promising," Kaluna said sarcastically.

"Your ultimate goal is the same as all the other settlers," Mereth said, continuing without acknowledging Kaluna's skepticism. "You will continue making contact with the loose network of Stewards until you find my lead contact, Pluto. He should be making arrangements for your arrival."

"Another branded horseman to dictate our lives?" Kaluna asked more seriously.

"No," Mereth said patiently. "Pluto has his own ways."

"Well, we can't find him if we don't leave," Sembado replied. "When will that be?"

"Out of respect for your support and effort," Mereth said slowly, taking unusual care in her word choice, "I wanted you to have a say in when you will leave. Having said that, we will have everything ready for our next team to depart in three days."

Kaluna made absolutely no effort in concealing her exasperated gasp; she flopped her hands in her lap with frustration.

"Well, what would you have me suggest?" Mereth suddenly spat with recrimination. "Do you have any idea how much criticism and blame I have already received from my people for being so lenient with you bunch?"

"Oh my God, you're right," Kaluna mocked. "That does sound like terrible circumstances. Good thing you aren't sixty-five yet. They might just do you in!"

Kaluna left the group in slack-jawed awe and marched away to her tented quarters. Sembado's stomach turned as he took in the look of pure disgust on Mereth's wrinkled face. His heart raced and his guts churned. He jumped up and ran after Kaluna before anyone could stop him.

Sembado traced the outside row in the small village of tents; each held at least one family of escapees from the sub-aquatic complex he used to call home. He heard arguing in one, playful laughter came from another. He turned in to his left, cutting across a row of tent openings. He navigated the series of familiar twists and turns as he slowly closed in on his and Kaluna's designated tent. They had moved from the lodge in an attempt to live in fresher air. While the salty sea breeze moved through the camp regularly, the tightest of quarters had provided a smell so noxious that it rendered the fresh air meaningless. He threw open the flap of their little triangular prism to find Kaluna angrily stuffing belongings into a canvas ruck sack.

"Well, there's no point packing now if we aren't going to leave for a couple days," Sembado said as he fidgeted nervously.

"Seriously, Sembado?" Kaluna replied angrily, whipping her head around to glare in disbelief. "That's the best you can offer right now? Why did you even follow me back? Because you thought you had to?"

Sembado's stomach turned hot and rolled over yet again. The pace at which he was losing control of his surroundings seemed to be accelerating at an alarming rate.

"I just don't get why you can't compromise a little," Sembado said meekly. "We won't have to deal with her forever."

"Compromise?" Kaluna rebuked. "They have a deekin' age limit, Sembado! Your grandpa would have been too old to live here. They would have *let him pass*. You know Mahana's not far from that old either. And that's just their solution for the elderly. That's just a taste. Population control. These rules are crazy. What I don't get is how you can just roll over like this."

"I'm not rolling over," Sembado snapped back. "I understand that these rules are harsh, but at least they have a means to an end."

"What does that even mean?" Kaluna asked. "So did the IFCG. It's all the same, Sembado! *They* are all the same."

"I don't agree. I think these people have a long term, sustainable thing, and they're willing to fight for it," Sembado stated passionately. "Did our whole experience bringing the Spring and Elephants together teach you nothing? We have to compromise when we can. We have to be willing to bend."

"Not on this, you idiot!" Kaluna shouted. "These are people's lives, Sem! You don't compromise people's lives."

"That's their whole point though," Sembado yelled back. His bionic leg shuttered. "Not compromising on human life is why this whole thing had to happen in the first place. Every single person was treated like the future of the human race depended on their survival."

"Did they put something in your water?" Kaluna asked bitterly. "Letting old people live out their life until they die of natural causes and keeping children with their mothers did not cause overcrowding. Now, I'm fine with people having to be more responsible and conscientious about birth rates and making the environment a priority, but this is ridiculous. This is not compromise. Us living by their heartless laws is not compromise. Us agreeing to live this lifestyle, but doing it our way is. That's what you and I said, that's what we agreed to, and that's what we're going to do!"

Sembado did not respond, but bit the insides of his cheeks and breathed heavily out of his nose. Kaluna too went quiet, and continued packing her bag as they sat in silence. Sembado dropped his head into his hands and tried to process where he was, what was happening, and what he could do about it. He thought of the long trek ahead of him as well as the long journey he had just made. He could not imagine doing either one without Kaluna.

"We can't let these people come between us," Sembado said quietly.

Kaluna stopped packing to listen, but did not make eye contact.

"We can't do what we do without each other," Sembado continued. "I can't do what I do without you. I don't want to. We're going to have a hard enough time with all of this, even without things to argue about, and I don't care about their rules enough to let it get between us."

Kaluna consented with a slow and silent head nod as she finished filling her canvas bag. She looked around at their meager surroundings and her sparse possessions, let out a deep sigh, and looked at Sembado.

"Are you tired? I'm tired," she said, slumping down on her little, squishy mattress.

Sembado secured the front of the tent and yawned deeply. He crawled on his hands and knees to his own sleeping pad, shuffled it up against Kaluna's, and flopped down on his stomach. He curled up next to her so that their faces were nearly aligned.

"Yes," he said quietly, reaching up and blowing out their little oil lamp. "I'm very tired."

The bedlam of the surrounding tents had tapered off to near quiet. Sembado and Kaluna laid in silence as insects sang outside in the waning twilight. Kaluna searched in the dark for Sembado's hand and gripped it softly when she found it.

"Sembado?" she said in a soft address.

"Yeah?" he replied sleepily.

"Sorry for calling you an idiot," she whispered.

Chapter Nine
Head East, Young Man

The next few days were a blur of preparation and activity. Sembado and Kaluna were directed to the main lodge where pre-trip medical screenings were taking place very early on the day before they were to leave. The walk had become a familiar one as they moved up the front steps and through the large wooden doors. They followed a line of people to the make-shift medical ward which had been converted into a series of examination spaces with sheets of fabric hanging from the ceiling. Sembado shuffled forward groggily while Kaluna stood with her eyes closed, her hands held a steaming cup of coffee in front of her face.

"Sembado! Kaluna!" a voice called, rousing them both from their early morning haze. They looked up to see one of their more cheery class instructors waving them forward in line. They moved around a mass of people, some children, and met the young woman as she was guiding people to available exam spaces.

"Good morning, guys," she said, shaking both of their hands energetically. "We'll get you two through here quickly. Most of these families can go together anyways.

85

Oh, I almost forgot! These are the new citizens that have been chosen as your villagers," she added loudly, indicating the group she had just ushered past. They numbered about two dozen in total. They looked ahead in curiosity as the instructor's address had been quite public. Some of the children stared at Sembado's bio-mechanical leg, looked up at his eyes, and then hid their faces behind their parents in embarrassment.

"We'll take our same place in line," Kaluna said, sipping her coffee. "If they'll move through quickly then we don't mind waiting our turn."

Sembado got the distinct feeling that Kaluna had stated her position a little more loudly than usual. Her point was not lost as multiple adults expressed gratitude at the humility as Sembado and Kaluna moved to the back of the line. The instructor stayed where she was, but her bright and shining smile was replaced with a sheepish and quizzical expression.

Indeed, the line did move quickly as whole families where examined at once. Soon, Kaluna's turn came and she was moved forward into one of the sheeted spaces. Sembado went right after and was directed to a separate location. He pushed the sheet aside, letting it flop behind him as he passed. The space contained a small bed, a chair, and a table covered in a host of equipment and tools. The examiner entered and started pouring over a clipboard and checklist. He was an older man with a long gray pony tail pulled tightly across his otherwise balding head.

"Alright, we're going to do a quick physical and then take a blood sample. Are you sexually active?" the examiner asked rapidly. But before Sembado could respond, the old man added, "Oh, never mind. You're a village leader. You aren't allowed to mate right now, so keep it in your pants," he said with a chuckle, cuffing Sembado on the shoulder. "So we'll skip *that* sample. Go ahead and take off your shirt."

He moved around Sembado with his stethoscope and small magnifying scope. He paused when he got to Sembado's neck, and saw the choker collar and wireless synapse transmitter for his bionic leg.

"Interesting necklace," he commented. "Never seen one like that."

"It goes to this," Sembado said, wiggling his powered leg dramatically.

"Well, hey now!" the examiner said, moving around to Sembado's front and taking a close look at his leg. "That's pretty slick. I have to admit, I've been pretty mesmerized by all the gadgets you water folk have brought up with you, but this has to take the cake."

The examiner finished looking Sembado over and asked him a series of routine family history questions.

"Well, that's it for me," the old man said. "Everything looks fine. Your lungs sound great. I'll send in my little vampire in just a second," he chuckled, smacking the sheet out of the way.

He was quickly replaced by a young woman with a rudimentary phlebotomy kit.

"You can put your shirt back on," she giggled as she prepared her needle. The blood was drawn and processed within minutes. Sembado was ushered back out, and found Kaluna waiting for him at the front doors.

"Everything go okay?" he asked.

"Yeah," she responded incredulously.

"Did they ask you the sex thing also?" he asked with a smirk. "My examiner said I wasn't allowed 'to mate.'"

"They told me that too," Kaluna said. "But I can't have children."

"Well, we're not supposed to anyways," Sembado said. "Not that I mean you and me would, but you know…"

"No," Kaluna said, shaking her head. "I mean I *can't*. The medical people back in the complex told me that when I turned fourteen. Something in that part of my body doesn't work right."

"Oh," Sembado said, genuinely surprised. "I didn't know that."

"Well, deeks, Sembado. It's not just something I break the ice with," she laughed. "It's not like I'm the most maternal candidate anyways so this worked out fine. I can't have them *and* I'm not allowed. Perfect," she added flippantly.

***

The rest of their last day was spent going over maps of the surrounding area and the lands beyond to the east.

They finished the last lectures in a way-finding series, and were given all of their leadership information, including detailed profiles of every man, woman, and child that would accompany them. Their last task of the day was securing and organizing the food and supplies each of their villagers would carry. They were provided an additional working tent while they portioned and packed the designated rations for each person based on their age, size, and nutritional requirements. In addition to food, a limited amount of medicinal bandages and salves was provided as well as a dozen primitive weapons. Kaluna chose a very painful looking saber while Sembado opted to use his leg if they encountered trouble.

They both wanted to stay up and prep well past midnight, but they agreed as much rest as possible would be the prudent choice. Sleep did not come easy, but after an hour of ever-less frequent whispers, they were both out cold.

Their rest did not last as they were both awoken at dawn by a blood curdling scream and subsequent commotion. They dressed quickly and collected their belongings before leaving the tent. Outside was a scene of subdued panic. People milled about, craning their necks for a view of something beyond the tent town. A verbal altercation and crying was coming from the lodge. Sembado and Kaluna checked their supply tent before heading to the epicenter of the action. They rounded the last tent to see a crowd circled around some mounted horsemen. Mereth stood at the top of the lodge steps, looking on with a stony grimace. Sembado and Kaluna pushed through the crowd to get a better look, and were shocked to see a man lying between the horsemen with two arrows in his back. There was a trail in the dirt showing how he had been dragged to his current location. A woman cowered at his side and wept. A pool of blood began to spread from beneath him. Two women stepped tentatively out of the encircling mass; first one and then the other. They slowly approached the weeping woman and tried to console her as they guided her away. The lead horseman gave her the courtesy of being out of earshot before addressing the surrounding throng.

"This man stole food and was attempting to leave in at unsanctioned time and direction," the horseman stated to his audience. His streaky blonde hair sparkled in the sun as his mount sauntered in place. "We asked him to stop several times, but he would not listen. We must abide the rule of law or there will be no order. Without order and sensibility, this way of life does not work. We will give you what you need, and send you where you need to go, but we cannot help you if you make this man's choice. Please abide the rules. I know they are sometimes difficult, but stewardship is sacrifice."

The crowd parted, allowing the two horsemen to circle their steeds to the west as they rode off toward the beach.

"Let's get the hell out of here," Kaluna whispered in Sembado's ear. They pushed back through the crowd as the others milled about in place to chat and gossip about what had just transpired. A group of men congregated to move the arrowed corpse.

Sembado and Kaluna gathered their group at the supply tent and handed out the provisions.

"Now, we've been through our own training just as you all have," Sembado called to the group. "Some of you already had some helpful skillsets that have been polished and improved. Mera, you will be in charge of our medical supplies, salves, and remedies."

He handed the bag of supplies to the woman named Mera. She took it happily and threw the straps over each arm. She pulled her tightly curled black hair out from between the bag and her back. She pulled and twisted the kinky locks into a dense mass behind her head and secured it with a small loop of fabric.

"Okay, weapons," Sembado announced. "When I call your name, please come forward and Kaluna will give you the weapon that has been paired with your abilities. Not everyone will need one, but the ones who do get them are responsible for at least three other people."

Eight men and three women walked forward, one by one, as Sembado called their names. Next to each of their names, he and Kaluna had scribbled notes from their file about their skills. A few of the weapons, like the hatchet and machete, would double as tools for building and were paired with their users accordingly. The remaining packs of food and supplies were distributed and by mid-morning, they were saying their goodbyes.

Mahana and Jain had come to bid them farewell. The great brown islander had tears running down his face as he embraced his niece and said a prayer.

"Dis is duh secon' time I gotta say shoots to ya. Ain't any easie'a if i's gonna be duh las'," he blubbered as he squeezed Kaluna tight.

Mereth and the instructors had also come out to send them off. It had become a near weekly ceremony, but this one was different. The old woman slowly approached Sembado and Kaluna and put a hand on each of their shoulders.

"No matter what disagreements we've had while you've been here," she said, clearing her throat as her emotions betrayed her, "you two have shown more promise and potential than anyone I've seen." She paused as she considered her next words, which she directed more intently at Kaluna. "Heed the rules," she said before pausing. "But follow your gut. That is paramount."

She hugged each of them, and sent them down a line of their instructors who wished them well with handshakes and encouragements.

Kaluna bid Mahana one more emotional farewell before she turned to join Sembado at the front of the pack. A small squad of horsemen escorted their traveling party around the north side of the bay and to the foot of the eastern hills. They wished them additional luck as Sembado and Kaluna started to climb the grassy slopes, a crowd of twenty-six men, women, and children right at their heels.

Chapter Ten
The Easy Part's Over

The strenuous morning hike gave way to a leisurely afternoon stroll for the travelling party as they traced the tops of the winding green hills east of San Diego. The sides of the small mountains fell away to deep ravines that could be seen stretching down into the valleys on either side. There were five children in the group. The two boys, ages ten and twelve, ran along and teased the two younger girls, who were seven and eleven. Meanwhile, the fifteen-year-old girl, Lenee, walked along with the adults and tried to appear as disinterested in the playful antics as she could manage. As the younger girls ran ahead of the group, their playful shrieks turned to desperate screams for help. Three armed men joined Sembado and Kaluna as they hustled around a rocky outcrop ahead. There they found the two girls had fallen onto their backs while just feet away, a very large and angry-looking mountain lion glared menacingly. Sembado, Kaluna, and the others quickly moved between the girls and the cat. Within moments, more of the party appeared around the bend. One of the mothers' high pitched screams was enough to convince the puma that the odds had turned against it. With a low moan and a hiss, it turned and scaled down the rocky ledge to the rear. Sembado led the group of guardians to the edge where they watched the mountain lion trot across centuries of accumulated fallen rocks and disappear into a wooded thicket nearby. The two young girls and their male counterparts decided not to play their chasing game for the rest of the day.

***

Ten hours of good progress found them approaching the base of the mountains that they could once only see on the horizon. Their trail took them right past a lake and the crumbled dam which once made it even larger. The youngest girl was being carried by her father, and a quick poll from the party found Sembado and Kaluna scouting for a bed-down zone for the night. Small portions of their provisions were dealt out while a few of the adults were sent to scour the landscape for additional roots, greens, and berries. A small fire was erected and lit with a striking stone. Sembado found it very clear how much the people enjoyed having assignments and duties. He and Kaluna sat around the fire with the others as they slowly talked through the mountain lion encounter, the day's other, less exciting events, and who would be first in the night watch rotation. Three of the weapon-wielders would stand watch at a time, each being relieved at different increments. Sembado volunteered to be one of the first three and he borrowed Kaluna's blade while she bedded down until her turn at watch. The energy in the camp slowly faded until all but the watchmen were asleep, and the fire's glowing embers were minimally stoked.

Sembado sat nearby, the fire's radiant glow warming his tired limbs. The other two on watch, a man named Neemus and a woman named Violet, sat and quietly craned their heads. They, like Sembado, were finding it difficult to not react to every crack, pop, and whistle that came from their foreign surroundings. The moon, which was waxing in the final week of September, cast just enough light to create monsters out of nothing; silhouetted specters that danced at the edge of the fire's reach. More haunting still was the way the white moonlight shimmered off the rippled surface of the nearby water. Every once in a while, a splash at the lake's edge would elicit another call of, "The hell was that?!"

Near midnight, Sembado had Neemus call his replacement first. He stirred a man called Viliano from an uneasy dream. Viliano grumbled and pouted for the remainder of his shift. An hour after Neemus retired, Sembado advised Violet to find and wake her replacement. Not long after that man reported for watch duty, Sembado went to Kaluna's resting place and woke her gently with a slow shake of her shoulder. She opened her eyes silently and sat up, taking the blade from Sembado's hand, and joined the two men that sat around the fire. Sembado lowered himself into Kaluna's bedding; it was still warm. He was asleep before his body fully settled on the ground.

***

The morning sun had just crested the eastern mountains and glared in on Sembado's eyelids, beckoning for him to wake. He opened his eyes just to slam them shut again. He tried rolling to a position better suited to avoid the glare, but Kaluna was tucked so tightly up against him that he could not move without disturbing her.

"Hey," he said, his eyes still closed against the sun's persistent beams, "you gotta move."

Kaluna groaned in protest but rolled away just enough to secure his freedom. Sembado sat up and stretched. The camp was slowly coming to life. Some of the children still lay curled and clinging to their mothers. Sembado moved slowly about the camp. He greeted those who were just waking, and sent those that were already alert out on gathering missions for breakfast. He sent a man with a spear and his wife to try and gather some fish from the lake. By the time Kaluna finally rose, Sembado had the camp abuzz with activity. The fire had been fully stoked and chunks of slightly charred catfish were being passed around. Kaluna found a seat near the children who were chatting happily.

"You have to be careful though, Tillie," one of the boys called to his sister. "Dad said he saw a dozen rattlesnakes when he went to go fish! They'll wanna bite ya even more than that puma!"

"That's enough, Olbie!" the father called from his seat, but Kaluna could overhear him and his wife describing their rattle snake encounters to Sembado and the others.

"They just look so…mean!" the woman said, making a sour face.

"They let ya know when you're getting too close, though," the man added.

"Then let's make sure to not wander off without an armed escort," Sembado declared. "Even if you have to go to the bathroom, make sure someone is nearby. I know it's not convenient or private, but…stewardship is sacrifice," he said with a chuckle. The camp joined him in a light-hearted response. Kaluna shook her head when he looked her way.

***

The camp was packed up by late morning with spirits high and hunger sated. Sembado and Kaluna continued driving their squad east toward the chain of mountains that stretched from north to south. Their goal was to close more distance to the ridgeline but to work around the southern tip, which the map showed would taper off within two days' journey. They had been warned that, beyond the mountains, the surroundings would become hot and dry. Not far into that region, the Stewards had actually dug a series of tunnels over the last few decades. The tunnels would allow protection from the sun and heat during the day.

It was later afternoon and Sembado was walking at the front of the group, a spearman at his side, while Kaluna was flanking the group's midsection. Sembado was just beginning to pass a dense collection of tall shrubs when a man suddenly came into view. He was just twenty feet ahead, crouched under a shady tree. His eyes looked lost and longing as he took in the traveling party. As more of the group became aware of the man's presence, more of the guards took post in the front. The man slowly stood and stepped out of the shade. The sun highlighted the dark, rich smears that lay across his tattered, threadbare tunic. The stains were a ghastly combination of red and brown. His beard was overgrown and matted; his hair was a wild mop behind which his eyes peered, lingering far too long on the women and children. Sembado's stomach turned as his genuine curiosity morphed to very certain distrust of this odd, troubled character.

"We must ask you to make a wide pass," Sembado stated clearly. His guards bristled at his sides. The man's wild eyes darted from the children to Sembado. He curled his cracked and bleeding lips into an unfortunate-looking smile. His teeth were revealed as sparse chips of yellow and brown.

"You're the ones travellin," the man said. His voice was high and cracked and loathsome. "But you all look so well fed," he continued. "Perhaps you have room in your party for one more?"

Sembado replied with a stoic and silent head nod 'no.'

The man's eyes dropped ever so slowly to Sembado's feet before shooting wildly around to the smaller party members.

"Then perhaps you'd be able to spare some of your party for me?" the man said with a smile. Sembado's stomach went cold as his armed followers moved forward with him. The unarmed adults shielded the children from the stranger's view.

"I can't have that and I think you know it," Sembado said dryly. "Now, we will pass with a wide berth. You *were* here first. You will not follow us if you value your life."

"But I don't," the man said darkly, clenching his fists and curling his lips. His yellowed eyes were piercing behind his gray and brown tangle of a bowl cut.

Sembado and his guards held their position, weapons drawn, while the others moved past, making sure to always keep themselves between the children and the stranger.

Once the rest of the team had passed, Sembado and his guards backed away from the man slowly, but the stranger made pursuit. He matched their steady pace step-for-step as they tried to make meaningful distance away from him.

"You think you can pass through the wild without paying your toll?" the man growled in his sharp, whistling voice. "You stewards think you're above me, but you're not."

As Sembado and his guards slowed their line to a halt, Kaluna led the other adults and the children down a path to the south.

"We're all animals," the man said. "Just clever, ugly animals. If you don't eat me, then something else will and, if I don't eat you, then maybe I'll settle for one of those beautiful children."

The stranger made a sad and desperate attempt to break into a sprint and circumvent Sembado's defense. His malnutrition showed as he slowly and clumsily lumbered toward the father who was still carrying his fishing spear. A look of fear, rage, and panic flashed across the spearman's face just before he planted his back foot and drove his spear deep into the stranger's chest. The rest of the defenders gasped in unison as the excessive force sent the dirty hermit's frail frame backwards into the air. He landed in a lifeless heap; the spear lay off at an awkward angle. The spearman stood in place, his hands shaking as he tried to process what had just happened.

"I...he...wanted the children," the man said with an adrenaline-fueled stutter. His dark brown skin glistened in the sun.

"It's okay," Sembado said, belying his racing pulse. "He was not in a good way. If anything, you...put him out of his misery."

He walked to the stranger's body with the spearman at his side. Even from a few feet away, the man's body smelled of sharp, pungent odors and weeks of dried urine.

The spearman rolled the body over with his foot to better remove the spear when the stranger suddenly gasped and clawed one more time, spewing blood into the air. The spearman cried out in surprise, grabbing the handle of spear and jabbing the stranger's face and chest several more times until Sembado and another man could pull him away. He recoiled in a tearful fit of disgust.

"This is not what I thought it would be," he cried, his entire body shaking uncontrollably. "Wild beasts and depraved lunatics pursuing my children...I'd rather be back in the Complex. This is unlivable!"

The man rejected Sembado's consolation and marched away into the brush to be by himself.

The trail was silent for the rest of the day.

Chapter Eleven
Titus's Little Shack Of Hope

By the fourth day of walking, they were passing the sloped lowlands that built up the southern tail of the mountain range. Sembado and the others plodded along quietly. Any and all excitement that the children had contributed to the beginning of the journey was all but dead. Sembado and Kaluna's only reprieve in their responsibilities came in the form of food being more readily available than assumed. But, while the party remained well fed, spirits and morale had fallen beyond average since the encounter with the crazy stranger.

Sembado walked along in the sunny glare of the afternoon heat. He had grown accustomed to a nearly ever present headache from his insufficient hydration. Ahead in the distance, he saw a surprisingly stark contrast between the loose green shrubs through which the party currently walked and the even less dense weeds of the desertscape beyond. The line between the two regions seemed almost comically obvious, a vector shooting due south from the end of the mountain ridge that died to their left.

At Kaluna's behest, they took a break in the shade of some nearby overgrowth. The children were quiet and subdued; the youngest girl, Tillie, was nearly lethargic. Small amounts of water were accumulated from everyone's rations to provide her with a few meager gulps. The group medic, Mera, mixed a thin paste of ingredients and fed a small amount to Tillie. The little girl made a disgusted expression and buried her face in her mother's arm.

When the sun had fallen further behind them, Sembado and Kaluna drove the group back to their ever drier trail. The shrubs that were once ten or twelve feet tall had become small, dry bushes of three and four feet. There was absolute silence, save for the sound of crunching rocks and quietly groaning children. Sembado closed his eyes against the setting sun's reflection off of the rocks and sand, but as soon as he shut his eyes, his head would bob and swim. It took more concentration than he could muster to allocate more power to his bionic leg. On top of that, the sun and sand seemed to be rendering the electric limb less and less functional or efficient. Indeed, the sandy transition seemed to take everyone by surprise, and proved to be a much harder adversary than they thought. Hours of dragging along in the afternoon sun had even provided some in the party ample time to decide how and why Sembado and Kaluna were doing a terrible job. As night began to fall, the bickering got worse. Assigning purpose and function to the travelers seemed to no longer translate to fulfillment but burden. Sembado and Kaluna retreated to a private corner of the camp while the others begrudgingly breathed life into a fire which threw flickering shadows deep into the arid surroundings.

"This is not good," Sembado said wearily.

"I'd say we need to take a break for a day, but we can't here," Kaluna responded. "This could cause some serious damage. We *need* to get to those tunnels."

"Yeah," Sembado agreed, "but that'll require we push them a little harder. According to the map, they are still a day away."

"Well, let's just tell everyone about them so that they have the same incentive we do," Kaluna replied.

Sembado dropped his head to her shoulder in response. They remained distant from the rest of group until the night watch rotations began.

Sometime after midnight, Sembado was woken unceremoniously by one of the others. The man did not wait before shuffling off to find his own rest. Sembado was immediately struck by the chill in the air. He quickly moved toward the fire, which was being stoked by the other watchmen. The others looked at Sembado with humorless expressions but not contempt. He could tell that they weren't angry with him, just the situation. He leaned his head back and took in the incredible stellar spectacle that sprawled above them in the sky. The moon had set below the horizon but the stars shown brilliantly against their inky black backdrop. Sembado felt his mouth bend involuntarily into a weak smile as he took in all of the shapes and constellations.

"Do you know any of the names?" one of the other men asked quietly.

"Nope," Sembado said without looking down. "I think Kaluna might."

Some snapping sounds in the near distance suddenly broke their concentration. Sembado looked all around. The shadows of the fire made murky phantoms out of every bush and rock. His heart raced every time he thought he saw something, but then it would melt back into obscurity. Each time Sembado got comfortable enough to do some more stargazing, he would hear another noise. Each one seemed closer than the last. He felt tormented and thought of the crazy stranger. The remainder of his watch duty was a fitful panic of paranoia. When he traded shifts with the next person, falling asleep proved to be his biggest challenge yet.

The next morning, Sembado and Kaluna announced their intentions, their target, and explained the purpose of the tunnels. Their message was well received compared to the previous day and some semblance of morale had been restored.

They trudged on through the morning. Beyond them in the distance, a small structure appeared. As they approached it, it took on the shape of a wooden shack. Sembado called for the guards to move ahead and he took a recon party closer. The little wooden building had a flat roof, one door, and no windows. The door was propped open with a large brick. Sembado circled around the shack until he could see through the doorway. Some movement inside prompted his group to tense back and hold their ground. Suddenly, a face appeared. It belonged to a little old man. His beard was white and yellow; his hair was the same, but with a hat perched on top. He was much more groomed than the crazy stranger, but his skin was far darker, sun beat, and wrinkled. He appeared to have no teeth.

"New passersby?" he called. His husky words whistled through his gums.

"Yes," Sembado replied firmly.

"Headed for the tunnels?" the man asked.

Sembado and his guards exchanged looks and brief affirmations before responding.

"Yes," Sembado stated.

The old man shook his head and disappeared into the shack. He peeked his head back out a moment later.

"Well, come on in," he called.

Sembado's group moved forward slowly; they weren't trusting of the man just yet. As they approached the door, they could hear him fumbling or tinkering inside.

"Surprised to see another group so soon," the man said as Sembado and his team carefully accumulated by the door.

A quick peak inside revealed a very simple existence: a bed, a table, and a chair. The old man's belongings were humble but well organized. He was digging through a box of papers. From this distance, Sembado could see he wore small round spectacles. He had set his hat on the table. Sembado looked back outside and waved to where Kaluna and the others were hiding. By the time they arrived at the shack, the old man was going over a map of the local area with Sembado.

"Yer gonna have to clear these next two ridges," he said, smacking his lips and gums. His eyes twinkled behind his glasses as the children were filed in, out of the sun.

"Well, my goodness," he said with a chuckle. "Ain't seen no children on this trail for a very long time."

He stood up to greet everyone else. He was just about Kaluna's height. He shook hands and patted the children on the head.

"That old bat in Mission Bay must really be short on space," he said with a chuckle as he leaned over a pile of papers. "I'm Titus, by the way. Now, where ya'll passing through to? The tunnels go a ways. Don't want to take a wrong turn. It's a long way back if you go down the wrong one."

"We're supposed to continue east until we find a man named Pluto," Sembado replied.

Titus straightened up and stared at the rickety boards that made up the walls of his shack.

"Oh," he said with a hollow sigh. He turned to face Sembado and the others, scratching his beard. His little blue eyes blinked furiously behind his glasses. He grabbed a paper to his left without looking and pulled an old stub of a pencil from his pocket. He plopped down at his desk and began scrawling furiously across the aged parchment.

"Well, you'll wanna be usin' number four then," he said, quickly scribbling numbers next to the lines. He presented the wrinkled, yellow paper. On it was a simple sketch of the tunnel network as it spread north and east.

"See, four here, it winds past all this other stuff and will take ya east," he said, pointing with his stubby, crooked finger. "Well, go on and take that. I can always draw another one."

Titus let them escape the sun in his shack as long as they wanted. At one point, he dug through an old tin and revealed some small sweet cookies for the children.

"Now, the tunnels are gonna break before the rough river," Titus advised, pointing out a line on the map to Sembado. "That's the Colorada'. She's slowed down a bit, goin' into the fall. You should find some Stewards there guardin' the river crossing in Yuma. But ya'll best beware down in them tunnels. Can't keep them cleared at all, it seems. I'm warning you, I say. Some that know them have even elected to take the heat to avoid whatever stranger things you might find lurking."

Sembado felt the eyes of his party burning into him from every direction. The traumatized father named Timm stepped out silently. Sembado looked back just in time to catch Titus sneaking a finger behind his lenses to wipe away some tears.

"You all seem like a sturdy bunch though," he said with a throaty laugh, mussing one of the children's hair playfully. "Pretty well armed too."

The old man teetered back and forth between his piled belongings, offering what he could to the different party members.

"No, really," Sembado said, refusing a collection of antique compasses. "We really only need the one, but thank you so much, Titus. We really should move out. The sun's beyond overhead and I would like to get to the tunnel entrances as early as possible tomorrow."

Titus continued to force little trinkets and tools on them, but Sembado and Kaluna had finally corralled the others outside. But before Sembado could leave the shack, Titus grabbed his wrist. Sembado looked down at the deminuative old man, but he was looking out at the group as Kaluna started them back on the trail.

"Just remember, boy," Titus said without looking up. "They can't never take yer mind. That's always yers...no matter what."

He let go of Sembado's arm and gave him a soft, reassuring pat on the shoulder.

"Go on, now," Titus added quietly, "ya'll got a ways ahead of ya."

Sembado walked out into the sun, stopped, and turned.

"Thank you, Titus," he said, barely able to see, for the sun glaring in his squinting eyes. "You've given us hope."

He trotted after the others, his bionic leg buzzing slightly from its effort.

"I'm sorry for that," Titus whispered to himself.

Chapter Twelve
The Low, Low Road

The visit with Titus had spirits soaring. Most of the children were nearly playful again except for young Tillie who stayed at her mother's side through that evening's campfire. Kaluna even took pity on the little girl and brushed her frizzy brown hair into a more manageable bun. The excited buzz was worse among the adults who recognized the relief to be offered by the tunnels more than the children did. Most of the travelers remained awake well into the nightwatch's first shift.

Sembado chuckled to himself as he watched the paler travelers take turns visiting with the medic, Mera, as she used up nearly all of the available aloe paste on their red and blistering skin. He thought back to when he himself had first arrived at the surface and Kaluna had done the same for him. Mera played her role well as the conservative ward of the remedies, but even she acknowledged what little need they would have for the aloe vera once they made their way into the sunless passages.

By midnight, only a few extraneous bodies sat around the fire with Sembado and the other two watchmen. The conversation had slowly grown quiet. With the prompting of the next watch rotation, the additional travelers made their way to a resting place. Soon after, Kaluna came and laid a hand on Sembado's shoulder. He tilted his head to the side, letting his cheek pin her hand to his body. She slowly pulled her hand away and ran it through his long, shaggy mane.

"Go get some sleep," she whispered.

Sembado reused Kaluna's resting place but, despite his comfort in her residual warmth, he found trouble falling asleep. He was just as excited, anxious, and expecting to make his way into the tunnels as the others. He impatiently exhaled, burying his face in Kaluna's sleeping blanket. He wished his mind and body would follow his desire for sleep, but both his heart and brain seemed to be following the same driving beat. He inhaled as peacefully as he could. The smell of Kaluna's body filled his nose. Even in the gritty, uncomfortable abuse the last week had provided, Kaluna's things smelled beyond pleasant to Sembado. He did not want to acknowledge the intoxication it caused in him for the drive that he knew would reawaken. She had made it clear several times that they could not pull that thread and that she herself was not as interested. Regardless, the smell that filled his nose and lungs seemed to travel directly to his brain. It was just engrossing and comforting enough to block out everything else. Sembado's heart rate dropped, his eyes grew heavy, and his breathing slowed. But despite the steady, determined pleasure signals his heart was sending his brain, one random thought burrowed its way in just before he fell asleep. Deep in his mind, he heard old Titus's raspy voice mutter out, *"They can't never take yer mind."*

***

The tunnels were lighter than Sembado thought they would be with portholes to the surface bringing sunlight down at regular intervals but the protection from the sun was twofold. Not only were they avoiding the burns of the direct sunlight, but the air temperature was nearly thirty degrees cooler. Sembado walked along at the front of the pack. His leg was yearning to make longer strides but he kept the pace regular and manageable for the children. Suddenly, little Tillie took off past him like a bullet. Her parents called after her but she tore ahead in a dead sprint. Sembado volunteered to go catch her and broke into the heavy trot that his bionic leg pined for. The sand and grit were blown from the joints as he fully exercised all of its degrees of freedom for the first time since being discovered by Cistern and his men. He picked up the pace, wanting to intercept the little girl as quickly as possible. She sprinted just ahead, the vertical rays of light highlighting her each time she passed one. Sembado called out to her, but she did not respond. He ran harder; his powered leg pushed with more force, compensating as it took on more of the load. He yelled for Tillie to stop, this time using more power and anger in his tone. The little girl looked back over her shoulder but did not slow down.

Sembado grew less patient by the second. He dug in with his bio-mechanical limb, kicking sand up behind him, and his gait transformed to a nearly one-legged leap. The powered leg responded to his mood as he became more upset with Tillie's insolence. Suddenly, the tunnel made an unexpected turn. Tillie disappeared around the corner. Sembado made one giant leap, landing hard with his bionic leg but ready to spring off in the new direction. Just as he landed and turned, his heart stopped. Tillie was nowhere to be seen but had been replaced by the crazy hermit from the mountain pass. The dirty, mangled stranger held the spear in one hand, blood ran from the holes in his chest and face. Sembado was petrified with fear as the creepy rambler quickly closed the distance between them. His beady eyes seemed to glow in the dark. He grinned his awful grin; blood trickled from his chapped lips.

"Stewardship is sacrifice," he said in a wild, high-pitched howl.

Sembado woke up whimpering. Kaluna was trying to snuggle in next to him. He jumped when he saw her so close.

"What the hell are you doing?" she asked incredulously. "You were whining in your sleep."

"I had a bad dream," Sembado said defensively, sliding his body over to give her room.

She did not respond but rolled over herself. She laid her head on his bicep and remained quiet. Sembado burrowed in next to her, breathed the smell of her hair in deeply, and reluctantly went back to sleep.

The group could not have been more eager to leave the next morning, Sembado as much as anyone. Some even elected to skip their food in anticipation of realizing the tunnels' promise as soon as possible. Sembado gathered Kaluna and some of the older travelers to look over the hand-drawn map to the tunnels that old Titus had given him. Together, they determined what visible landmarks coincided with the symbols and clues scribbled out across the tattered yellow sheet. A rocky outcrop was shown on the map to be towering over the entrance of the first tunnel. They climbed a nearby hill and looked out to the south and east.

"There! Over there," Kaluna said, pointing to a large pile of massive stones.

"Let's move out," Sembado replied. As the others returned to camp to ready the group for travel, Sembado remained at the hill, thinking over his disturbing and frustrating dream. His mechanical leg shuddered. He closed his eyes and took several slow, deep breaths. Behind him, the camp was ready to move. At Kaluna's command, they set forward toward the pile of boulders. The distance was a close and easy one, but Sembado and Kaluna commanded the guards to keep a watch out for man or animal. They moved steadily across the open terrain, like a platoon of soldiers with a purposeful marching tempo.

Sembado felt the group's tense posture relax as they stepped into the shadows of the boulder pile. He saw no signs of an entrance and continued to march the group around the circumference of the rocky protrusion.

"Here!" called one of the men.

The group swung around as one to view a rickety old door which appeared to be propped against the rocks. It looked as if it were taken right off of Titus's little hut. The guards moved forward slowly, the spearmen took the lead. Sembado stepped forward and pulled the door's rope handle gently at first but it held fast. He gave it another, firmer tug and, sure enough, the door swung open, revealing a shadowing entrance that moved downward quickly. Sembado inched inside, leading with his bionic leg, should he need to use it. The dirt floor dropped more quickly than the ceiling so that, by the time Sembado and the guards had reached the bottom of the entrance slope, the ceiling was nearly twelve feet high. Sembado continued his cautious shuffle inward; his guards were so close behind him that their weapons jutted out past him on either side. He tried not to stumble over the undulating path that was worn in the sandy floor. The walls were lined with vertical wooden timbers that stood at ten foot intervals. He followed the timbers upward to the continuous line of planks that made up the ceiling. The smallest amount of sand was raining through the cracks, nearly a grain at a time. Unlike the skylights from Sembado's nightmare, the light from the open door behind them offered only minimal illumination for the path ahead.

Sembado stopped short; his guards stiffened in response. Not very far ahead, shady figures moved in and out of the light.

"What is it? Do you see something?" Kaluna asked from behind them. Sembado and the guards all shouted in surprise, turning their attention and their weapons on Kaluna. The rest of the travelers stood right behind her.

"Deeks, Luna," Sembado shouted. "You can't just sneak up on us!"

He turned back around, remembering the lurking figures ahead. As his eyes continued to adjust to the dim setting, he realized the shapes he saw were just the shadows being cast by Kaluna and the others. He took the opportunity to prepare the party for the lightless path ahead.

"Alright," he called over the murmuring and chatter. "We're going to have to use our lanterns, but we must use as few as possible and make them last." The Stewards had provided them eight small oil lanterns for their journey. Sembado and Kaluna decided that only two would be necessary to begin with. Sembado took another moment to compose himself, padded his leading shoulder with some extraneous garments, and lit the first lantern. One of the travelers went back up the slope to close the entrance door as Kaluna transferred the flame to the second lantern. She decided to carry the lantern at the middle of the group and handed her small blade over to Sembado. With everyone's consent, he moved out, carrying the lantern in one hand,

Kaluna's blade in the other, and continuing to lead with his bionic leg.

Their initial progress was slow as the group got accustomed to the limiting pace, tight quarters, and near darkness. Sembado held the lantern as high as he could, but felt a burning sensation in some arm muscles that he hadn't strained in some time. The glow of the lantern was pretty meager, casting meaningful light a mere fifteen feet, a dim haze lay beyond that. His inner ear and equilibrium gave him the distinct feeling that they were still moving on a downward slope, albeit an ever so gentle one. The longer they moved, the more confidence they gained, and soon they were walking at a confident stride that the sun and heat would not have allowed on the surface. The newness of the tunnel experience was apparent: neither adult nor child made a noise for the first few hours. They took a short break at what Sembado guessed was high noon. The men and women took turns relieving themselves, a treasured modesty offered by the near darkness. They moved a little further down from their makeshift latrine in order to eat and rest. The group crowded around the glowing lanterns in two huddled masses, a short stretch of darkness separating the two bunches. They sat in near silence, the only sound coming from the near constant breeze that blew down the corridor from somewhere ahead.

Through the dim murk created by the old brass oil lamps, Sembado could just make out the silhouette of Kaluna's face and torso as she sat in the other group. Her dark brown hair draped over her neck and shoulders. It had finally returned to its former length. The light of the nearest lantern twinkled off her jade colored eyes. She turned and looked at him. They shared their private exchange for just a moment.

"We need to keep moving," she called softly.

The travelers complied and those with weapons moved to the front with Sembado so they could renew their structured march forward. They made quick progress after their break. After just a few minutes, Sembado felt his pace adjust as the floor's downward slope terminated into a steady, horizontal surface. He looked back briefly to see that the light that had once poured through the loosely structured entrance door was now a faint pinprick behind them. They were plodding along quickly when, all of a sudden, they heard a noise ahead. Sembado slowed down; the guards behind him were careful to hold their weapons away from each other as they piled up behind their leader. Sembado froze as the noise was repeated very close ahead.

That sounds like words. Like someone speaking!

Sembado directed his team to pack together but fan out so that they would form a solid line of defense across the width of the tunnel. The guards with shorter weapons stood fast and formed the front line while the spearmen stood behind the first row, ready to strike over their companions' shoulders. Sembado flexed his grip on Kaluna's short blade. He turned the diminutive sword over

118

in his right hand, the oil lantern dangled in his left. On Sembado's command, they started to inch forward. He picked his bionic leg up just enough to not drag sand on the earthen floor. The electric limb buzzed as his cerebral anticipation tickled its transceiver. He held the lantern as high as possible as they moved forward. His eyes strained in the dimness, but then he saw them: over a dozen little floating reflections of light. They bobbed and blinked.

Blinked...

Sembado had to force himself to breathe as his mind put together the puzzle that his eyes were feeding it. There were at least five or six human beings standing in the darkness, just beyond his lantern's reach, and they looked beyond crazy. The eyes became noses, mouths, and necks. Soon, eight grown men were shuffling at them with dark, lifeless eyes. The beady little soul-windows were outlined by gaunt, sallow sockets and cheeks. The skin was not taught and light, but sickly and thin. The shadows under their eyes first appeared grey, but additional lantern light would have them painted a burning, infectious hue of red. The creepers were just ten feet away when Sembado finally spoke.

"Please leave us alone," Sembado said flatly.

The creepers' eyes flared and they whispered and hissed, but they did not stop. The guards tensed and prepared for their first move while Sembado warmed up his leg by slowly cycling it in the air three times. One of the creepers stepped forward faster than the others. He reached out for Sembado and snarled. Before anyone else could move, Sembado planted his human foot, braced himself against the others, and picked his bionic leg up to his chest. He grimaced and tried not to clench his teeth as he released the full power of his kick directly into the creeper's chest. The surrounding guards' footing slid, but they held Sembado fast as they watched in wonder at the results of his thunderous strike. The creeper's weak frame had buckled inward, even as it was lifted off its feet and into the air. The body hit the ground with such force that the head whipped back against the floor with a sickening pop. The man's crumpled body lay at the feet of his pack-mates. They were just starting to hiss and spit and yell obscenities at Sembado's team, but they became distracted with the available flesh that had just been delivered at their feet. Sembado and his team looked on in utter disgust as the pack of creepers started to rend the meat right from their brother's bones. They were so busy fighting and clawing at each other that they did not notice Sembado and his guards approaching with haste. In just a few bloody, poorly lit moments, the creepers had been dispatched. Sembado asked Kaluna to hold the others back while he and the guards aligned the creepers' corpses off to one side of the passage. They tried to block the view of the creepers' bodies as Kaluna, the children, and the other adults passed. But despite their best effort to shield the children's view of the bodies, Sembado and his guards did not realize how much blood spray, strife, and struggle they wore on their grizzly faces, which were perfectly showcased by the lantern's glow. The terrified children remained inconsolable for several hours as the troop stumbled into the cool, tense darkness.

Part Two
Free Will

Chapter Thirteen
Death Race

Without the ambient light to transition from day to night, Sembado and Kaluna's group had lost track of when they were sleeping and when they were moving. They continued to take regular breaks to eat, sleep, and relieve themselves, but Sembado was convinced that they were making better progress than they had in the sun's glaring heat. Even on the third day when they had encountered three more groups of ghostly vagabonds, Sembado insisted that this was the wiser path. He believed it in his heart, but each attack made convincing the others increasingly more difficult. The third day also marked the first time they had passed a branch tunnel. It disappeared into inky blackness on the north side of the main passage. Just a few more hours of travel had them pass through three additional forks in the path. Each time, they stayed to the right as their tunnel moved ever eastward.

The fourth day in the tunnels found their spirits slightly recovered. The team's eyes had completely adjusted to the darkness and they had not encountered any creepers for twenty-four hours. They noticed also that the path was undulating more than usual. Sembado hung his lantern low to his feet to investigate the uneven terrain. The sandy floor carried strange tracks that ran in parallel lines down the length of the passage. They were nearly geometric in appearance, regular and uniform. The adults guessed at the cause quietly between one another but no one could formulate a reasonable conclusion for the strange, repetitive marks. The pattern continued down the passage until it abruptly swerved to one side and then into a perpendicular tunnel that branched off to the north. The travelers gathered at the intersection and puzzled over the nature of the zigzagged design.

Sembado exchanged a bewildered look with Kaluna; her face wore a more troubled expression. Just as he was about to address her concerned look, a soft brushing sensation tickled his shoulder. He craned his neck to see a small amount of sand had fallen from the ceiling and was accumulating on his shoulder. He looked up at where the sand had fallen. The trickle of fine grains had stopped cascading from between the ceiling planks for just a moment. Sembado stared at the leaking cracks with curiosity. He felt a weak rumble inside the passage and the sand began to fall anew. Again the sand stopped but another soft pulse of air pressure and a faint buzzing noise caused the trickle to begin. The other nearby adults were just as captivated as Sembado as they stood and stared at the shower of sand. The sound of the vibrations grew in pitch until it was a steady, gritty whine. Sembado looked down slowly from the ceiling as the sound grew louder still. It emanated from the tunnel that branched to the north. He peered in vain into the darkness, holding his little lantern as high as he could. The light lit the next ten feet but then something else glimmered beyond that. Sembado squinted into the deep dark blackness until he saw it. A bright light that grew larger. He instinctively retreated, grabbing the arms of the nearest bodies and pushing them away from the northerly tunnel. The noise grew louder with the lights. Sembado turned and ushered his people away from the approaching light.

"Grab the children," he called, "and start running east!"

He waited until everyone else had passed before completely turning his back on the light and breaking into a run himself. The sandy floor shifted and slipped under the beating feet. The already stifling air filled with dust and grit as they ran away from the ever-growing threat. The bouncing lantern light painted the passage walls in shadows of chaos, haste, and fear. The flashing patterns the lights made were almost nauseating. Through the turmoil, Sembado could just barely see that the next three people that ran ahead of him were all armed guardians.

"Timm," Sembado called out to the young father who had stabbed the crazy hermit in the face. "I need your spear!"

Timm continued running, the glow from the pursuer's light just starting to highlight his neck and back.

"Timm, please!" Sembado shouted.

A muffled thud indicated that Timm had dropped the spear to the ground without slowing his sprinting gait.

Sembado nearly tripped over the wooden pole but was able to grab it with one hand just as he skidded to a stop. He turned to face the light, which had split into two ghostly orbs that careened toward him. He bounced the spear off his hand, finding its balance point while he firmly planted his bionic foot. The lights drew nearer as the echo of the growling bedlam climbed to a painful crescendo. Sembado tensed his body all at once before taking one small hop and launching the spear with all the strength his body could muster and all the power his prosthetic would supply. The spear sailed forward, nearly forty feet, and stuck just above the two beaming circles with a wet pop. A terrible shrieking noise, like a dying animal, reverberated down the tunnel as the lights swerved back and forth before driving straight into the wall of the tunnel. A tremendous boom echoed down the passage; copious amounts of sand rained down from the ceiling. Sembado stumbled backwards as he retreated from the calamity. He slowly climbed to his feet as he acknowledged the uncomfortable ringing that filled his ears. He shuffled forward to retrieve the spear from its target. A small fire flickered to life as a thick, acrid smell met Sembado's nose. The flames were still meager but their light was enough to highlight the thick smoke that climbed to the ceiling of the passage and immediately started spreading back over Sembado's head. In the light of the growing fire, Sembado could see the twisted framework of some kind of vehicle. Its ruggedly treaded tires were as mangled as the crumpled corpse that lay across the handle bars. His face was twisted and obscured. The spear lay buried halfway through his chest. Sembado gave the sharpened wooden pole one apprehensive tug before abandoning the smoky scene but he had to pause just feet away and hack out the soot that filled his mouth and throat. Sembado gagged and wretched as a nasty, gooey mucous clung to the base of his tongue. Tears filled his eyes and his powered prosthetic hummed. Suddenly, half a dozen hands grabbed Sembado's arms and neck. He tried to kick away, but was barely able to breathe.

"Sembado, stop," Kaluna called. "We're trying to get you outta here. We need to move!"

Kaluna and the others struggled to drag Sembado the nearly one hundred feet to fresher air. His powered prosthetic kicked and thrashed all the way. The wireless transceiver at the base of his neck was sending his leg all the wild, anxiety inducing messages that ran through his brain as he fought to breathe and see. The burning sensation that his prosthetic's power supply inflicted on his left thigh had just surpassed the discomfort of his eyes and lungs. His bionic appendage's overactive motion was actually searing his flesh for the first time in weeks. Sembado cried out as the others continued to struggle with his oscillating mass. He felt the practical half of his consciousness fight through the animalistic reflexes of his human instinct.

You can do something about this, you idiot. The prosthetic is your slave, not your master!

128

Sembado lifted his hand to the back of his neck; he had to weasel it in between the arms of those who dragged him. His hand blindly wrestled with the strap that held the transceiver tight against the back of his neck. Finally, he found the Velcro fastener and with one firm yank, he freed himself from the electronic torment. The choker and transceiver assembly lay limp in his hand; his bionic leg followed suit. It immediately collapsed against the dirt floor and the others were able to quicken their pace, dragging Sembado away from the burning vehicle and the charred corpse that lay across it.

Fresher air began to fill Sembado's lungs as the concerned tone of the children's whining could be heard just ahead; they had caught up with the others. At Sembado's emphatic request, the others stood him up on his right leg and allowed him to help as two of the men propped him up on their shoulders. Sembado's irritated eyes could just make out Kaluna's silhouette in the murky lantern light. She gave him one last stony grimace before turning ahead and trotting up to the front of the pack. Their travelling party moved ahead with desperate purpose. Despite the continued ringing in his ears, Sembado could still hear a muffled version of the undulating roar of some other distant vehicle. The climbing pitch seemed to have a direct relationship with the speed and desperation with which the party fled. Sembado tried to block out the panic inducing fear and uncertainty that betrayed his reason, heart rate, and focus. Through all his pain and muddled senses, a single discomfort stuck out to him: the muscles in his right calf and thigh were burning with cramping pain. With his bionic limb dragging dead in the dirt, it became uncomfortably clear how much of the load the powered leg normally provided. Sembado's right leg had been slowly atrophying with the left leg's mechanical might slowly compensating more and more. Sembado tried to play his part but soon his right leg completely seized and he reluctantly accepted more help. Two more men were called to lift and carry his legs so that his body was outstretched between four of his compatriots.

The pulsing scream of the pursuing vehicle multiplied to two and then three. Sembado and Kaluna's team was being driven like a herd of prey; their feet pounded the earthen floor harder by the minute. Sembado craned his neck from his uncomfortable perch and looked around to see the growing glow of the tunnel's end. The smoky haze had thinned but was spreading so that its ghostly presence stretched its crooked fingers across the promising conclusion that lay ahead.

One by one, the children were picked up as their little legs failed to keep pace. The light of the tunnel's end grew to a glaring reflection on the curving passage walls. They rounded one last corner and Sembado's eyes were dazzled by a blinding white beam that shined from beyond. The team slowed to a near stop as the blinding sunlight overwhelmed their eyes. Their stumbling gait made only humble progress but the din of the chasing engines had nearly died as well. Sembado leaned his head back over the shoulders of the men who carried him. Even with his vision bouncing and inverted, he could distinctly make out the sight of one of their pursuers peaking the nose of his all-terrain vehicle around the last bend. The hood and fenders were highlighted bright, oxidized orange in the glaring sunlight. The rider contorted his twisted, sallow face against the bright daylight; another rider had just joined his side.

Sembado and Kaluna's team slowly moved out into the sunlight. The warmth and brightness were overwhelming, but welcomed after the cold and claustrophobic tunnel network. Sembado held his eyes shut against the sun which beat directly down on his face. Even behind his tightly clenched eyelids, the white circle danced and multiplied into blue and yellow orbs that haunted his mind's eyes. Sembado stole a glance at the entrance of the tunnel. At this distance, it was but a funny little hole in the side of a rocky ridge. He could not see the men who chased them but a steady black chain of smoke was already rising out of the tunnel; it stretched straight up in the stagnant desert air.

Kaluna led the team to another collection of boulders nearby. It was covered in shady crevasses. Sembado's rear view afforded him the chance to watch the smoke steadily grow darker and heavier. It climbed into the sky and slowly spread so that it took on the appearance of a giant black funnel. Suddenly, the vehicles and their riders blasted out of the opening. They rocketed forward, one performing an acrobatic flight as he zoomed away from the sooty mess. They roared their engines and zigzagged as they gained their bearings as well as the current location and heading of Sembado and Kaluna's party.

Kaluna and the others were just getting the children settled in behind the larger rocks in the mound while Sembado's carriers deposited him at the foot of the incline. One of the men helped him hobble to the top while the others were handed extra weapons and prepared for the worst. The riders circled the base of the rocky hill and revved their engines loudly. One produced a rusty chain and whipped it around his head carelessly. It bounced here and there, sending loose pieces of plastic and rust into the air. Sembado limped to where Kaluna sat. He consulted with her as briefly as he could; the surrounding attackers exhibited more menacing behaviors by the minute.

"We must do something," Kaluna called over the racket of the engines. "We can't just sit here and wait to be picked!"

"Do we even have anything for a barricade?" Sembado replied. The transceiver necklace dangled in his clenched fist.

"Barricade?" Kaluna scoffed. "We're out in the wide open! We need a deekin' counter assault, Sem!"

Their armed comrades made a commotion as the chain-wielding rider began creeping the front wheels of his engine up the lowest crag. They tried to fend him off with their spears and axes but he stood vertically on a sturdy set of pegs and swung the chain around his head with one hand, cracking it off the front of his vehicle. He goosed the throttle with the other hand, making the vehicle hop up and down angrily. The jolting rubber tires startled one of Sembado's defenders. The young man lost his purchase; his legs kicked out from under him and he landed hard on his lower back. The attacking rider wasted no time, swinging his body around the side of the vehicle and lashing out with the chain. His first strike lay across the fallen man's chest and ribs with a sickeningly hollow whack. The immobilized man was barely able to get his arm up in defense when the second blow arrived. The chain wrapped around the fallen man's forearm just as the attacker backed his vehicle off the rocks, dragging his victim off the ledge to land in a dusty heap. Two others jumped down to their cohort's rescue but the jeering riders were already closing in.

Sembado watched from above, helpless, while Kaluna tried calling out commands to the others. He looked around for anything that could ease their current predicament.

An escape! Anything!

Below, the riders had kicked all three men to the ground. They struck and beat them relentlessly. Blood was flung high into the air. The women and children screamed. Sembado averted his view from the sickening scene that played out against his will. When he did look, a glaring bright light shot painfully across his eyes. He raised his arm to block the sun but the glare continued. It was then that he realized that the dazzling beam was coming from the ground. He squinted his eyes and looked harder. A handful of sparkling reflections was racing across the sparse desert rockscape, a streaming cloud of dust swirling in their wake. The dust cloud paled in comparison to the ever expanding black plume that still billowed from the hidden passage. The bright reflections appeared larger as they drew closer. Some veered back and forth in the sand. Their pursuing dust clouds wiggled in response.

A blood curdling scream won the battle for Sembado's focus as he looked back at the unraveling scene below. The three men who were being beaten had succumbed to their wounds and lay limp and lifeless while their attackers moved on to terrorizing the women, children, and other men who sought shelter in the rocks. The remaining warriors made a valiant effort as their smoke-stained assailants drew ever closer.

The glimmering sun spots dazzled Sembado's eyes yet again. To his horror, they had quickly transformed into additional roughly built vehicles which hopped and swerved across the terrain. More striking was the silence with which the new vehicle arrived, even as they approached a dangerously close distance. Sembado and Kaluna instinctively grabbed each other's hands as the new vehicles quickly approached the explosive scene at hand.

The warriors, the children, and the rocks they desperately cowered behind were suddenly illuminated by the sunlight that had refracted off of the new vehicles. Large white spots of light swirled across their terrified faces. The attackers took notice, craning their necks around in an instant.

The riders of the reflective vehicles stood up out of the open framed tops with weapons drawn. Each held a rugged looking assault rifle. One of them stood on the back half of the vehicle and manned what appeared to be a small cannon which was mounted on the chassis.

"Mind freaks," one of the smoky attackers yelled, the pinkness of his tongue and mouth were highlighted against his dark and sooty face. He scurried to the nearest vehicle and quickly mounted it.

The call was repeated until the entire troop of bandits was made aware of the new arrivals. The soot covered men had not even clamored half way to their rides when the shooting erupted.

Sembado furrowed his brow at the sound but watched in wide-eyed awe, horror, and disbelief as each bullet struck its target. They popped with a flash of blue, leaving one foot spherical cavities in their place. A quick and noisy barrage reduced the attacking men to a pile of indiscernible body parts. One of the shooters whistled and pointed. The first attacker to retreat had already motored his vehicle a hundred yards away. The man that controlled the large, mounted power rifle immediately took aim, trained his weapon in a slow leading arc, and fired three rounds in rapid succession. The third shot made contact with a brilliant blue orb engulfing the entire vehicle. The escaping motorist suddenly ceased to exist. His ride veered off to the right and rolled to a stop.

Sembado and his team cowered as they awaited their fate. The shooters turned their rifles quickly but instead of firing on the huddled group, they shared a brief victory call and then got to work surveying the damage.

"You can come down," one of the men called to Sembado and Kaluna's group. "They're all gone."

"Not completely," a rifle-bearing woman jeered, kicking a disembodied leg.

"That's enough, Seyra," the man called as he climbed to the hood of his vehicle to get a better view of the surrounding area. When he seemed sure the horizon was free of more vehicles, he turned his disapproving gaze toward the column of smoke that climbed out of the nearby tunnel. It had died down to a wispy acrid trace. The man shook his head and sneered.

"Disgusting ingrates," he said aloud, spitting on the partial corpse at his feet. "Fossil fuels? What century is this? These barbarians should be thankful that we killed them as humanely as we did. The chemicals put off by those fumes have certainly shortened their life enough that they were already on borrowed time."

Sembado and Kaluna remained at their high perch. She helped him secure him cerebral transceiver and make adjustments to his bionic leg.

"*I didn't think they had those weapons up here,*" Kaluna whispered to Sembado. "*The San Diego Stewards didn't.*"

Sembado merely shrugged his shoulders, a bewildered look on his face. Kaluna responded with a terse gasp, grabbed him by the hand, and led him down to where their followers were slowly introducing themselves to their saviors. Kaluna slid down the last large rock, a drop that was taller than her. Sembado took advantage of his regained mobility, taking a foot-first dive from the ledge and landing skillfully on his prosthetic.

"That's an interesting leg you got there," the leader of the shooters said to Sembado. His tone was more matter-of-fact than Sembado expected, neither disapproving nor confrontational.

"Those are some interesting weapons you got *there*," Kaluna responded.

"More forgiving than theirs," the man said, using his toe to rustle a chain that a severed limb still gripped.

"To an extent," Kaluna responded. "We didn't think they existed up here. Thought they were too technological for the Stewards."

The surrounding gunmen abandoned their tasks to straighten up and stare at the odd little woman who questioned their leader. For his part, the man smirked at Kaluna's candid language and bristling honesty.

"You may be confusing us with our puritan brothers and sisters on the coast," the man said to Kaluna. "These weapons are a means to an end, that's all. They are tools. We neither love nor hate them. We *use* them."

"To kill other people?" Sembado asked boldly, impassioned by the return of the indifferent lethality of the blue spheres.

"A natural order," the man scoffed. "Is that not one of humans' primary purposes? Just because I use advanced weapons does not mean I am devoid of the Stewards' ethos. If human beings do not kill each other, then who will?"

Sembado and Kaluna's followers shuffled and fidgeted nervously while the Stewards returned to scavenging.

"Then why did you stop these marauders from killing us?" Sembado asked.

"We didn't," the man replied with a bemused smile. "We stopped them from using these death machines and pumping their unwanted soot into the atmosphere. Why, we could see that column of smoke from miles away. You're lucky really. If we hadn't seen the smoke, half of you would be dead by now. But that's just the cold, hard truth…"

"That can't be your only justification for saving us," Kaluna replied, scornfully interrupting the man's cocky quip. "That's *ridiculous*."

He looked at Kaluna and sighed.

"Of course we were meaning to save you. Seeders are necessary in maintaining homeostasis and biodiversity. But I need you to understand that our use of these guns and powered vehicles does not make our commitment to protect our flora and fauna any weaker. If anything, it allows us to weed and prune more efficiently than our seaside cousins. Do you understand?"

"Yes," Sembado replied, staying Kaluna's response with a firm touch of her shoulder. They redirected their attention to their mourning followers. Every man, woman, and child knelt over the bodies of their slain defenders. The gruesome nature of the injuries made the horrors of the tunnels a distant, tolerable memory.

The Stewards allowed them just enough time to dig shallow graves for their brothers. A pile of loose stones completed the hasty burials. All three men left widows behind, one a grieving child. Little Tillie was inconsolable for the remainder of the day.

Chapter Fourteen
Autumnal Equinox

The solar powered Stewards provided Sembado and Kaluna's traveling party guidance and protection for the rest of the day. In the early twilight, they came to the rolling Colorado River, just like old Titus had described. The Stewards were greeted kindly by their ford-guarding brethren. Sembado and Kaluna's posse was observed with indifference. The Stewards conferred with each other quietly. Sembado looked on awkwardly as he was sure they were openly discussing his leg. After they appeared to reach some kind of agreement, the leader of the motorized regiment returned to Sembado and Kaluna.

"You will camp on this side of the river tonight," he said. "You will be permitted to cross in the morning. We will stay as well so that we do not drain our cells."

"That will be fine," Sembado said coolly. "By the way, I don't think I ever caught your name," he added, extending his hand.

"I don't think I ever gave it," the man replied dryly. He spun around without further remark and returned to his private discussion with the river guards.

"I don't think I *want* it," Kaluna whispered in Sembado's ear.

He laughed it off but could not deny the burning heat of rejection, thankful that the light of the setting sun would obscure his reddening embarrassment.

"Let's get the group ready for sleep and watch," he replied, thankfully accepting Kaluna's reassuring embrace.

***

The next morning was a flurry of activity. The group was roused just as the sun was creeping over the horizon. No special attention or accommodation was spared for the children. The Stewards practically pushed and prodded the harried travelers right up to the river's bank.

A heavy, braided rope had been suspended between the two sides, each attached to a heavy, round post. Its catenary curve swung and swayed in the breeze. Below it, a line of small boulders had been rolled into the rushing water at even spaces so that the water crashed and flowed around their ever smoothing curves.

Sembado took the lead, gripping the rope with both hands as he carefully shuffled his feet forward: first the natural one, and then its bionic mate.

"Best load the rope with no more'n five," one of the river guards shouted. "N' that's includin' child'n!"

Sembado heard the man clearly but struggled to respond with much more than a clumsy head nod. Before he knew it, he was contemplating the first slippery stone. As usual, his bionic leg offered infinitely more control and

141

poise than its biological counterpart, but soon Sembado had scurried across a dozen of the perilous gaps. He glanced back to see the crowd watching in nervous silence. Mera the medic was now inching her way onto the first rock. Sembado continued onward, the need to accommodate the others providing the necessary incentive for him to make meaningful progress. Sembado looked across to the other side. A handful of stewards waited to help him to the other shore; their concerned expressions immediately making them appear more caring and interested than the indifferent river guards on the west side of the water. It was only then that Sembado heard the screaming behind him. When he looked back he realized that the river guards' fretful appearances were due to the medic, Mera, hanging off the rope into the full flow of the river. The man that crossed behind her was hurrying forward as quickly as he could, and called for Sembado's help. Sembado pivoted on his bionic leg and made a reckless dive forward. He maintained a minimal grip on the rope as he sprung ahead again. Each jump cleared two whole intervals between the large rocks. He reached Mera just before the other man, and together they pulled her back onto the rock. The three of them were quite crowded, but Sembado allowed Mera to cower on the rock for a few more minutes before he moved back ahead. He used his jumping technique to reach the far side. His heart rate and temper had only just come up to speed. The awaiting stewards tried to help him onto the sandy bank, but he refused their assistance, choosing instead to turn and guide

Mera to a dry, safe footing. She clung to Sembado in sopping desperation, relenting only when the stewards peeled her white knuckled hands away. Sembado was freed from her frazzled clutches just in time to assist his next follower off of the perilous crossing. One by one, he and his future villagers received their teammates, consoling those who had also taken an unwilling plunge in the unforgiving rapids.

Sembado's chest swelled when he finally saw Kaluna deftly crossing the rocks. Her poise and skill painted his heart with relief, affection, and reverence all at the same time. She had even waited a few beats behind the others so that her crossing was not slowed by their lumbering and nervous pace. Her mouth was clenched firm with concentration but the light in her eyes revealed the true delight that Kaluna's inner spirit took in such a challenge. She was neither scared nor comfortable but she was being forced to actually try. It was a rare treat for a young lady who had seldom been presented with challenges worthy of her talents. The motion of each cat-like spring made Sembado's spirit soar higher and when her first foot was planted on the wet, sandy bank, he reached out to her hand and pulled her in close. She did not resist, choosing instead to embrace him heartily. There damp frames pressed against each other tightly. Sembado could feel the thundering patter of Kaluna's heart as it raced in her chest. Her head was turned to the side and tucked up under his chin; her wet hair felt cool and relieving against the ambient heat. They stayed embraced for several more minutes, using the increasing intervals of Kaluna's breath as a guide for the appropriateness of their interaction. It seemed that Sembado and Kalunas's heart rates were inversely proportionate: the longer they held each other, hers slowed down and his sped up. When they released their grip on one another, Sembado found it quite necessary to spend an elongated moment of solitude near the riverbank, very eager for his arousal to be a little less obvious.

As the excitement of the crossing died down, one of the river guards hailed the traveling party's attention.

"Folks!" a woman called in a loud and husky voice. "On behalf of the village of Yuma, I would like to welcome you all to the territory of Arizona! The challenging river crossing you just conquered represents the first in many trials you will face on your way east. And while I am glad that you all made it, I must emphasize how insignificant it will seem when you compare it to your future endeavors. This was but a small taste of the hardships to come and it would be immoral of me to deceive you in expecting otherwise."

The noise of the rushing river was deafening as a somber hush fell over the group. The woman's face showed remorse for the truth she was liable to bare but she continued on with determined certainty.

"I must speak with your village leaders," she shouted over the raging rapids.

Sembado worked his way to the front of the crowd where Kaluna was already waiting. The woman reached into a loosely woven bag that hung from one shoulder. Its simple, net-like weave was made from colorfully dyed twine, a geometric pattern surrounding a rudimentary rendering of the sun. Out of the bag, she produced a small clipboard, paper, and a stubby charcoal pencil.

"May I have your names, please?" the woman asked. Her words were squeaky and strained, the gravelly nature of her voice was a poor match for the quiet intimacy of the conversation.

Sembado and Kaluna provided their information and the woman quickly poured over her documents.

"Ah, here," she said, pointing to a set of hastily scrawled lines. "You will head to Albuquerque. Do you have a compass?"

Kaluna produced a little round compass attached to a safety pin from her bag.

"Okay," the woman said, "with this one, you get this arrow to line up here. That means you are heading due north. But you'll want to turn it until you're lined up with the '70' there. Do you see that? If you keep it on '70' the whole way, you should run into the refuge just north of Albuquerque. That will be about three more weeks but then you'll be done. That will be your winter destination. They don't send out seeders till the spring," she croaked.

She and her guards allowed Sembado and Kaluna's group a prolonged, late-morning rest due to their troubled crossing.

"It sure can take a lot out of ya, huh?" the hoarse woman asked Mera as they sat in small circles. Kaluna nodded lightly. She sat cross-legged next to Sembado.

"I'm just glad you're okay," Sembado replied, patting Mera on the back. "I don't want to sound selfish but life would have been a lot harder without you."

"No, I get it," Mera said with a faint smile. "It's good to be of use. But I'm not gonna lie, I sure am looking forward to a few months rest in Albuqueque."

"I don't mean to ruin your expectations," the river guard said as she walked by, "but they'll be having you do something all winter, either work or class."

Disappointment spread across Mera's face as she looked down at her food scraps.

"But you're right," the woman added quickly, seeing the discomfort her words had caused. "At least it won't be wandering a desert full of creeps."

They sat in silence for the remainder of their rest. Soon, the river guards called for their attention.

"We are just starting to set eastern shadows," the woman called loudly in her rich, natural timbre. "I'm sorry, but I must insist that you continue on your journey."

"Does it seem like the days are going by faster?" Sembado asked. "Even with all the activity, I feel like this morning rushed by."

"They are getting shorter, Sem," Kaluna replied. "That's what happens as winter approaches."

Sembado leaned his head on Kaluna's shoulder with a deep sigh.

"Oh stop," she whispered. "You have to set an example."

Chapter Fifteen
High Anxiety

As the days quickly passed, Sembado and Kaluna had driven their team steadily eastward and a little north. At first, Sembado obsessively checked the reading on the compass every few minutes but Kaluna eventually convinced him to find a large tree, hill, or other landmark to use as a guide between readings.

The daily temperatures had dropped nearly twenty degrees from the time they entered the tunnels and they had refashioned their clothing around their heads and shoulders for better protection from the sun. Their ability to walk during the day had even allowed for more hunting and trapping but frequent breaks at a nearby river were still required to stay hydrated. Despite their continued hardships, even the children had started to laugh and play again, inventing silly games with dirt clods and brush.

A week into their journey from the river found the ground beginning to change. The ever present cracked dirt and sand began to slope upward ever so slightly. Miles ahead, they now saw the earth climbing up a steady incline. They forged ahead, resting a little longer each night. The brilliant stars kept the night watch company.

Another few days brought an odd silence to the group. Everyone, even the children, had foregone their energetic chatter as their breathing had become more labored. Sembado himself was stricken by frequent dizzy spells and noticed the temperature of his prosthetic slowly climbing as it compensated for his body which had mysteriously started to struggle with the climb. The nauseating disorientation peaked and the entire party agreed to take a day's rest.

Sembado sat under the shade of a large shrub. He teetered in place, moaning, as he struggled to control his breathing, stomach, and equilibrium. Kaluna sat at his side in near silence.

"Do you think it was something we all ate?" Sembado asked. "Or maybe the water? Should we be boiling it? I almost feel hung over."

"Elevation," Kaluna said softly. "I think we may be a lot higher than we think."

"What?" Sembado replied with a wincing grimace, his face contorted by the pain of the day's third headache.

"When I was a little girl, Mahana took me to the peak of Mauna Kea on our big island. It took us two days and when we got to the top, I collapsed. When I woke up, he and the others were happily sitting around a fire but I felt just like this only worse. My stomach and head hurt, I couldn't breathe, and I couldn't stand up. I tried to tell Mahana I was sick and needed to go back down but he told me to rest. I laid against him for a day and a night before I started to feel better but eventually I adjusted just like they had."

"But why is it happening?" Sembado begged, pushing his thumbs against his temples.

"Because the air isn't as thick," Kaluna replied. "Mahana told me it's like going closer to the surface when you're under water. The pressure isn't as bad, right? Air acts the same way as water. When we're down near the ocean, it's as heavy as can be, but when you move up a mountain, it's like getting closer to the surface."

Sembado closed his eyes as they contorted in pain and confusion.

"Well, that's just fascinating," he said sarcastically.

"I think it would be a good idea if we rested a second day," Kaluna suggested. "Especially for the children."

***

Kaluna's prediction came true and within forty-eight hours, every adult had recovered and most of the children were on their way. The smaller children were carried for another day until the intrigue of the hike proved too much for their curiosity.

The continued acclimation slowly nurtured the group's confidence and the children frolicked and reveled in each new discovery as the adults trudged along with carefully guarded optimism.

Despite his followers' defiantly happy dispositions, Sembado found himself in an overpowering funk. After all of the tribulations he had experienced since traveling to the surface with Kaluna, his endearing hope was at its end. While the men and women around him continued to regard their trials as dark exceptions to a normally favorable rule, Sembado began settling into the bitter reality that his life would never be easy again. As the days ticked by, he grew more upset at how pessimistic he had become. He began resenting those around him for enjoying their journey. He even started to experience thoughts of blame toward Kaluna for teaching him how to be distant and jaded.

If it wasn't for her lead, I might still be able to hope for the best. But no. She refuses to enjoy anything. She doesn't know how to just let someone have their ignorant bliss. These people wouldn't know struggle anyway. A few crazy marauders on smoking carts? My opportunities to be disappointed in others started way before we ever breached the surface. The single-minded ideologues that couldn't see past their own egos. The perverted justifications for mass murder and restrictive controls. Personally witnessing those abuses was far more traumatizing than seeing a raving lunatic was for these people. At least the lunatics and madmen are easy to identify. They're strangers and they're bad and if we didn't kill them, they would have hurt us. That's easy. That's black and white. That's justifiable. They don't know what it's like to see the nuances. The personal faces. Faces that have history and meaning and love suddenly betray you. Deranged desert hermits are easy. You can put them in a box. You can compartmentalize that. These people don't know what it's like to be betrayed. They simply saw a civil war and an uprising. They don't know. And even still, here they are as happy as could be. Don't they know this isn't going to last? Don't they know something terrible is always just around the corner? Idiots…

Sembado's face felt tight as the muscles settled into the glowering sneer that his dark thoughts had slowly spread across his face. The days of walking finally brought them the relief of shade offered by some sparse pine trees but each new excitement from the children and others about a new type of tree or animal made Sembado feel even more bitter. He struggled to keep his thoughts from becoming words as he continued finding opportunities to ruin the others' wonder and joy. In a last ditch effort to vent his frustration, he chose instead to move ahead of the group. He kicked off with his powered leg and began trotting through the trees at a measured pace. His prosthetic pushed him forward with quick pumps of energy and he spent the next several days and nights ahead of Kaluna and the others but just within earshot.

The days of solitude proved helpful. Sembado's quiet reflection on himself, Kaluna, and the others made him realize that he alone was responsible for his outlook on life and that he should be happy for the others for being as delightfully unaware as he used to be. After much thought, hard truths and a remorseful spirit brought him back to the group. Or rather, he slowed his pace until they could catch up with him. The other adults kept a respectful distance while Sembado and Kaluna quickly found themselves walking beside one another.

"I'm sorry for being so…actually distant the past few days," Sembado said quietly.

"It's okay," Kaluna replied. "I didn't want to be around you while you pouted anyways."

Sembado scoffed in protest but he turned to see Kaluna was actually wearing a smirk.

"Oh, come on," she said. "If I had to apologize every time I was acting aloof, then it's all I would do."

Sembado emitted an involuntary, loving chuckle at her candidness.

"Just don't leave me back here with the adults again, huh? The kids I can handle," Kaluna joked, reaching out for Sembado's hand.

"Yeah, sure," he replied, squeezing her hand lightly.

***

Fair weather and favorable conditions continued to follow the travelling party as they approached what they believed to be the last few days of their journey. The ever increasing pine tree cover had also allowed for extended days of travel as the fatigue of the sun had been significantly reduced.

"Well, this is day twenty-one," Kaluna said, as she, Sembado, and a few others peered down into the next valley from a high, rocky ledge.

"What about that over there?" one of the men called, pointing off to the distance.

Indeed, a small wisp of smoke could be seen trailing out of the hilly landscape as it floated up into the deep azure heavens above. Sembado and Kaluna double checked the compass and confirmed that the position of the smoke made sense with where they thought they should be going.

Even Sembado and Kaluna could not contain their excitement as they passed more and more signs and evidence of recent human activity. As the day slowly faded to evening, the number of smoke plumes quickly multiplied ahead and to their periphery. With one last exhilarating thrill, Sembado and Kaluna crested the next slope with just enough dying daylight to feast their eyes on the sprawling sanctuary as it stretched into the foothills where Albuquerque once stood.

Chapter 16
The Larder And The Forbidden Beyond

Sembado and Kaluna marched forward into the village of small tents and adobe lodges that were bathed with the bluish white light of the full October moon. Their followers were close behind, the children guarded in the center of the pack. Groups of four or five villagers were gathered around most of the fires. They regarded Sembado's clan curiously but did not appear concerned. Two young boys rushed by from one camp to another. Their crowing laughter echoed into the twilight as a brisk night chill settled over the refuge of travelers. The novelty of their surroundings started to fade as Sembado, Kaluna, and the others started to question where they were going and to whom they needed to speak.

Just then, a small pack of horsemen came thundering in from the wild. They slowed their mounts to a trot as they passed the encampments. Seeing Sembado and Kaluna's group wandering aimlessly, one of the horsemen peeled off to meet them.

"Ya'll the new seeders?" he called in a light, boyish voice. He used an accent that Sembado had never heard

155

before. It was some kind of slow drawl. It seemed to match his awkward combination of long, tangled hair and high cut bangs.

"Yes," Sembado stated clearly.

"Come around here then," the man said, turning his horse about and leading them off in a new direction. The funky stench of rough alcohol wafted in the air behind him.

They walked north along the base of the mountains with the ridge on their right. The moonlight highlighted every crack and crevice on the western slope so that the rocky incline appeared nearly polka dotted. The young man led them up a gravel path incline and into a thicker copse of trees. At the top, there was a clearing with a cul-de-sac of log cabins. There were ten in all. One of the chimneys had a steady stream of smoke rising from it. The orange flicker of firelight danced in one small window.

"Looks like they're all at Caspen's there," the horseman said, pointing to the illuminated cabin. "Ya'll can go knock. He likes to meet the new seeders when they arrive. He'll get ya a place to settle in. There're only two spaces left. Guess that means only one more group of seeders before the cold comes. Well, go on then and knock. My name is Churlen but everyone calls me Chut. Welcome to the Larder. See ya'll around. I gotta be gettin' my horse up for the night."

The young man named Chut trotted his horse back down the gravel slope as Sembado and Kaluna approached the front door of the cabin. Just as they reached the stoop, the door jerked open. A small group of people stood inside, preparing to leave.

"Oh!" a man in the doorway said. "You must be the new seeders. Welcome! Oh, was that Chut? I needed to talk to him. Oh, just a moment please."

He quickly tended to his guests as they worked their way out of the cabin. Each man and woman greeted Sembado and Kaluna as they squeezed past. Their cordial salutations continued out into the moonlight as they greeted the rest of the travelling party.

"Hello," the man said again, extending an open hand to Sembado and then Kaluna. The firelight behind him highlighted his mop of curly blonde hair, giving it the appearance of looped wheat. "My name is Pluto Caspenelli," the man stated, "but Caspen is just fine."

"You folks are keen on nicknames, huh?" Sembado quipped before he could catch himself. Caspen laughed in response but mostly because Kaluna had given Sembado a quick cuff on the arm.

"Just me and Chut actually," Caspen replied with a smile. "Everyone else seems content with what their mother's gave them. Speaking of which! I'm sorry but I still don't know what to call you."

"I'm Sembado Grey and this is my..." Sembado stuttered awkwardly as he tried to think of the appropriate expression for his and Kaluna's relationship.

"My name is Kaluna Kalani," Kaluna interrupted, returning Caspen's firm handshake.

"A beautiful name for a beautiful girl," Caspen replied with a smile.

Kaluna's neutral expression showed neither distaste nor flattery. It was as if she hadn't even heard him. Sembado avoided eye contact with everyone.

"Yes, well," Caspen recovered skillfully, "as is tradition for our seeders on their first night, you all will be staying as our guests here on the Circle. It appears your party is already being divvied up among my neighbors. You two are welcome to stay with me."

Kaluna remained silent.

"Uh, yeah. That will be just fine," Sembado said quickly. "Thank you for your hospitality."

"Well, after a long journey and all the hard work ahead of you, the least we can do is give you one night of creature comforts. The others will be accommodated in kind. Please come in!"

Caspen led them into the cabin. The humble outer appearance belied the warm and spacious interior with an ample great room and roughhewn doors to other rooms on two walls. A large fireplace composed entirely of hardened mud glowed bright orange at the far end of the space. Beautifully crafted tables and chairs were positioned in a ring around the center of the room.

"You'll have to pardon the clutter," Caspen said, grunting with labor as he reorganized the dense furniture. "Our weekly gathering was concluding just as you arrived."

"Discussing where we will be shipped off to next?" Kaluna asked casually as she moved between the cushioned chairs.

"No, not yet," Caspen chuckled. "We've already sent out the last wave of seeders for the year. That was back in July. But they're planning on settling pretty close. North Texas if I can remember right. No, the rest of you are staying the winter. We're expecting the last group a couple weeks behind you all actually."

Kaluna did not respond but continued to move around the room. She stopped to look over the small trinkets and knick knacks that cluttered the mantle.

Sembado helped Caspen return the furniture to its rightful layout before they both took their seats across from one another. Sembado hadn't leaned back in a cushioned chair since he was in a submarine. The soft support of the chair cupped his back in a way that made his head feel distant and weightless. He took a long moment to savor the pain-free luxury.

"I don't think this is what we were expecting," he said quietly with his eyes just barely closed.

"Well, of course not," Caspen replied. "Most of the seeders are out there in tents. If you're lucky, you'll get one of the mud huts that were built by some of the more ambitious travelers. These are the only cabins for over a hundred miles."

"And why the special exception?" Kaluna asked, walking over to take a seat next to Sembado.

"There's no exception," Caspen replied, stretching his arms out along the back of the loveseat that he was sprawled across. "You are welcome to build one of these when you get to your settlement sight. You just can't have one here. The cabins here on the Circle are home to the only permanent residents of the Larder."

"We heard that before," Kaluna said. "Why is it called that? What does it mean?"

"A larder is an old name for a store cupboard. A pantry. This place is like a larder for villagers. We have all the ingredients to make a successful village and successful villagers. We also have the recipe," he added with a wink.

"But didn't we go through all that in San Diego?" Sembado replied.

"San Diego?" Caspen laughed. "Those people are living a dream. They don't know what we do out here. How we make their fantasy come to life. They don't have to worry about the cold or the heat or even preserving food for a dry season. Now, don't get me wrong. We're still living our simple life and I have patrols holding the villages accountable year round, but we're going to teach you real skills and real lessons. We're not going to waste your time teaching you some hokey catch phrases."

Kaluna exchanged a look with Sembado that bordered on bemusement. He did not respond but sat quietly and actively enjoyed his plush accommodations while he still could.

"You both look very tired," Caspen concluded, rising from the loveseat. "Let me show you to a spare bed."

Kaluna got up first with Sembado reluctantly prying himself from the exceedingly comfortable chair. They followed Caspen to one of the doors across the room. He opened it with a slow creak to reveal a quaint little bedroom that was dimly lit by a small lantern and the excess light from the hearth behind them. The lantern sat on a tall, slender, three-legged stool. The stool stood next to a log-built four post bed. It had two round pillows and a series of light animal hides.

"I think this will do," Caspen said warmly. "It certainly accommodated my wife and I."

"Where is she?" Sembado asked innocently.

"Uh, she passed away a few years ago," Caspen stated matter-of-factly, "giving birth to our son."

"Oh, I'm sorry, I didn't..." Sembado stuttered.

"Oh, you're fine," Caspen said with a sigh. "That's how life is here, these days. It's not all creature comforts and cozy chairs. Remember that."

He took another minute to situate Sembado and Kaluna before bidding them a good night.

***

The next morning found long lines at the cabins' outhouses but the women and girls were especially excited to have somewhere to sit down with privacy. The citizens of the Circle served a hearty and generous breakfast out of a sprawling outdoor kitchen. Fresh chicken eggs and a mild green salsa were another welcomed treat after over a month of roots and charred jack rabbit meat.

Afterward, Caspen led Sembado, Kaluna, and their followers back down the hill to the main encampment while his neighbors cleaned up.

"This could be every day for you if you really work hard," Caspen said as he, Sembado, and Kaluna walked ahead of the rest of the group. "Now, it sounds like you all will end up somewhere with an actual winter. That has its pros and cons just like anything else. You're going to have some rough months where this will seem like paradise. But you will also be allotted seeds, chickens, and a few other things that those coastal dreamers see as unfair. I'll warn you though: looking after chickens and crops can be just as much work as hunting and gathering. It certainly takes more planning and organization."

"I have to be honest," Sembado said as they walked out from under the pines' shade. The sun warmed his skin as it broke through the cloudy ceiling above. "You seem so much more easygoing than the woman who runs San Diego. No offense to her."

"Who, Mereth?" Caspen laughed.

"Do you know her well?" Kaluna asked.

"And then some," Caspen said, rolling his eyes. "She pretty much raised me. With that meat-head Cistern always nipping at my heels."

"He's running patrols up and down the coast now," said Sembado.

"Oh, I know," Caspen replied. "He was just a kid when I left but, dear God, he was obsessed. He hated the fact that I didn't want the patrols and that Mereth would allow a rule-bender like me to move all the way out here. He acts like those damn patrols are so important, like he was chosen for that. But Mereth has told me straight up that she only distracts him with that because he wouldn't be able to handle his own village."

"Whatta ya mean, rule-bender?" Kaluna asked.

Caspen looked around to see how far back the followers were. His expression became a little more serious as he leaned into Sembado and Kaluna's personal space. "The thing I don't think Mereth and her henchmen understand," Caspen whispered, "is that you don't *have* to make your followers bend to your will around the clock. It's just unnecessary stress, right?"

Sembado nodded his head in agreement. Kaluna reserved her judgement.

"I mean, look," Caspen continued in a hurried whisper, his pale yellow locks bouncing like golden ringlets in the sun. "What's the point? You two come from the ocean cities, right?"

Again, Sembado nodded while Kaluna remained silent.

"So then you know what it's like to have authoritarians breathing down your necks all the time. Did that make you any…*better* of a citizen? Did it make you choose to do it their way or *have* to do it their way? That's how Mereth is running things with her enforcers on the coast. All muscle, all the time. Now, being from where you're from, you are

163

more than familiar with the kind of technology that can be used to keep an eye on people. Again, I'm not talking about controlling them. Just making sure they're doing what you've asked them to...and nothing more."

Sembado and Kaluna exchanged a concerned look that Caspen seemed to anticipate.

"Oh, come on," he said with hushed exasperation. "Even Mereth and her goons are using drones out there. I'm the one that suggested them. That's most of what I'm talking about. But where they have adopted a purist opinion on stewarding, me and my folks have a more realistic approach."

Sembado gave Caspen an intrigued look but the procession had already worked its way down into the sprawling encampment. Caspen was forced to quickly curtail his persuading, choosing instead to greet the friendlier inhabitants who approached to say hello.

***

Sembado and Kaluna's travelling party was assigned a sector of the camp and given some rudimentary supplies to establish themselves for the winter. Additional goods were shipped in weekly and any additional needs were met with donations from the other campers. Their neighboring settlers were all kind and approachable, and the children found an army of playmates.

Volunteers for a search team were sent to find the last of the winter seeders but, after two weeks, the effort was abandoned. News of scattered belongings came in through the network of mountain scouts.

The adults were put on rotating duties and by November 1, Sembado and Kaluna's followers were among the most adjusted and helpful of the newcomers. Sembado was happy to see them thrive on the purpose provided by the Larder but he noticed that he and especially Kaluna were not spending as much time with the villagers as he thought they should. The two of them were encouraged to spend more time with the other village leaders, but there still seemed to be some kind of cultural barrier, even with the leaders that came from the Complex. Besides Kaluna, the only other person Sembado could really find a connection with was Caspen. His candid honesty was a breath of fresh air from the double talking Sembado had encountered within the rest of the Steward movement.

He rose early one brisk November morning to meet with Caspen before the day's activities were underway. They met in the Circle where the cabin dwellers were eating breakfast. Caspen led Sembado down a path he had never been down. It led out of the back of the Circle and further into the piney grove.

"I don't know," Sembado said as they walked along. The pine needles cracked and popped underfoot. "I try to be honest and direct with the other village leaders about my past and how I feel about unnecessary rules. You know, the kind of stuff that you've said about Mereth and Cistern, but they don't seem to quite understand or, at the very least, they are pretending to play dumb or something. It makes me feel isolated and distant. Kaluna's even worse."

"I can imagine," Caspen said dryly. "You know, you two have a unique perspective on things. You played such a special role in liberating the Complex and have had so many encounters that the others couldn't even imagine. Your view of reality is raw and pure."

Morning song birds swooped overhead and chattered happily from the branches as Caspen seemed to choose his next words carefully.

"Sembado, I do things differently than Mereth," said Caspen. "The part you played in that uprising was intimidating to Mereth. It made her suspicious of your intentions. But it doesn't scare me. If anything, I am intrigued. But people like her don't get intrigued. They get scared. They are afraid of losing control or of their rules falling apart. That someone will color outside the lines. But I'm different. There are things that I allow people to have and do that would make her hair stand on end."

The trees ahead were increasingly marked by posted signs. Caspen led Sembado past them, each one carrying a similar warning:

DO NOT PASS – RESTRICTED AREA – TURN BACK

Caspen continued talking as they approached a gate which interrupted a wire fence. It continued into the woods on either side of the gate.

"You'll find that the world is so full of extremes," he said as he lifted the gate latch and led Sembado forward. As they moved through the opening, a quick crunching of pine needles produced a mounted marksman who swiftly rode out of nowhere. His weatherworn poncho billowed in the breeze.

"Yo, there, Caspen," the man called. "Just keepin' watch."

"Thank you, Gordo," Caspen replied. "Just giving a tour."

The concerned look did not fade from the man named Gordo's dark face. His bristly black mustache accentuated the downturned shape of his mouth. He continued watching Caspen and Sembado until they were out of sight.

"Down in the Complex, you people were obsessed with technology and instant gratification," Caspen continued. "Out on the coast, they only live for the day and swear off anything that makes life easy. Well, I'm not a huge fan of extremes. I prefer some balance in life, don't you agree?"

Sembado nodded in the affirmative as he followed Caspen through a thicket of dense vegetation.

"I thought so," Caspen continued. "You understand what it takes to survive. You know that committing yourself to one path only limits your options. But here's where I'm coming from: I don't want to be a good steward because of the warm fuzzies it gives me inside or because I think it's my solemn duty. I want to be a good steward because it's a means to an end. A way to survive."

Caspen pushed through the final branches of low hanging brush and held them back so that Sembado could pass as well. As Sembado pushed past, he found himself on the edge of a large clearing. A hundred yards, away there were dozens of neatly organized structures: large wooden buildings with solar arrays on each roof.

"What...what is this?" Sembado asked.

"This is what I want for you," Caspen replied. "All the rest of those village leaders will go off to form some struggling tribe and beat rocks against rocks until they can claw their way to some semblance of a society and village. But you and Kaluna are different. You know this is all a game. It's always a game. Just with different players and by a different name."

"But what are these buildings?" Sembado asked pointedly.

"Some grow food. Some make power. Some house workers," Caspen said casually.

"But that's way more room than a hundred villagers," Sembado said.

"Are you serious?" Caspen laughed. "Have you been listening? Forget the one hundred cap. Those random rules don't apply to guys like you and me. We know we can't over populate like before, but village population caps? That's just a way for the coastal extremists to scare their followers into submission. Do you think I could do what I need to do here without this? House all these people for four months while we wait for the north to thaw? Where do you think those *shipments* of food are coming from? You think those are care packages from Mereth?"

"I guess I assumed you were trading with the village networks," Sembado said, shrugging his shoulders.

"How?" Caspen asked impatiently. "Even the villages that are *allowed* to farm and preserve are only just making ends meet when they play by the rules. They don't have anything to spare. There isn't a single other settlement like mine in the world. Not that I know of. I have no one to trade with so I have to make it for myself. For all of those travelers. But all that is gonna change."

Sembado stared out in awe at Caspen's ambitious ingenuity. He looked back to see that Caspen had his hand extended for a handshake.

"Come on," Caspen said. "This is the easiest decision you've ever had to make."

Sembado looked down at the extended hand.

"Caspen," Sembado said smugly, "I'm afraid you're right."

Chapter 17
Not So Friendly Fire

Sembado tried to explain every detail of his conversation with Caspen to Kaluna as they ate dinner that night but no matter how hard he tried, she did not seem to agree with their conclusion.

"I'm also annoyed that you didn't even think to bring me along," Kaluna said under her breath as the racket of the nearby camps echoed off the surrounding hills. "Did you really think I wouldn't care to be included?"

"I don't know," Sembado said softly. "I guess I just thought...I don't know what I was thinking. It was just something I wanted to ask him and I didn't realize he was going to take me to that other camp."

"It sounds like a lot more than a camp," Kaluna said bitterly. "And how are we supposed to move all those people and resources without alerting those that aren't in on it?"

"I...I don't know," Sembado said.

"Are all of those workers in on this?" Kaluna asked more pointedly.

"I don't know," Sembado said forcefully.

"Don't snap at me," Kaluna scolded. "You're the one that's not thinking this through."

"You've always got the right idea, don't you?" Sembado asked, his frustrations boiling over. "You always have it figured out! Everything and everyone!"

He stood up quickly with his last assertion, his spark of anger shooting his prosthetic up harder than he intended. The fiery outburst drew the attention of the surrounding campers. Before Kaluna could protest further, Sembado stomped away.

He quickly walked out of the dense encampment and into the unadulterated moonlight. The crisp bite of the evening chill was soothing on his hot skin. He continued walking until the late evening din of the Larder was out of earshot. He found a bare patch of dirt to sit down on with a large rock to lean against. He let out a deep sigh as he plopped down, his back nearly slapping against the boulder. He looked up into the starry night; the bright white pinpricks seemed to jump off their infinite inky backdrop. The summit of the nearby mountain ridge was the only thing bold enough to impose itself on the celestial splendor. Sembado unclenched his teeth. He felt so angry just for being angry. Two years ago, happiness was almost the only emotion he needed. Once in a while, his parents would be disappointed but not often. And then, when he got mixed up with the Elephants' revolution, fear and sadness became common sentiments. But it wasn't until his endeavors with his bionic prosthetic that Sembado had to contend with anger. With great effort, he had finally started to master the control of his rage. He knew when it was coming and how to make it pass but his frustrations with Kaluna were a new obstacle wholly their own. The longer Sembado spent around her, the more frustrated he became with her incessant skepticism and moody responses.

We have worked well as a team, but is that because she's gotten used to me just rolling over whenever she puts her foot down? I get so annoyed with her treating her opinion like the only logical decision. Like it must be the correct choice because Kaluna *says it is. And she wonders why I went and talked to Caspen without her. She probably wouldn't have let me go in the first place. I hate feeling like this, but it's her fault!*

Sembado sat and sulked while the moon slowly moved across the sky. He let out another sigh and rested his head back against the boulder.

Suddenly, a muffled crack rang into the night. The sound of a single gunshot reverberated off the rocks all around him. Sembado stood up and immediately started back toward the center of the Larder. He used his prosthetic to make a quickened pace and soon the sounds of commotion and chaos could be heard spreading through the camp. Sembado trotted past the first few fires. Men and women were lighting torches as he passed.

"Was it an animal?" a woman called.

"Not sure," her husband replied.

172

"It came from inside the camp!" yelled someone else.

Sembado's electric leg quickly carried him back to his tent. There, he found Kaluna and a few others taking stock of weapons and supplies.

"What is it? What's going on?" Sembado asked between heavy breaths.

"A man has been shot," Kaluna said as she dug through her belongings and produced a large knife. "By Chut."

"Chut?" Sembado repeated. "Wha...why? What happened?"

"I don't know!" Kaluna snapped, whipping around with the knife in hand. "But everyone is agitated and it's getting worse by the minute. Would you *please* stop asking questions and just let me know that you have my back?"

"Yeah...yes," Sembado said. "I'm here for you. Always."

"Well, let's go figure this out before these idiots pass the point of no return," Kaluna replied.

Sembado followed her out of their immediate camp and into the largest common path. Kaluna tucked the knife in a sheath on her hip as they moved. The epicenter of the bedlam was near the stony path that led up to Caspen's circle. Kaluna followed in Sembado's wake as he pushed through the loosely packed crowd that had formed. Chut was visible above the others as he remained perched upon his steed. Not far off to his side, a group of people tended to a man with a bullet wound clean through his left shoulder. It was Caspen's forest guard, Gordo. The blood flow had been stopped but Gordo's usual chestnut complexion had already faded to a pale umber.

"I told you it weren't me!" Chut yelled. "If ya'll'd shut up a minute, you could see that my shooter still has six!"

"Dammit, Chut, then who was it?" a woman demanded. "Stop playin' yer damn games!"

"Playin', hell," Chut snapped back. "They got me and my damn horse boxed in. Can a fella at least get some room?"

"So you can run off, I bet," a man called.

"I didn't do it!" Chut bellowed.

"Have you been drinkin' again, Chut?" someone chided.

"Sure smells like it," chorused two others.

Sembado was already regretting moving up so close. The scene around Chut's horse was growing ever more confined. The surrounding crowd jostled and pushed him and Kaluna further ahead as a torch-wielding stranger to their left lost his footing and stumbled forward. The thrashing flames nearly singed Kaluna's hair just before the horse reared in fear, pitching poor Chut to one side. He landed hard on his back with all his breath leaving his lungs in one guttural wheeze. The horse's bridle was secured as it landed and the animal was led away as its rider moaned and rolled where he had been left.

"Dammit, Chut!" one of his female detractors called. "You always make everything so damned difficult!"

Two men went over and helped Chut to his feet but not before one of them could wrestle the young man's six shooter off his hip. Chut was still too winded to protest. The man gingerly pointed the revolver away from the mob as he operated the cylinder release. He turned back around to the crowd, the paleness of his face exaggerated by the many flickering torches.

"Ah, shit!" the man proclaimed, his white face framing in his panicked, bug eyes. "Chut's got six live ones here!"

An energetic murmur spread through the gathering as fast as the discovery could be shared.

"We've got a shooter on the loose!" a nearby boy yelled before his father could cover his mouth.

The murmur turned to concerned chatter and some folks peeled off to head back to their camps. Chut was dragged off to be consoled as Sembado and Kaluna moved closer to where Gordo was still being treated.

"Ya still with us, Gordy?" a woman asked, putting pressure on the gunshot wound. Gordo moaned in response, his eyes dancing behind their lids.

"Let's get 'em up, then," a man said, and he and a friend propped Gordo's arms around their shoulders.

Once vertical, Gordo's bloodshot eyes rolled open and bobbed around from face to face. He made a raspy, disgusting noise as he cleared the back of his throat and spat a wad of thick, discolored phlegm at Sembado's feet.

"Did you at least get a look at who done it?" the woman asked.

Gordo's eyes focused for the first time as he took in the looming blackness of the mountain steps to the east. A orange flash from the mountain side was followed quickly with a sudden zipping noise that led right up to Gordo's face. With a quick snap, another gunshot popped through his forehead, out a large hole in the back of his head, and exploded the rough bark of a pine tree behind him. The gruesome display was supplemented with the crack and ring of distant rifle fire.

The woman screamed as the men abandoned Gordo's corpse in order to drag the beleaguered sister to safety. The remaining onlookers scattered in an anxious flurry. A cry of panic spread through the camp. Sembado grabbed Kaluna under her arms and, with a single kick, leapt behind a pine tree that stood four yards away. When they landed, she had already produced her knife from its sheath but held back behind the tree while the others assessed the threat from the hills.

"Shoulda known," one of the men called from behind a rock. "Haven't seen 'em in weeks."

"Who?" Kaluna yelled. "Who is it?"

"Goddang fiends!" the man cried. "Those effin' hill folk."

Sembado stood behind Kaluna as they remained frozen behind the tree. The front of his body faced her back in full but his face was turned to one side. His cheek was pressed against the braided swirl that sat upon her head. They remained silent as the nervous discourse fled back to the main encampment. But as that noise faded, it was replaced by a quick paced rumbling. The sound was accompanied by a vibration that rumbled the very earth as well as the tree to which Sembado and Kaluna desperately clung.

Sembado turned as the noise gained a definition behind him. A flashing through the trees revealed an entire brigade of driving cavaliers charging hard through their piney surroundings. Caspen led the charge and, as they cleared the trees, he pulled a very large pump shotgun from a saddle holster and slid the action forward and back. With a fluid motion that belied his rough and rugged mount, he quickly shouldered the gun and drew a bead into the brush of the nearest foothills.

Sembado peaked around the tree just in time to see a bright flash accompany the large bang of the gun. He craned his neck a bit further just in time to catch sight of a dozen blue flashes as they lit up the hill side; each sphere was the size of a grown man's chest. The silent response indicated a miss so Caspen pumped the action and fired again. But his second volley yielded nothing.

"Find them!" Caspen shouted to the other horsemen. "I want them dead! I want them all dead!"

He quickly doubled back to where Sembado, Kaluna, and the others had gathered around Gordo's remains. He dismounted the horse at a trot and handed its bridle off to one of his followers. He made determined strides right up to where Gordo's body lay and fell to one knee.

"Gordo," he muttered.

Sembado and Kaluna stood in silent respect with the others.

"This wasn't just an assassination," Caspen said quietly. "This was retribution."

"For what?" Sembado asked. "Who did this?"

"The outcasts that live in the hills," Caspen replied as he ran his hand across Gordo's motionless chest. "Gordo had been cracking down on their looting and pilfering of our supplies."

"Are these the same crazy people that we had trouble with the whole way here?" Sembado asked.

"No," Caspen replied, reaching out for help to stand. Sembado quickly stepped forward to oblige.

"Those were cannibals and oil-fueled psychotics," he continued. "These folk were stewards. Some still are, I guess, but they have been exiled from my camp and others because they broke one rule or another. Now, they envy what they're missing and so we have to run off a raiding party once in a while. A few months ago, Gordo started to push for a tougher response but I wouldn't let him. We kept losing tents...supplies...food. So I finally gave him authority to come down hard on the looters. Gordo did just that and ended up maiming an entire band of marauders. Most of the poor bastards were so mangled by our electronic weapons that they were asking for mercy kill and Gordo and his men did not hesitate to oblige. Well, the others are back. And they're not happy about what happened."

The group stood in silence around the bloody display at their feet. One of the women wept into another's shoulder. Caspen let out a deep sigh and turned to walk back toward his cabin.

"Where are you going?" Sembado called.

"To get a shovel," Caspen yelled over his shoulder. "Gordo's dead because of me."

***

Sembado and Kaluna stayed up late that night discussing what had happened. They sat propped against each other next to a dwindling campfire. The other campers had retired to their tents, and Kaluna was now dosing off against Sembado's shoulder. He lifted his arm to relieve the pressure point where her head was focused, and she settled into the crook of his bicep and chest. Sembado lovingly rolled his eyes and settled his outstretched grasp around her frame.

Why do I get so worked up? And why am I so surprised that she always plays the strong and silent card? That's what she does. That's who she is. Get over it, Sem. I mean come on. She has to put up with your whiney attitude, and she still comes back for more. It's okay to want to see where Caspen takes this...apprenticeship, but you have got to accept that Kaluna isn't always going to be one hundred percent on board.

Sembado sat and embraced the peaceful calm after a tumultuous evening. Even the fire's crackling pops had grown softer. He carefully shifted the weight of his head until he had found a cozy and comfortable way to prop it against Kaluna's. He pulled her in tight as he gazed at the twinkling spectacle above. The moon had drifted out of sight, but the stars' brilliant radiance never stopped amazing him. Since they had arrived at the Larder and settled into a normal routine, Sembado had made taking in the stars a priority. Each night, he tried to figure the amount of time he had been above water but finally calculated he would have thousands of peaceful, starry nights to make up for all the years spent in the Complex. But with Kaluna snuggled in at his side, he decided then and there that there was no better way to make up all those years. He closed his eyes and let his consciousness drift inside his head. Somewhere in the distance, a coyote whined and yipped. Sembado had grown fond of the animals' night noises. He relaxed his face into a gentle smile and drifted off to a surprisingly pleasant sleep.

Chapter 18
The Root Cellar

The next day, Caspen's followers petitioned against his initial denial to hold a funeral service for Gordo. Caspen stood silently in the morning sun with a bitter sneer and wetness in his bloodshot eyes while each citizen of the Circle took a turn bidding farewell. Several of the common followers stood patiently in line to stand at the foot of Gordo's mounded grave and give a blubbering address. After approximately two hours, Caspen gave up and walked away from the unrelenting spectacle. With Kaluna's nonverbal consent, Sembado departed as well. He discreetly followed Caspen up the rocky slope to the Circle, and caught up just as Caspen had reached his front door.

"Hey," Sembado said softly.

Caspen stopped at the door with his hand on the latch. He let out a deep sigh and dropped his head against the door.

"Yeah, look, Sem," Caspen said, his head still pressed firmly against the plank-built door. "It's not your fault but I *really* don't want to do this right now."

"I know it's not easy being at the top," Sembado said. "Everybody looks to you but you have nowhere to turn."

Caspen quickly pushed off the door and turned on Sembado. His reddened eyes were wide with anger, giving him a wild, vicious appearance. He threw his hands up and pushed Sembado backward with all his weight. Sembado nearly fell but his bionic prosthetic adjusted at lightning speed to place itself under his center of gravity. The sudden movement pulled a muscle in his adjoining thigh. The prosthetic's glowing warmth pulsed against his amputated stump. He remained in his awkward position while Caspen released a torrent of verbal abuse.

"I *had* somewhere to turn!" he shouted. "But he's buried out there with all those idiots gawking around! He was my friend. My closest ally. I don't have a back-up. And sorry, man, but it's not you! You and me, we aren't friends. We aren't buds. I need you to move this thing along. That's all. So don't try cozying up because I don't want to get close. That's not what you're for. That's not how I'm going to use you, get it? Do you get that you are just some piece in my puzzle? Do you think you're special? Huh?"

"No," Sembado muttered as he adjusted his weight and stretched out his throbbing quadriceps.

"Because I showed you my hidden powerhouses?" Caspen asked as he drew closer. His upturned lip painted his face in a dark shade of disgust.

"No," Sembado said more firmly, planting his organic foot in the dirt.

"Then why do think you're so freakin' special?" Caspen screamed, whipping a concealed handgun off his waist and waving it in the air.

"I DON'T!" Sembado roared just before he planted his bionic foot on Caspen's chest. He gritted his teeth in concentration as he attempted to regulate the power of his kick. With success, he was able to propel Caspen backward just enough to unsettle him. Caspen was able to land on both feet but still broke the impact by bending one knee. He trained his wild eyes on Sembado but remained down as he fought desperately to refill his lungs. Sembado wasted no time in advancing to a regular talking distance before accosting Caspen with his own caustic retort. His angry grimace revealed the heroic effort required to suppress his prosthetic's enraging feedback.

"I don't think I'm special!" Sembado hissed pointedly. "I'm just trying to do what I think is right!"

He stepped back and took a deep breath, looking around to ensure their privacy was sustained.

"You're the one who thinks you're above the law!" Sembado snapped. "You're the one who thinks he's special! Not me! What did I do? Try to help you out? So you think you're so unique that it takes an extraordinary person just to be your confidant? Are you that deeking vane? I'm sorry Gordo went out like that."

Caspen narrowed his eyes but then he dropped them. He struggled to maintain eye contact as Sembado continued his spirited address.

"I really am. But I lost my best friend in my arms at the same time I lost this," Sembado continued, stomping his bionic foot powerfully. Caspen regarded the leg ominously.

"So I *do* get it," Sembado said bitterly. "If you wanna be alone…fine! But don't make it this whole thing that it's not."

He turned and marched away before Caspen could respond. His bionic leg made short hops in his gait as he struggled to calm it down.

***

Sembado stared at the ceiling of his canvas tent. He had forgone the evening meal to seclude himself from further conflict. The sun had fallen and the nighttime fires made a myriad of shadows dance against the material. Despite all of his critiques, he had to admit that the yellowed fabric was excellent at retaining stains. Brown spots and black blotches made up an intricate and off-putting design that made his frustrations fester. His hands were folded under his head but the pressure had become uncomfortable. He slid his palms out from under his head and let them rest on the meager sleeping mat that he and Kaluna shared. He let out a deep sigh as he relived his exchange with Caspen yet again.

Kaluna pulled the flap of the tent open and popped her head inside.

"Have you been in here this whole time?" she asked. She started to move inside without waiting for a response and secured the flap behind her.

"I got in a fight with Caspen," Sembado said flatly.

"Aw, that's too bad," Kaluna mocked. "Move over. It's starting to get cold out and those people just wanted to stand around forever and weep."

"No," Sembado said. "I mean a physical fight. I kicked him in the chest."

"Oh," Kaluna said with surprise. She stopped settling down on their sleeping mat for just a moment. "Did you hurt him?"

"No," Sembado said quietly.

"Huh," Kaluna replied, continuing to find a comfortable position as she curled up against Sembado's ribs. "Well, I guess you two will work it out...or you won't. What happened?"

"I don't know," Sembado sighed. "He was worked up about Gordo and I started getting angry when he accused me of thinking I was *special*."

"Special?" Kaluna repeated.

"Yeah," Sembado said. "And specifically because he thinks I think I get to automatically be in his inner circle. Like that's something special all by itself."

Kaluna rested her face against Sembado's arm but said nothing.

"Well, don't you think that's ridiculous?" Sembado asked.

"I think it's ridiculous that he thinks you feel that way," Kaluna responded. "I don't think it's ridiculous that he's that conceited. Why are you so surprised?"

"I…I don't know," Sembado said, flailing his hands.

"I do," Kaluna said calmly. "It's because even after all of the terrible personalities we've encountered, you still expect the best of people."

She did not say it as an insult or even regard it as a weakness. She stated it as plainly as one describes the sky as blue. They breathed in concert as the cold hard truth sunk into Sembado's tightening chest. He tried to release the tension with another sigh, but it didn't work.

"Well, what am I supposed to do?" he finally sputtered. "I've been struggling not to lose that. Do you want me to lose that? Seriously!"

"Sembado," Kaluna sighed. "It doesn't have to be all or nothing. I know I'm less trusting than you. And I know that gets old for you. But at this point, I'm just sick of setting myself up for failure, ya know? You and I understand each other very well but we've been operating in very different realities since we met. I'm not saying mine is the real one or that yours is wrong. But they are *very* different."

Sembado said nothing but turned onto his side so that he was facing Kaluna and could drape one arm across her torso. She responded by rolling into him, her head tucked just under his chin.

"I don't think you know how close I am to giving up on that," Sembado said quietly, barely audible. "That hope. Those expectations."

"Please don't," Kaluna whispered.

***

Sembado and Kaluna kept to themselves the next morning. They ate an early breakfast before taking an exhilarating hike through the brisk mountain air to the south and east. They returned well after the sun had started to fall and found a herald sitting by the opening of their tent.

"Caspen would like to see you," the young man stuttered as he clamored to his feet. "Both of you."

Sembado and Kaluna exchanged a glance and a shrug before following the messenger through the greater Larder to the Circle beyond. He walked them right up to Caspen's front door before making an awkward kind of bow and running back to the main encampment.

Sembado gave Kaluna one more look before knocking firmly on the door to Caspen's cabin. A response of some kind echoed from within. Sembado paused a moment longer before the muffled invitation was repeated. He opened the door and he and Kaluna slowly walked in.

Caspen was in the main room facing the hearth. The fireplace hosted a small blaze. The room was comfortably warm against the soft bite of the outside air.

"You're welcome to come have a seat," Caspen offered, "but I have somewhere I'd like to take you. So if you'd rather skip the pleasantries, we can get straight to business."

The silence in the room was an awkward, ringing cry. It fed the tension so that it swelled to palpable conflict in seconds. Kaluna gently set an elbow into Sembado's side. He clicked his tongue and responded with pursed lips but then a soft sigh.

"I'm sorry I kicked you," Sembado said to the room.

"It's nothing I didn't deserve," Caspen said, rising from his chair to turn and face them.

"I respect what you did," Caspen continued. "*And* what you said. I'm not used to people speaking their minds to me and you were right. Being in control of an operation like this is a lot of work. But it only gets harder when you try to do it alone. Gordo was my closest friend and I will miss him. But he was also a vital part of this operation and I will struggle to maintain status quo around here without someone to step up into his role. Please, have a seat."

Caspen motioned for them to join him at the center of the room. Sembado and Kaluna moved in slowly and sat down on the love seat while Caspen chose one of the rough hewn easy chairs across from them.

"Sembado, I've already discussed this with you," Caspen said, turning his gaze to Kaluna. "But I want to make sure Kaluna is on the same page."

"Sembado's already filled me in," Kaluna assured him.

Caspen chuckled in response.

"You really don't like wasting time or words, do you?" he asked Kaluna.

She responded by shaking her head.

Caspen laughed again.

"Look, you two live with your eyes open. Wider than any seeder I've ever met. Now, granted, most of the new folk coming through here have come from your underwater cage. But even compared to the people who have been born and raised as stewards, you two have a clearer picture of what this really is. I need that."

Caspen took a deep breath and looked at Sembado.

"And not just as part of my game," he said earnestly. "I need it to make this work. I need it to survive."

He got up and moved behind his chair, slowly pacing around the rugged furniture.

"What I'm asking is for you two to abandon any winter preparations for a traditional village and to stay on to apprentice under me. When I think you are ready *and* I can find someone to take your place, then you will move on to recreate my facilities in your own territory to the east."

Sembado looked into Kaluna's eyes but she withheld any obvious response while Caspen looked them over.

Caspen replied for her, saying, "I understand you need to discuss this. While I can still add weight to my side of the scale, I will have you know that Gordo was a resident of the Circle here and left behind a cabin which he had all to himself. The residence would be yours immediately. Included would be a seat for each of you at my regular council gatherings. Now still, I understand this is only

189

more to discuss. While I'm waiting for your reply, I actually have more to show you. I mean, even if you turn down Gordo's position, you're still my ideal candidates to host the replica of my endeavors here. Please come with me. I think you'll like this."

Sembado and Kaluna rose again and followed Caspen across the room. To Sembado's surprise, Caspen led them past the front door, which he locked, before he moved into a corner of the great room where the floor was raised a step higher than the rest. He walked up to an old dusty rug that lay on the raised floor. The rug was a rough weave of colored threads, animal fibers, and other natural materials. The irregular symmetry of its handmade appearance was only accentuated by its worn and tattered ends. Caspen grabbed the rug and flopped it over on itself. A small cloud of dust shot past his feet and settled on the planked floor beyond. Kaluna reached out and squeezed Sembado's hand. Where the rug had been, there was a heavy framed trap door with a large iron hasp and a padlock securing the latch. Caspen produced a key from his pocket and knelt down beside the lock. As he fumbled with the mechanism, Kaluna squeezed Sembado's hand harder. He tried to reassure her by placing his hand on her back but it did not seem to help.

"I gotta remember to oil this thing more often," Caspen said when the lock finally clicked open.

He removed the hasp and lifted the trap door to one side. Opening the hatch revealed a rusty spiral staircase which disappeared into the darkness below. Caspen rose and fetched an oil-fueled lantern before returning to the hole and leading the way down the twisted steps. Sembado went next with Kaluna hesitantly in tow.

The staircase fell away quickly. Each step was nearly a foot interval to the next. Sembado braced himself on all sides as he descended the precarious flight. Despite the large distance between steps, Sembado still had to duck his head to clear the planking of the raised floor. Even still, if it had not been for the extended ceiling that the raised floor offered, Sembado would have had to nearly sit down to clear the final awkward step before the stairway completely cleared the ground level of the cabin. Sembado strained his eyes painfully; Caspen's lantern afforded only minimal vision at the bottom of the stairs compared to the glow of the fireplace above. By the time they had reached the bottom, Kaluna's hand was planted firmly on the top of Sembado's head as she steadied her descent.

Sembado stepped off the last stair tread on to the dirt floor. Caspen waited for Kaluna to land before he reached for a nearby object. Out of the shadows, he pulled a crooked staff, on the end of which he fixed his lantern. He held the staff close to his belly as they started their way down a wood planked tunnel. Sembado noticed that, aside from its diminutive size, it was very similar to the desert tunnels they survived just weeks before. The biggest difference was the accuracy and skill with which the framework and planking had been placed. The tunnel's steady slope downward made Sembado lean back against Kaluna as he concentrated on not walking any faster than

Caspen. Kaluna kept one hand pressed against Sembado's back; the other she swiped lightly against the walls.

"This is very weird," Kaluna whispered softly in Sembado's ear.

"It's just a little bit further ahead," Caspen called from ahead. His pace had quickened as the tunnel floor had leveled out.

Sembado also sped up to match his speed to Caspen's. Kaluna held a handful of his shirt so that she could keep up.

Caspen's lantern highlighted an apparent dead end as the tunnel was truncated by another planked wall. Sembado and Kaluna slowed their steps as they continued to question Caspen's intentions. It wasn't until they saw a dark shadow develop on one wall that they realized the tunnel did not dead end but, in fact, made an abrupt turn to the right. Caspen paused at the turn and looked back at Sembado and Kaluna, who were now twenty feet behind.

"What are you doing?" he asked. "It's just up here."

Sembado led Kaluna to the corner just as Caspen disappeared around it. They poked their head's around to see Caspen up ahead at an actual dead end. He stood at a door. Its smooth steel finish immediately made it stick out against the earthen and wood appointments which surrounded it. Caspen produced another key but waited for Sembado and Kaluna to approach before fitting it in the door's deadbolt.

"You'll have to come up close," Caspen said. "We don't like to keep this door open any longer than we have to."

Sembado nearly dragged Kaluna up to Caspen's back while he pulled the door firmly, turned the lock, and popped the latch. A sealed hiss was released when he pushed the door open; an odd but familiar smell rushed out with it. The olfactory memory raced through Sembado's head as Caspen pushed the door open. A flood of bright light glared across Sembado and Kaluna's eyes. Caspen had them move quickly inside as he extinguished his lantern and abandoned it in the tunnel. Sembado and Kaluna had to cram themselves into the room so that Caspen could shut the door behind them.

"Sorry," Caspen offered. "I usually only come through here alone."

The room was just big enough for the three of them to stand. Sembado and Kaluna balked at the pristine concrete floor, walls, and ceiling as Caspen shuffled by to get to the next door. Sembado put his hand across his eyes as he tried to stare at the small metal conduit and electric light that were fastened to the ceiling. He suddenly realized that the smell he recognized was that of warm, burnt air as it radiated from electrical circuits. He and Kaluna had only a moment to marvel at the modern convenience before Caspen had the next door unlocked and open. It led to another well lit, concrete space. This one was much larger and featured a bank of metal lockers and benches on one side. A man sat at the bench and changed into a crisp

193

uniform and boots. A pile of tattered clothes and sandals lay at his feet. He looked up and greeted Caspen but his smile faded as his eyes landed on Sembado and Kaluna.

"It's okay, Vern," Caspen said. "These two are the new recruits I told you about."

The man tried to form a welcoming smile but it came across more like an uncomfortable grimace. He quickly finished changing and beat them out of the room by way of a doorway ahead.

Kaluna nudged Sembado as they walked through the locker room. She tried to discretely point out that the lockers were numbered one through forty.

"Yes," Caspen commented. "You will find that it takes many bodies to keep this place running. The numbers are a little misleading though. They usually only work in shifts of four at a time. It's important to keep their presence here a mystery to the others. They are absent from the others every few days. Normal hunting parties are a good cover. Of course, then we have to actually produce game to help sell the ruse."

"Why keep any of it from any of them?" Kaluna chimed in from the rear.

"Mostly because they don't need to know, if I'm being honest," Caspen replied. "Additionally, if word got out about what I've created, then I would be facing stiff condemnation from the other stewards. Or worse, they would want a piece of what I have."

"Those hill folk know, don't they?" Sembado asked.

"Only pieces," Caspen replied as he led them through the doorway at the far end of the room. They stepped out into a hallway that branched off in both directions. Sembado followed Caspen to the left. Kaluna kept a firm grip of his hand as they walked.

"I'm sorry," Sembado said as they briskly walked the hall, "but can you just tell us what this is?"

Caspen chuckled as he stopped along a series of large, plate windows that flanked the right side of the hallway.

"Why don't you see for yourself?" he said with a smirk.

Sembado and Kaluna stepped up to the glass and looked in to the adjacent room. They stared in wonder at the bank of technicians, men and women, who sat with their backs to the windows. The man named Vern was just settling into one of the consoles. In front of him were countless computer monitors and control boards. Each of the stations was a step below the one behind it so that the floor fell away from the ceiling. The geometry of the space made the opposite wall a tall, theatre size expanse which was covered in large viewing screens. Each one showed the rapid, jerking perspective of a different flying drone. One surveyed the rocky desert crags to the west. Another flew through the heavily wooded canyons to the north. The screens quickly rotated between drones every few seconds. The technicians clicked and scrolled across a number of additional information pages at their individual consoles. One smaller monitor at the top center of the large wall did not change. A stream of data and charts flashed across it with regular updates. Graphs depicting some sort of power production and consumption were being compared in real time.

Caspen wore a delighted smile as he watched Sembado and Kaluna watch the screens.

"It's a lot to take in, I know," he said coolly.

"How…?" Sembado stammered. "Where did you get these components?"

"Are you serious?" Caspen replied. "I've been working on this for almost thirty years. Do you know what kind of smuggling I had to do to get this stuff past Mereth? She's literally been my main impediment since I started."

"But who would you smuggle with?" Kaluna asked.

"With the Complex government," Caspen said matter-of-factly.

Sembado and Kaluna could not conceal their emotional response to Caspen's response.

"Oh, stop," Caspen said calmly. "I only worked with those creeps to get what I needed. Don't you get it? They didn't have the control for this kind of lifestyle. And Mereth doesn't have the vision. This is the happy middle ground you two have been searching for. Order and control with a purpose."

Sembado and Kaluna looked back to the screens. One of the drone feeds had been selected for further review. The camera flew over a meadow clearing in a forest and revealed a burgeoning village that teemed with life. Its inhabitants moved together as one while they erected the framework for the first structure in their camp.

"Do you see how hard they try?" Caspen asked. "That right there is why I can't completely condemn what Mereth and her muscle are doing. Look at them. Those people care for this...thing. They really think their actions are going to make a difference. She was always very good at making people feel special."

The drone monitored the villagers' progress a moment longer before turning and flying in another direction. As it did, the camera feed quickly switched to another location.

"But this can't be much different from Mereth's plan," Sembado said. "They use those exact same drones out on the coast."

"No," Caspen replied. "Theirs are different. They have little, solar powered, single pilot controls to look over a ridge or through some dense canopy. My technicians monitor thousands of these things. And their functions go far beyond some simple recon mission. See, if Cistern or another one of Mereth's goons catches sight of something with their drones, they still have to hunt down the perpetrator and lay some hands on them. Each one of my drones packs its own punch if a guilty party is observed in the act. I don't have time nor care to waste the manpower to run down some sorry sot and talk to him about what he did wrong. It's just easier this way."

Caspen tapped on the glass until Vern turned around to look. Caspen signaled to him by swirling a clenched fist in a tight circle and then miming an explosion by quickly opening his hand.

Vern nodded obediently and turned back to his console. He repeatedly pressed a button on his control board, cycling through the camera feeds at a dizzying pace. He stopped on a live feed of a rocky canyon. Shrubs and grass dotted a backdrop of reddish orange boulders. The drone rotated fifteen degrees every few seconds until Vern pressed another button and sent the small aerial shooting off in a straight line. He slowly dropped altitude as the camera's perspective raced along. A trail of dust rose ahead in the distance. Vern increased the speed of the drone and set it after the cloud of orange dirt. Within moments, Vern's monitor showed an all-terrain vehicle like the one that chased Sembado through the tunnels. It raced across the desert landscape, black smoke spewing from the poorly fashioned exhaust. Vern swung the drone out to one side, affording a clear profile shot of the driver. The driver immediately took notice and he nervously regarded the flying camera as he accelerated down the canyon floor. The camera closed in from the side as Vern easily matched pace with his swerving prey. The drone approached twenty feet then ten then five. The driver's face was now visible under his mat of hair and large, tinted goggles. He looked unequivocally horrified as he produced a twisted club which he swung widely at the drone. Vern steadied the camera for a moment longer before pressing another button. The camera lit up with a blue flash for just a moment before Vern pulled it back a few feet. The perspective change offered a view of the entire vehicle as it slowed to a veering stop. The drone also came to a complete stop as Vern surveyed the damage. The vehicle remained running while the drone's flash attack had reduced the driver to a bloody pair of legs. With his head and entire torso dissolved by the sphere, his hands still clung to the steering yolk.

Vern looked over his shoulder with a pallid expression and returned to his regular observation duties. Kaluna gasped and turned to look away. Sembado averted his eyes as well.

"Oh, come on," Caspen chided. "You're going to get worked up about a dirt bag like that? That was literally one of the people whose chest you threw a spear into."

"Yeah," Sembado retorted. "Because they were bearing down and ready to attack!"

"And I'm just preventing that from happening again," Caspen replied angrily. "Wanna guess why that last group of seeders didn't make it in? Because freaks like this are allowed to roam the earth. I'm just putting him out of his misery and doing the environment a favor by keeping the carbon output down."

"You have to understand that this isn't easy for us," Kaluna argued. "Even if we end up agreeing with you, this is something that most people would struggle with. We *hate* those things. We've seen people we know and love destroyed by them. I know you know that."

Caspen did not respond but clenched his teeth, bit his lip, and let out a deep sigh through his nose. He stared at Kaluna and then to Vern's monitor before dropping his eyes to the floor.

"That step isn't necessary to my process," he admitted. "But it will remain available."

"Why are you so certain that they must die?" Sembado demanded. "How do you know that exact man there was guilty? Of what? Driving an oil-fueled machine? What else has he done?"

"What good does keeping him alive do?" Caspen countered. "What good is there in exercising judgment or restraint? The world is literally better off without that creep and his roadster. What benefit does he provide?"

"That doesn't say anything about his character," Kaluna insisted. "But it does speak *volumes* about yours. Why do you act as if others' actions are heinous enough to force you to respond? Are they really that bad? And are you really that righteous?"

"Again," Caspen said with punctuated diction, "I ask…what purpose did he serve?"

"What benefit do any of us serve then?" Kaluna shot back, throwing up her hands in exasperation.

"I provide purpose!" Caspen snapped bitterly. "That is the only commodity left. When the playing field has been leveled and everyone is forced to fight and claw for their food and shelter, they still have a nagging call deep inside them for what's next. If I could catch enough food for today *and* tomorrow, what would I do then? If my goal is for the world to be here tomorrow, then I *must* keep as many people as I can from asking themselves that question. There is no inspiration. That leads to industry. And industry destroys stewardship. And without stewardship, there is no tomorrow. That should be the real stewards' motto. That's the sad truth of it. Stewardship is sacrifice because we're sacrificing an enriching, happy existence so that we can actually have a tomorrow to dream about. That's it. Dreaming is dangerous. I tried explaining that to Mereth but all she can see is her pie in the sky fantasy about hugging trees and singing to plants. A green earth for generations to come has a very simple price: boredom. Your underwater masters understood that and they tried to defeat it with entertainment. My system also focuses on the boredom, but I have some more purposeful antidotes."

"Like what?" Kaluna demanded.

"These folks sitting at these consoles are a good example," Caspen replied. "They know what they're doing is secret and they keep it from the others. Now, do I really need them watching these drones twenty-four hours a day? Probably not. Whats the risk? I might miss one or two infractions? But what else is happening here? They have a role. They have a secret that they feel dedicated to keeping. They have *purpose*. And if you don't give them an explicit task, people make their own. It's one of our only remaining instincts. You gotta keep yourself busy! Throughout history, leaders have used gods, farming, industry, education, consumerism, war. The list goes on. Each one had its time but the distractions never last. People keep asking questions until the puppeteers get uncomfortable."

"But why do you think it's so important to keep them distracted?" Kaluna asked. "I wasn't plugged in like Sembado and the others when I lived under water."

"Did you not suffer for it?" Caspen shot back. "Did you not feel constantly unsatisfied? Unfulfilled? Without the promise of tomorrow... the expectations of progress... the hope of dreams... what did you *live* for? Seriously! I'm asking you. What made you wake up and want to get out of bed every morning? What has ever done that for you?"

Kaluna's immediate response was a stony silence but then she quietly provided a reply.

"That tomorrow would be different from the day before," she whispered.

"Exactly," Caspen said excitedly. "You know exactly what I'm talking about. It's what brought you and Sembado here. He awoke from that fog and you were waiting for him. And the two of you could not *wait* to get the hell out of that place because there was no challenge left and therefore no purpose. So why would we just limit ourselves or our followers on the principle of stewardship alone? That's never been enough. The box has been opened. When people lived this way thousands of years ago, ignorance was bliss. But now, the knowledge of what's missing can become an immobilizing depression. So I must keep them busy above all else. For their sake, and for a sustainable future."

Caspen crossed his arms while he waited for any further objections. Kaluna and Sembado exchanged a glance, but mostly looked at the floor or the giant monitors in the next room.

"I have to admit that your intentions really do seem noble," Kaluna said earnestly. "But I have yet to see who provides oversight. Who watches these watchers?" she asked, motioning to Vern and the others.

"I do," Caspen replied matter-of-factly.

"Yeah, okay. I get that," Kaluna replied quickly. "But who watches you?"

Caspen appeared thoughtful, as if genuinely interested in the concept of oversight. But it was clear that it had never been a burden he had had to suffer and he did not seem interested in starting.

"I do have my council at the Circle," he suggested. "But their decisions and input are only part of my considerations when making a judgement. What poor decisions can really be made? The commoners are supposed to be struggling. If my choice happens to make life easier, then it's an added bonus for them. But if it makes living life a terrible, difficult thing, then they have no reason to be surprised."

"So that makes me question what the entire goal is here," Kaluna said firmly. "To make seeders successful or to make their mission an arduous journey?"

"Neither," Caspen said with a chuckle. "We are simply supposed to facilitate their endeavors. Sometimes it's easier than expected. Sometimes it's not. But my experience is that it rarely falls in the middle."

"I just don't know why you wouldn't try and make things more manageable for them," Kaluna replied.

"Yes you do," Caspen responded belligerently. "Because then manageable is the expectation. And that can never be allowed. This lifestyle is *not* manageable. It's difficult! It's very, very difficult. For some people…it's impossible."

Kaluna sighed deeply and was about to begin another objection when a great commotion erupted behind the glass of the observation room.

Sembado was the first to notice and quickly called Kaluna and Caspen's attention to the bright red warning screens and hurried activity of the posted sentinels. Vern was the first to look over his shoulder. He purposefully made bug-eyed visual contact with Caspen before returning to his many screens and drone controls. Caspen pushed past Sembado and Kaluna as he quickly made his way into the observation room. Sembado and Kaluna followed quickly behind. They barely reached the watch floor's door before it latched and locked behind them.

Chapter 19
Fire Fight

"Whatta we got?" Caspen called out to his team as Sembado and Kaluna shuffled in behind him.

"Hill folk," the woman at the first computer called over her shoulder.

"They're makin' a hell of a move," Vern added.

"Show me," Caspen ordered.

Vern clicked a few keys and sent a drone feed to one of the large screens at the front of the room. The camera hovered for a moment as it transitioned to infrared. Where the murky twilight had shown only pixilated shadows a moment before, the camera's night vision suddenly highlighted dozens of ghostly figures. The heavily armed assailants moved through a thick pine grove. Several of them carried idling flamethrowers. The tube-shaped weapons flickered brightly in the grayscale display.

"Where are they?" Caspen demanded.

"East of the north camp, moving west," Vern responded. He clicked a few more buttons and brought up an overhead map of the surrounding terrain. Their current location was marked on the map, with Caspen's mysterious work houses shown to the north. Vern zoomed in on the trees that surrounded the work camp to the east.

"There," he said, selecting an icon on the map that indicated the drone's position. "They're right there."

"I'm heading out," Caspen said flatly. "You give me support when the time comes. Watch your flyers against that fire."

"Yes, sir," Vern and the others replied obediently.

Caspen turned and marched out. He grabbed Sembado by the shirt as he passed and dragged him along. Kaluna followed just behind.

"Well, I hope this well formed squad of marauders is guilty enough for the punishment I'm about to inflict," Caspen snapped sarcastically as he led Sembado and Kaluna back through the root cellar at a hastened pace.

Sembado glanced at Kaluna but she was avoiding eye contact. They continued through the dirt passages that led to Caspen's cabin. When they breached the planked floor, the main room was already a flurry of activity. Several of Caspen's council waited expectantly.

"Well, don't let me keep you," Caspen shouted. "For God's sake, move!"

The collective blew out of the cabin's door to an entire stable worth of horses that were being held outside by a group of nervous attendants. Caspen and a few others chose individual mounts while the rest, Sembado and Kaluna included, climbed into a large, four-wheeled wagon which was fastened to two massive stallions. As they piled in, Sembado and Kaluna were handed rifles.

Each one had an electric light fastened to the muzzle. Caspen shouted a war cry to the others before racing off to the north. Each rider shot forward until a single file line was streaming out of the Circle. The wagon was the last to rocket forward but, with a simple snap of the reins, the two large horses pulled forward with enough force to plant every single passenger on their rear.

"Hold on," the driver called.

"It's too late for that, ya jackass," one of the passengers chided as he climbed back to one knee.

Sembado dragged himself up to a similar position. The stock of his gun rested on the timber rails that formed the sides of the wagon. Kaluna knelt just in front of him, her elbow pinned against his chest as she struggled against the forward acceleration.

The wagon barreled forward at breakneck speed. The eight hooves of its locomotive benefactors rolled like unrelenting thunder as they beat against the dirt path. Sembado looked over Kaluna's head to see the bright white beams of the other soldiers' rifle lights hectically bouncing off the evergreen canopy above like some kind of deadly, outdoor discotheque. He closed his eyes against the flashing mayhem but the jarring experience offered by the wagon's severe lack of suspension made him immediately nauseous. He opened his eyes just in time to see their passage through the gate which Gordo had guarded just days before. An anxious looking sentry stood at the opening and watched the spectacle roll by, his ghostly face fading into the night behind them.

Sembado leaned his head back and took a deep breath. Twinkling pinpricks of starlight shined through the pine boughs above as the density of their branches became sparser. The clearing was getting closer. He looked back down. The path had widened to nearly twelve feet and the riders ahead had condensed and were now riding three abreast. Only Caspen remained alone as he drove his horse just ahead of the others.

"One last check and prep!" the man at the front of the wagon shouted. The other passengers checked their rifles' actions, turned on their flashlights, and fitted the butts firmly into their armpits. Sembado and Kaluna quickly emulated the sequence. In the glare that the lights reflected off the surroundings, Sembado could see Kaluna's face as she looked back at him. Her stunning green eyes and beautiful brown skin defied the unflattering motion of the surrounding chaos. Her mouth was pulled into its usual terse purse but her eyes were wide with apprehension.

"It's okay," Sembado said firmly through the din. "These people are trying to kill us."

She closed her eyes and planted her head against his chest so that they could bounce and buck as one.

"That doesn't help," she said softly.

"I'm sorry," Sembado replied, motioning ahead with his eyes. "But you're not gonna get any better than that right now."

Kaluna followed the implication of his body language out ahead of the wagon as the tree line stopped to their flank and opened to the wide clearing that accommodated

Caspen's work houses. Ahead and to the right, the edge of the clearing was already ablaze. The flame-wielding hill folk were hard at work setting fire to as much of the pine needle-laden ground as possible. In their sights were also any surrounding structures or defensive drone attacks. Their assault rifle-carrying brothers also loosened one three-round burst after another into the air. Each of their successful strikes against the propellered contraptions was signaled by a premature burst of blue light.

Sembado's expectation of battle heightened as they drew closer. His anticipation manifested itself as labored breathing just as a rapid series of buzzing sounds blasted past the wagon very near to his face. Dozens of drones were being flagged to counter the hill folk's mounting offensive. He watched the assaulting enemies' movement slow to a stop as they focused their gunfire and flame attacks against the ceaseless waves of drones. The far edge of the clearing was truly illuminated in orange and blue as the assailants continued to belch columns of fire against the drones' flashing blue orb attacks. The display of contrasting warfare was awe inspiring as hundreds of premature drone detonations now formed a near cocoon around the attackers.

As Caspen led the cavalry closer, he drew a bead with his rifle and shot. His sights rang true as one of the flame-wielding attackers crumpled and fell. With his demise, the impending drone attacks grew closer. Caspen aimed again and fired along with the next row of horsemen. Another

209

line of hill folk fell but the endless stream of drones continued.

Sembado refitted his rifle against his shoulder as the wagon approached the impending disorder. He took aim at one of the attackers but just before he fired, one of the wagon's wheels struck a large rock and tossed its passengers several feet into the air. The wagon landed with a loud crash. Sembado reached for anything firm to avoid being tossed out the back. The only purchase his flailing hand could find was Kaluna's outstretched arm. She reached out to hold Sembado tight as the driver slowed the horses in response to the unexpected obstruction. By the time Sembado could recover and re-sight his rifle, Caspen and the other horsemen had nearly encircled the dying assault. While the counter assault of drones was slowing, the remaining copters were enough to overwhelm the few remaining hill folk. Sembado grimaced as the last few assailants conceded to the dazzling onslaught of blue flashes.

Caspen slowed his circling cavaliers as the wagon drew up behind them. Some of the riders dismounted to finish stomping out the errant flames that crawled through the dense undergrowth. Others discharged their weapons in an effort to commit mercy kills against their enemies who had not fully succumbed to their wounds.

Sembado and Kaluna waited on the wagon as the others piled off and began surveying the battle zone on foot. The ground was littered with hundreds of drone components. They crunched underfoot as the soldiers walked through the mess. Several operational drones hovered in place as the site was secured. One of the awaiting flyers buzzed down within arm's reach of Caspen. He looked up into its camera and circled his finger overhead.

"Form a perimeter and search the rest of the woods," he said to the drone's pilot.

The drone quickly buzzed away followed by all the remaining copters in the area.

Caspen turned his horse around so that he could look directly at Sembado and Kaluna.

"I hope you can now appreciate what a destructive menace these people are," he said stoically. "I have worked *way* too hard for myself and my people to see this place destroyed by some directionless psychos."

The surrounding soldiers turned to face Sembado and Kaluna as Caspen continued addressing them.

"If mother nature were to wipe us off the map, then I would happily embrace my demise. But there ain't no way I'm gonna let these animals ruin this paradise."

His declaration was met with several hearty cheers throughout the crowd.

Chapter 20
Settling Down Doesn't Mean Settling

As news of the attack spread, Sembado and Kaluna quickly came to realize that it was the largest and most overt of its kind that the citizens of the Circle had ever seen. Caspen was very effective in using the attack to embolden his followers and after daily propositions, he was even successful in convincing Sembado and Kaluna to take up residence in Gordo's vacant cabin on the Circle.

With their limited personal items and the cabin remaining furnished, it took less than a day for Sembado and Kaluna to become acquainted with their new home. Despite the fact that Kaluna's own hesitation was the biggest impediment to moving in, she quickly accepted the quiet and privacy that the little log house afforded them.

Sembado was nearly dismayed at how much Kaluna embraced their new lifestyle among Caspen and the citizens of the Circle. To his pleasurable surprise, their relatively domestic surroundings had even nurtured a budding physical relationship, the likes of which he had never known. Their winter schedule soon settled into a satisfying repetition of communing with the commoners, passionate council meetings, and amorous alone time in their cabin retreat.

They lay in the heavily built bed that served as a focal point in the one-room house. Across the room stood the other showcased feature, a sturdy pot belly stove which flickered its flames to the ever present draft of brisk air that seeped through the windows and walls. Sembado readjusted his neck against his lumpy, hand-made pillow while Kaluna curled up on her side and tucked herself against his torso. An intricate, patchwork quilt weighed down on them. The bottom corner was kicked off Sembado's bionic prosthetic; its power pack had pushed their cozy warmth past an uncomfortable and sweaty heat. Sembado's chest heaved before he released a long and noisy sigh.

"What's the matter?" Kaluna asked lazily.

"I don't know," Sembado responded. "This is the most relaxed and…comfortable we've been in as long as I can remember."

"Yeah," Kaluna said. "Even I can't find something wrong with this, though."

"Yeah," Sembado said, emitting a single laugh. "But for once, that's not enough for me. I just don't feel easy. I feel like I will be able to appreciate and enjoy this someday, but I can't right now."

"What do you mean?" Kaluna asked, turning her head to be propped on his chest.

"Like the world isn't right," he replied. "And deep down, I know it and I can't rest until it is."

They remained in silence while the echo of his truth-filled confession soaked into the wooden walls.

"Well," Kaluna said in her matter-of-fact style. "I guess there's just one thing for you to do about that."

"What's that?" Sembado asked.

"*Actually* do something about it," Kaluna replied with uncharacteristic sass.

"Well, that'd be real simple," Sembado snapped, lovingly. "As soon as I figure out what's bothering me, I'll let you know."

"Well obviously it was unexpectedly being sucked into warfare," said Kaluna. "Especially with those deekin' spheres being used more up here than we ever saw beneath the surface."

Sembado's stomach jolted him so abruptly at Kaluna's cold truth that he nearly jerked in discomfort.

"Does that mean you're uneasy about Caspen's methods?" she asked.

"No," Sembado replied resolutely. "That *was* an unsettling scene that night but I feel very confident in his direction and purpose. After all, the other doctrines and so called truths...even the other stewards...none of their messages resonated with me as purely and simply as Caspen's. He's the first one to admit at least part of his methodology is just part of some game...a ruse."

"Yeah," Kaluna countered skeptically. "But if *Fabian* had been straight forward about his motives, would that have made you feel better? Just because Caspen's honest

214

about who he is and what he does does not make him more noble. It just makes him an honest tyrant."

"I do not think Caspen is a *tyrant*," Sembado responded. "I will admit that he is harsh. He is very certain about his beliefs, and that he has little room for compromise. But think about it: those people were going to burn his camp to the ground. They were pretty clearly requesting that fate."

"That seems a little extreme," Kaluna shot back. She picked her head up off his chest and rolled onto her back so that they were both staring at the ceiling.

"I'm not saying I enjoyed it or that they even for sure deserved it," Sembado replied. "I'm just saying they didn't seem too innocent themselves. If it's one thing you and I have had to learn the hard way, it's that perfect, infallible people are pretty hard to find. The Stewards obviously have their issues, as did the Spring. The Elephants even had problems with compromise. Look at my grandfather! You know I loved him until the end but if we can't be honest about our flaws, our loved ones' flaws, and the flaws of our communities, then I think we are doomed to fail."

"Obviously I agree with you," Kaluna said with exasperation. "I wish you wouldn't get so dramatic as to compare Caspen to your grandfather, but I *do* get your point."

"And don't get me wrong," Sembado added. "Some of this is just me being sick of running from one bad leader to the next. A good part of me just wants to settle down and accept whatever crazy bastard we've been given at this point."

"I'll settle for that when that crazy bastard is you," Kaluna said flatly as she turned back against Sembado to share his warmth. "And not a moment sooner."

***

One brisk December evening found Sembado sitting in his easy chair across from the persistent heat of the old iron stove. He was waiting anxiously for Kaluna to arrive. The sun had gone down but she had promised to return by dusk. She was with a large group of women but Sembado took little comfort in the strength of numbers. The attacks from the hill folk had colored them a very capable people in Sembado's eyes and he worried any time Kaluna left his side for very long.

He sat and picked under his fingernails with meticulous detail. If he hadn't caught a glimpse of Kaluna's nimble body shooting past a nearby window, he would have picked his nails until they bled. He was up at the door before she could even open it.

"Where have you been?" he demanded before she had completely opened the door. His words fell flat when he observed the uncharacteristic look of dread on her face.

She answered with nothing but heavy, labored breathing which offered little relief to Sembado's concern as it quickly swelled to panic.

"Kaluna," he said firmly. "What happened? Where have you *been*?"

Kaluna motioned for him to help her sit down, and she leaned back in the chair while she attempted to control the pace of her breathing.

"Caspen," Kaluna said with her eyes closed.

"What about him?" Sembado asked. "Did he attack you? Did he *touch* you?"

"No," Kaluna said, indignantly shaking her head. "Caspen's work camp. I followed him down there."

"With the other women?" Sembado asked.

"No," Kaluna responded. "Let me finish a deekin' sentence!"

Sembado put a curled fist in between his teeth and bit down on the skin of his fingers.

"After the group retired for the night," Kaluna continued, "I saw Caspen acting suspicious. Checking over his shoulder, you know? So I followed him, and he walked all the way down to the work camp."

"Inside the buildings?" Sembado asked quickly.

Kaluna confirmed with a head nod while she took several more deep breaths.

"Did you follow him inside?" Sembado asked.

Kaluna paused before slowly shaking her head up and down. She closed her eyes and took a deep breath.

"Sembado, it's bad," she said quietly.

"What? Why?" he asked.

"It's some kind of weird, forced labor camp," Kaluna replied.

"What do you mean?" Sembado asked.

"Forced labor, Sembado," Kaluna repeated. "Like people *forced* to do work. What do you think I mean?"

"I mean in what way?" Sembado shot back.

"They are fixed to pedaled cycles," Kaluna replied hotly. "But they are hooked up to all kinds of wires. I think they are being forced to spin the cycles to create power."

"Forced how?" Sembado asked.

"Seriously, Sembado?" Kaluna snapped. "I don't know! It's not like I walked up and started interviewing them. I didn't decide to get a tutorial from Caspen while I was there."

"Well, I can't really picture what you mean," Sembado responded defensively.

"I wasn't in there very long," Kaluna replied less venomously. "One of the cyclists saw me and started making noise."

"Asking for help?" Sembado asked.

"Not exactly," Kaluna replied. "It was weird. Almost like he was alerting the guards."

"So maybe they weren't being forced then," Sembado suggested.

"I know what I saw," Kaluna replied firmly. "These people were clearly in pain."

"Well, there's only one way to find out," Sembado replied.

Kaluna looked at him with a furrowed brow. She clearly did not understand his intent.

"We could just ask Caspen what's going on," Sembado said.

"Oh yeah, great," Kaluna replied. "I'm sure he'd be happy to know I was secretly following him."

"Well, we don't have to put it like that," Sembado laughed. "I can just express curiosity about what those buildings are for."

"But doesn't it bother you that he hasn't volunteered this information yet?" Kaluna protested. "I mean, he has us living in his right-hand man's old house and going to council meetings but he hasn't explained what the giant freaky warehouses are for yet? Doesn't that bother you?"

"Not really," Sembado said, shrugging his shoulders. "He has told us a lot. He probably just hasn't gotten that far yet."

"Well, we're there," Kaluna said. "And I want an explanation. Think about it, Sembado. He said he wants us…wants you…to run a camp just like this, but he hasn't even revealed the whole thing to you? What have you agreed to? I hope you didn't agree to running people on death machines against their will!"

"Of course not," Sembado replied. "You're being ridiculous. I would never enforce what you're describing."

"I told you," Kaluna said, shaking her head. "I told you I didn't like this place."

"No you did not," Sembado argued. "We will figure out what's going on and I *will* demand an answer for you. But don't throw this all away because you snuck into this place without any context."

"I know what I saw," Kaluna said firmly, crossing her arms. "I know what I saw."

Chapter 21
The Kinetic Farm

After several days of debate and contentious speculation, Kaluna permitted Sembado to confront Caspen about the work camp. As he had suggested, Sembado planned to ask more general questions about the buildings and Caspen's facility as a whole in a feigned attempt to learn more about his eventual role as a camp master.

They met Caspen for tea just a few days before Christmas. They bundled up for the short trot across the Circle as the plummeting temperatures played host to some of the first snow of the year; the first snow of Sembado's life.

Caspen opened his door without greeting so that they could run inside and gather near the fire. He laughed as he brought over a tray of mugs and rudimentary tea sachets. A kettle steamed over the fire. Caspen used a bent hook of a pole to retrieve the kettle before setting it on the hearth to cool slightly.

"So, you want to know more about the business, huh?" he asked, gingerly handling the hot vessel.

"Well, yeah," Sembado replied hesitantly. "If it's okay with you. I'll have to know at some point, right?"

"No, it's fine," Caspen said, pouring the contents of the kettle over the packets of leaf fragments. "To be honest, I was planning on pushing the issue soon. I thought you two might be getting a little too comfortable here."

"Oh," Sembado said, looking to Kaluna to remedy his awkward pause.

"I said it's fine," Caspen laughed, handing them each a mug. "It's just funny you decided to come see me now without being pressed but that you didn't mention it sooner. I guess I've always been fascinated by the threshold of people's comfort zones, ya know? Like, at what point does someone stand up and scoot their seat away from a fire that's too hot? Or how long does an individual go without seeking distraction or…or purpose? I know there has to be a time period of recognizing that they're unhappy with their situation…and then assessing what the problem actually is. After that, you have to come up with a solution…a remedy. But it's that next part that I'm so curious about. Then what? What does it take for you to actually act?"

"That *is* interesting," Sembado replied.

"Well, you don't have to lie," Caspen laughed. "Now that I've said it out loud, it sounds incredibly boring. Or at least pretentious."

"Well, I can tell you that Kaluna and I have experienced exactly what you're describing," Sembado said as he observed his tea concentrate disperse through the hot water.

"And what have you found?" Caspen asked.

"To be honest, we have been enjoying the comforts of this lifestyle," Sembado answered. "But we've been clear with each other that we can't settle for this and that we can only *relax* for so long. I think we've just agreed that the break is over and we need to get to work."

Caspen nodded thoughtfully. He scratched at his coarse whiskers and took a sip of tea.

"So, to my point," he said looking from his tea to Sembado and back, "what do you think was the final straw for you wanting to move ahead? Like I said, it's just an odd fixation of mine."

"Well, for me, it was the discomfort of being of little use," Kaluna said. She looked at Sembado and touched his wrist gently.

"I'd have to agree with that," Sembado added. "Just knowing that we weren't actively improving anyone's situation but our own. We've seen too much grief to be able to accept comfort for ourselves while others suffer."

Caspen continued to nod enthusiastically.

"I hear ya," he said with an agreeably benign smile. "It's hard to enjoy luxuries when others' discomfort is so visible."

Sembado smiled in agreement but failed to speak any further words of wisdom. He was going to look to Kaluna for help but elected to consult his mug of tea instead.

Caspen responded to the lull in the conversation with his usual deftness.

"So you're ready to move ahead with our plan…is that it? You've agreed that you can't settle for less and now you want to move on to bigger and better things? Well, I've got them for you. But I think it would be easier if I show you instead of telling you."

Caspen set down his empty mug and cracked his neck. Sembado and Kaluna followed his lead and abandoned their mugs as well.

"I guess we've got a bit of a field trip ahead," Caspen said happily as he donned a heavy winter coat. "Are you two warm enough?"

With careful but persistent prodding, Caspen was able to outfit Sembado and Kaluna with more cold weather gear than either had ever seen. Once they were all ready to go, they ventured out to the north and into the woods beyond.

Caspen led them on the exact same path by which he had originally revealed the camp to Sembado. In place of Gordo and his mount, Caspen had over a dozen citizens posted along the trail, each within earshot of the next.

Sembado's breath shot out in thick bolts of vapor as he trudged quickly behind Caspen. Kaluna walked briskly at his side; her breaths were more rapid and harsh as she struggled to keep up with Sembado and Caspen's longer gaits.

Caspen led them across the expansive clearing unceremoniously. Their humble procession seemed wildly inadequate for the expansive rank of structures that stood proudly against the dreary winter blight. There were so many questions in Sembado's mind but he failed to verbalize any of them while he gawked in wonder at the scale of the facilities he walked between. The distance of his previous vantage point had belied the true size of the buildings. The smallest of them was a two story wooden lodge. It was surrounded by a host of large, timber framed power houses. Rudimentary flying buttresses had been employed to stiffen some of the side walls as some of their unbraced lengths reached heights of forty feet.

The larger buildings sat relatively close together so that when Sembado looked up while walking between, them, the two buildings appeared to be leaning toward each other. The disorienting illusion was not nearly as overwhelming as the undeniable heat that pulsed through the exterior breezeway. Sembado felt the warmth on his face and before they reached the next pair of behemoth buildings, beads of sweat started to form where his blazing red hair erupted from the top of his forehead.

Caspen turned and walked backwards as he led them.

"Welcome to my kinetic farm," he exclaimed excitedly with outstretched arms.

At the next intersection of structures, Caspen led them around a corner where a narrow exterior staircase began climbing the side of the building. Sembado took up the rear as Kaluna went just after Caspen. Like Sembado, Kaluna ran her hand along the building's exterior as they climbed. She discreetly turned her face back and pointed at the wall with her eyes. Sembado nodded in agreement as his hand also sensed the unreasonable amount of heat the wood cladding was emitting. The stairs ascended their full height without a landing; Sembado numbered their climb at just over fifty steps. His bionic limb hummed in eager anticipation by the time they mounted the top. The last step formed a small platform with a heavily secured door which led inside.

Sembado braced himself against the railing, the wall, and Kaluna while Caspen fumbled with a lock and key. A soft click and the squeak of the hasp preceded a blast of hot air. A cloud of steam billowed out of the doorway and into the frigid atmosphere. Caspen began unfastening his coat as he invited Sembado and Kaluna inside. They quickly removed their own garments as they shuffled into the stifling room that greeted them.

Caspen moved past them and flipped a switch on the wall. A dim light flickered to life on the ceiling and illuminated the small room. A desk and chair sat in one corner next to another door. The light reflected off large plate windows that boxed out the other three walls of the room. Caspen took Sembado and Kaluna's heavy outer layers as they shed one after another. He piled them on the desk and walked to the window that stood opposite of the exterior door. He looked down through the window and turned and smiled expectantly at Sembado and Kaluna. Kaluna took Sembado's hand in hers just before he led her to join Caspen. Sembado's initial view was straight out the window and showed the heavy framework of the building's roof and ceiling as it stretched out above the cavernous space below. As he approached the observation window, he gained more and more sight of the large space. Clouds of misty vapor rose from below. The large mass of steam diverged into dozens of individual columns as the source came into view. Sembado shuffled up to the window and the floor of the giant room became visible. The individual plumes of hot, moist air emanated from over one hundred people, each quickly pedaling the contraption they were mounted on. Sembado's emotional disgust was quickly washed with the memory of riding a bicycle through the underwater complex in a harried escape from unwitting pursuers. The machines below were nearly identical but lacked the actual spoked wheels and tires.

Kaluna gripped his hand tightly, almost to the point of discomfort. He shot a sideways glance to see small tears dribble down her face as she took in the industrial havoc below. Sembado looked back out the glass and noticed that besides the cyclists, there were a few overseeing attendants who roved between the workers. The overseers made adjustments to the machines as they walked by; some switched out chambers of liquids as they passed. The faces of the cyclists painted a grim picture of labored anguish. The attendants adjusted mouth guards to accommodate the cyclists' gritted teeth. Their hands were firmly gripped on the handles in front of them. Each one had a round helmet strapped to their head. A bundle of wires led from under the helmet to a control board at the back of the assembly. Their legs were freakishly muscular, a pair of disproportionate anomalies that made their toned and muscular upper bodies appear frail and atrophied when compared.

Sembado became aware that his heart was starting to race and his breathing became shallow and panicked. Kaluna's sweaty palm, the temperature of the observation room, and the spectacle of the human machine amalgam combined to simultaneously turn his stomach and overwhelm his consciousness. His eyes listed and his head slumped. The last image to clearly break through his muffled comprehension was the painted slogan that wrapped around the space below. The phrase was repeated in bright, bold letters and was visible from any angle:

'Work Makes One Free'

Part Three
Stewardship is Sacrifice

Chapter 22
Voluntary Reflexes

Sembado came to with his eyes still closed. His eyes drifted behind their lids, turned upward, while he became familiar with the anxiety inducing buzz that his stomach broadcasted to the rest of his body. His closed eyes caused his mental existence to bob in a disorienting, swimming sensation. He cracked his eyes open and the image of Caspen's haggard face materialized above him. His usual benign smile had been replaced with a downturned grimace. Kaluna stood over Caspen's shoulder. Her arms were crossed and she looked uncharacteristically pale and concerned. Her soft tears from before had evolved into streams of wetness which covered her face. Her red eyes and runny nose betrayed her beauty for the first time in Sembado's memory.

"There ya are," Caspen said softly, placing a hand on Sembado's forehead. "Man, you're warm. I didn't think you were going to take it like that. Let's sit you up."

He carefully pulled Sembado off his back and propped him against the wall below the plate window. Sembado began to slump again and his powered prosthetic reactively kicked and bounced on the floor.

"Whoa, careful now," Caspen said, bracing Sembado and lightly smacking his cheek.

Kaluna kept her distance. She cowered into the corner and slid down the wall into a sitting position with her arms crossed around her knees.

Once Sembado's eyes remained open and clear, Caspen sat down on the floor in front of him. He took in Sembado's pathetic attempt at recovery with a nearly loathsome glare. He looked over to Kaluna just as her teary gaze rose from the floor to look him directly in the eye. Her distraught panic transformed into a stony reflection of his disapproving scowl.

"I don't understand what you two expected," Caspen said flatly.

Sembado looked up at him in disbelief.

"Not this," Sembado said softly. "Not…slavery."

"Slavery?" Caspen replied incredulously. "Is that what you think this is?"

"What do you call it?" Sembado asked.

"Those people have volunteered for that duty," Caspen replied. "Not one person in that room is in there against their will."

"I don't believe you," Kaluna replied.

"That's because you don't want to," Caspen replied sharply. "You have no idea what you're talking about and you never freakin' listen."

Kaluna crossed her arms more firmly and looked away.

"Yeah, that's what I thought," Caspen snapped dryly.

"Leave her alone," Sembado said firmly.

"Don't do that," Caspen replied. "Don't enable her bad behavior. As long as she is absolutely unwilling to compromise and you defend that no matter what, then she is a liability to you. I could have explained all of this ahead of time but you two didn't give me a choice."

"What do you mean?" Sembado asked. "You had plenty of time to explain this."

"Not before she saw it for herself," Caspen said, quickly standing and pointing at Kaluna.

Sembado fell silent. Kaluna looked at Caspen with her mouth open.

"I'm not an idiot, little girl," he said angrily. "Nobody gets in or out of this place without me knowing. You should have asked and I would have explained. But no, Kaluna's gonna do what she wants. And then, on top of that, jump to conclusions about who I am, and what this is."

"How could this possibly be anything other than forced labor?" Kaluna shouted.

"Just because it doesn't occur to you, doesn't mean it's a lie," Caspen hissed, approaching Kaluna where she sat, towering over her. "You're *far* too young to have the whole world figured out. I don't care how wise beyond your years you think you are!"

Sembado quickly rose and moved between Caspen and Kaluna.

"That's not necessary," Sembado said, putting his hands up. "You don't need to be so close."

"Oh, *you* back off!" Caspen snapped. "The longer she goes without being put in her place, the worse that know-it-all attitude is gonna get."

"Give it a rest," Sembado said firmly, squaring his shoulders. "Are you going to continue to whine about her or tell us what the hell is going on down there? If you have such a simple explanation, then why haven't we heard it yet? Because you're not done pouting yet? Go on then!"

Caspen glared at Kaluna one last time before looking Sembado firmly in the eye. He turned and walked to the window again, looking down over his creation. He stood with his hands clasped behind his back for a few quiet moments. Sembado continued to stand between where Caspen stood and Kaluna sat. Caspen took a deep breath and spoke.

"They really are all volunteers," he said to the glass. "If they don't want to continue, we give them something else to do. But as long as they're committed, then I milk every drop of energy out of them."

"How?" Sembado asked firmly.

"We use small amounts of electrical input," Caspen replied. "And I mean really small amounts, to convert their stored energy from food and electrolyte solutions into larger amounts of electricity."

"How?" Sembado pressed harder.

"You think that leg of yours is so special," Caspen replied as he turned to address Sembado. "That technology has been around for years. I simply reversed the process. The cycles send low voltage signals, tiny pulses of electricity into the worker's brain which tells the legs to cycle."

"So you're electrocuting them," Sembado stated flatly.

"No," Caspen replied patiently. "I'm simply helping them push their bodies to their actual limits."

"Well, it's clearly still painful," Sembado replied. "Why would they agree to that?"

"Because they believe in this," Caspen replied. "It's a...sacrifice."

"You're putting me on," Sembado said sarcastically. "This is ridiculous. You're literally sucking the life out of these people!"

"No," Caspen replied more hotly. "They get on those bikes and they pedal. For hours, they can keep those things spinning. And when they get tired, they ask for a boost. *They ask for it*. So don't get mad at me."

"I don't believe you," Sembado said as he crossed his arms.

"I don't care," Caspen laughed. "You don't have to believe me. You can go ask them yourself."

Sembado dropped his arms and looked at Kaluna. She returned his longing stare with her own icy glare. He quietly approached her and offered a hand to help her up.

"Should we go see for ourselves?" he asked softly.

"I already have," she said, staring away to the floor.

"We don't have to do this for him," Sembado replied. "But this is our opportunity to get the real story."

"I don't want to go," Kaluna muttered.

"I know," Sembado replied. He crouched down on one knee so that their faces were at the same level.

"Please," he said softly. "This is our only option right now."

As she closed her tear filled eyes, her lids pressed out a fresh wave of salty drops. She opened them again and stared straight into Sembado's eyes. Her vivid green irises clashed with their bloodshot surroundings. Sembado was not accustomed to the quiet desperation. She reached up and put her arms around Sembado's neck. She closed her eyes so that she didn't have to look at Caspen.

"He can't make me believe anything I don't want to," Kaluna whispered ever so softly.

"I know," Sembado replied.

He let go of her and stood up, offering his hand to help her. Kaluna wiped away her tears and reached for his hand. Caspen waited patiently while Sembado consoled Kaluna one last time. She looked past him and glared at Caspen.

"Let's get this over with then," she said.

"This way," Caspen said, indicating the interior door in the corner.

He walked to the door and held it open for Sembado and Kaluna. They passed through and on to a new set of stairs just on the other side. Caspen closed the door behind them and ushered them down the zigzag steps that led to the workers' floor below. The sweet funk of perspiration hung in the air like a musky fog. Caspen strolled across the floor with Sembado and Kaluna close behind.

"Good day, Caspen," an attendant called as she replenished a liquid solution behind one of the cyclists.

"Molly," Caspen replied with a friendly nod.

The attendant scurried away with a giddy smile on her face. The cyclist didn't seem to notice. She stared ahead with a determined sneer on her face. She pumped the pedals of her generator smoothly. The machine appeared to have been custom fit to her splayed stance. Her massive thigh muscles would not have accommodated a narrower configuration. Sembado gawked at the ludicrous proportions of her legs to the rest of her modest frame. Her veiny feet were bare against the pedals, one toe wrapped in white medical tape. Her feet gave way to her thick ankles which led to grotesquely defined calves. The muscles were not only rigidly cut in shape but also astonishingly large. Her thighs were by far the greatest spectacle. Sembado had never seen anything like it. Her upper legs were over a foot in diameter. The tight black material that covered them was stretched and worn. Her small waist and stomach were exposed; a reasonably shaped figure in her upper body made the appearance of her lower limbs all the more asinine. Her concentration was inspiring. She did not look at Caspen, Sembado, or Kaluna as they approached. She stared straight ahead at the wall. It wasn't until they drew closer that Sembado noticed a regular twitching in her face. Every few moments, an irregular blinking was accompanied by a full facial spasm.

Kaluna slowly circled the young lady and took in her physique as well as the cumbersome mechanics and bundles of cables which made up the cycling station. Her dirty blonde hair was chopped short and loosely spiked about her head. The yellow peaks poked through the netted cap that was fitted over her hair. A group of tiny fibers were arrayed across the cap. They collected into a loosely bound bundle and snaked back to the machine. Her slender neck and delicate facial structure belied the gargantuan measurements that lay below her waist. Despite someone's great efforts to make her appearance an androgynous vision, she was decidedly feminine and undeniably beautiful.

Caspen signaled for an attendant's presence and pointed at the controls behind the young woman. The worker appeared within moments and did Caspen's bidding. A flurry of pushed buttons and twisted nobs had an immediate effect on the young cyclist's behavior. The repetitious twitching stopped at once and her honey-colored eyes darted around to take in Sembado and Kaluna's faces. She closed her eyes as waves of pain and discomfort appeared to wash over her. She deftly weathered the pain, barely gritting her teeth. Her eyes opened with a subtle force, a determined resilience that immediately resonated with Sembado. It was a look that he had seen countless times. A certainty. A fortitude that he hadn't seen in any other eyes except Kaluna's own green-hued gaze. It was only then that Sembado realized the cyclist's light brown eyes were locked with Kaluna's as she paced in front of the pedaling assembly.

"Draw back the concentrate a little more," Caspen demanded of the attendant.

The young man made the appropriate adjustments with the results becoming immediately evident as the female cyclist's revolutions per minute dropped to a steady idle. As her pedaling slowed, the confinement of her upper body movement was relaxed. She took in a deep breath and rolled her neck and shoulders. The attendant removed the netting and wires from over her hair. She turned her head for the first time in order to look Sembado up and down. Without comment, she looked to Caspen and waited obediently for further direction.

Chapter 23
Bristle While You Work

"Sembado," Caspen declared smugly, "This is Morgan."

Sembado observed the beautiful mutant with reverence. She returned his stare with indifference.

"And Morgan," Caspen continued. "This is Kaluna."

Kaluna locked eyes with the young woman named Morgan. Sembado could almost feel the animalistic tension swell before it broke into a wave of humanistic understanding. Kaluna slowly but surely approached the station and extended an outreached hand. Morgan looked from Kaluna to her hand and back before forcefully removing her grip from the cycle handle and sharing a firm handshake. The grip seemed to electrify both women but they relented simultaneously after a delayed embrace.

"You hit your quota for today?" Caspen asked.

"And then some," Morgan replied.

Caspen called an attendant back and made a quiet command. The serviceman complied, pressing several buttons in quick succession. Morgan's pace released to a free pedal and soon she kicked slower and slower. She placed her hands above her head as her legs kicked and convulsed into a slow, steady flail. The attendants hurried around. The spout of an upturned bottle of fluids was directed into Morgan's mouth. She accepted it willingly while slowly pushing her legs in a circle, her head craned back and to one side.

"Morgan is one of our most efficient generators," Caspen declared proudly. "Her caloric input boasts the most joules per pound of body weight of any cyclist I've ever seen. One hour of her ability can power fourteen of my drones for an entire day!"

Morgan's pedals slowed to a stop as she prepared to dismount her cycling station. She swung one leg over the center assembly so that both feet planted to one side of her equipment. She slowly rose to a full and erect position. She stood at almost the exact same height as Sembado. Her legs shook and twitched as she made steady strides forward. Sembado took a deep breath and held it in as her massive legs slowly closed the distance between them. He nervously attempted to replicate Kaluna's greeting. Again, Morgan looked from Sembado's hand to his awkwardly reassuring smirk and back. She paused for several seconds before returning his reluctant embrace.

"Nice to meet you," Sembado ventured, desperately avoiding her grotesque legs with his eyes.

"You wouldn't be the first to stare," Morgan replied matter-of-factly. "Even the people that aren't being creeps just don't understand how this is possible."

Sembado observed her lower body more freely. His earnest intake was allowed as genuine curiosity by

Morgan. Kaluna seemed much less understanding. She approached Sembado and forced him to focus his eyes upward. Morgan laughed at the awkward interaction.

"We've come here to ask you legitimate questions," Kaluna said directly to Morgan. "Questions Caspen may not want us to ask."

"I've told you," Caspen replied defiantly. "You are welcome to grill my laborers. They are fully dedicated to me, and fully dedicated to my cause. I dare you to find an anomaly."

Kaluna glared at Caspen defiantly before asking Morgan, "How old were you when you came to this place?"

"I have been integrated with the harvesting as long as I can remember," Morgan replied. "But I've only been pumping the pedals for five years now."

"And this is all you do?" Kaluna replied skeptically.

"This is all I *need* to do," Morgan replied. "The system helps me concentrate so that I don't have to worry about the things outside my abilities. That's such a typical human response. To try and control everything."

"And this isn't controlling everything?" Kaluna replied confidently. The smugness of the response was nearly masked by her indignation.

Morgan's body language became tense as she appeared at a loss for words for the first time. Caspen's confidence visibly wavered just as the veil of rehearsed responses began to do the same.

"There's more to life than having the most clever response," Morgan said, recovering her commanding posture.

"Like what?" Kaluna asked.

Morgan moved away from her cycling station without responding. An additional attendant joined the first as they eagerly attempted to hydrate and post-process her body from her day's sacrifice. She walked at a designed pace that allowed one of the attendants to stick a new bottle of electrolytes in her mouth while another ran an electrical impulse down her tightened muscle groups. Sembado and Kaluna excitedly kept stride with Morgan's powerful saunter as she approached one of the powerhouse's exterior doors.

"Do you ever wonder about the world outside?" Sembado quickly asked.

"No," Morgan replied flatly. "Does the world outside ever wonder about me?"

"You *must* wonder about your freedom and independence?" Kaluna protested.

Morgan turned and looked at Kaluna. The longing gaze hung for just a moment. Her eyes darted toward Caspen and Sembado before she lunged forward, approaching Kaluna in three powerful steps. She seemed to tower over Kaluna in a way that Sembado never could. She pointed at the slogan that outlined the room.

"I am free," Morgan growled. "Free of wonder. Free of scheming. Free of worry and concern. So watch your mouth."

She turned and lumbered away more purposefully. When she reached the exterior double doors, she blasted one open with a mighty kick. Her exhalation and body heat could be seen billowing into the cold day before the door swung closed behind her.

Kaluna did not move or speak, she simply regarded the doors tersely. Sembado stood equally quiet at her side. He turned and observed the rest of the room. There was absolutely no evidence that Morgan and Kaluna's exchange had just happened. Even the distractible attendants were too busy scurrying from station to station to notice. Sembado took a deep breath and looked at Caspen. Caspen returned his stare with an attempt at a comforting gaze. He nodded at Kaluna whose back was still turned to the room. Sembado shrugged his shoulders and sighed.

The exterior doors opened to let in another blast of daylight and cold air. A middle aged man waddled in. He was clearly also a cyclist; the dimensions of his legs were even more absurd than Morgan's. His grizzled face, graying temples, and rough beard stubble painted the portrait of a rugged and handsome older man. His legs forced an even more exaggerated gait than Morgan's. Each step was a labored effort to swing the weight of the next limb forward. He almost looked uncomfortable as he walked past Kaluna and Sembado. His large frame lumbered nearly a head taller than Sembado as he passed.

"Reight," Caspen called as the man approached. "Ready to knock it out?"

The man named Reight stretched and rolled his neck.

"Let's hit it, man," he replied in a deep, gravely voice.

"How's the heart?" Caspen asked.

"Doc says I've got a few more years," Reight said confidently.

"Good," Caspen replied encouragingly. "We don't want another scare like the last, huh?"

He held up an outstretched hand which Reight slapped firmly before approaching the empty machine Morgan had just vacated. Three attendants converged on the station and helped Reight mount his massive legs over the seat of the generator. Once seated, his ridiculous frame looked surprisingly appropriate amongst the electromechanical equipment.

Caspen watched the attendants finish integrating Reight before he turned and approached Sembado and Kaluna.

"See," he said softly. "These people are absolutely dedicated. I couldn't keep them away from here if I wanted to."

"Great," Kaluna snapped as she whipped around. "Congratulations on being a wildly successful and convincing brainwasher. A true accomplishment for sure."

Caspen's lip curled and his face distorted as he strode forward and grabbed Kaluna by the upper arm. She barely fought back as he marched her forward toward the exterior doors. Sembado followed quickly behind them, unable to reason with either of them.

Caspen dropped his leading shoulder and blew one of the exit doors open. He dragged Kaluna out into the biting cold and tossed her away. Sembado said nothing but took a moderating stance between them. Kaluna's fists were clinched at her side as she defiantly locked eyes with Caspen who was angrily pacing back and forth as he returned her icy energy.

"Is this going to stop or not?" Caspen shouted. "I have neither the time, energy, nor interest to put up with your pouty shit week after week. Either get with the program or you're out. There are *so many* reasons I can't abide your crap. Why do you insist on dragging Sembado down with you?"

"What?" Kaluna replied. "Is that what's going on?" She backed away from Sembado who stood dumbfounded between the two of them.

"Wha...no," Sembado said in distress. "I...you two have to..."

"Oh my God," Kaluna interrupted. "Are you defending him?"

"Oh, please," Caspen hissed. "You think your attitude and stubborn-ass position are beyond his judgment?"

"Hey!" Sembado yelled at Caspen. "You don't speak for me!"

"Do not," Caspen growled pointedly. "Do not defend her. Do not defend her behavior. Do not defend her actions. Do not defend her bullshit. You have so much more potential than this."

"Than what?" Kaluna asked. "Standing his ground for what he believes?"

"What *you* believe!" Caspen shouted.

"Hey!" Sembado screamed. "I think and act for myself, damn it! You two *both* need to stop!"

Caspen and Kaluna both stood and fumed silently. Sembado's use of such a shrill tone had temporarily knocked the wind from their sails.

"Caspen," Sembado said firmly, "I *will not* have you try and create a wedge between me and Kaluna. I will compromise. I will admit that she can be wrong but don't you dare try to bargain for me without her. It *will not* happen. Period. I'm sorry that she isn't as easy to indoctrinate as I am but I am so glad she's not. If you don't get over the challenge of convincing her, then we both walk. Period."

Caspen took a deep breath and huffed out a cloud of steamy defeat. He looked off down the corridor created by the closely spaced buildings.

"And Kaluna," Sembado continued, "We must compromise somewhere. *Somewhere*. We can't do this forever. Is this pretty? No. I don't think it is at all. I am truly repulsed. But these people are no more brainwashed than I was when I was living fat, dumb, and happy in the complex. Was blowing the lid off of that situation really the best way to serve those people? I'm not so sure. Caspen's putting a lot on the line by revealing so much to us. He's exposing so much in the hope that we won't betray his trust. I know how you feel about this right this minute, but I just can't walk away from this kind of offer when he's clearly trying so hard."

Kaluna relaxed her clenched jaw and tossed the weight of her head to the other side of her shoulders. She looked at Caspen and sighed. He returned her gaze and for a brief moment, they silently partook in another staring match. Sembado watched with increasing impatience. His bionic limb hummed and buzzed in place. He was just about to make another reprimanding outburst when Kaluna spoke.

"Well, we have to figure something out," she said, dropping her crossed arms to her sides. "We can't keep doing this, can we?"

"No," Caspen replied. "I don't think we can."

"So the expectation is that we will run a similar facility at our own camp?" she asked.

"That was my intention," Caspen responded earnestly.

"Can it be done without the electrodes?" she asked. "Can't we just let people give what they can on their own?"

"That's how mine started," Caspen answered. "My cyclists were actually the ones who asked for help to go further. It was actually that man, Reight, and Morgan's father that originally asked about it. This is the system that we developed to solve that problem."

"What is the problem, exactly?" Sembado asked. "Everyone has physical limitations – that's life."

"It's more mental, really," Caspen replied. "They reach a wall that they can't surpass – an emotional limit. Couple that with their tendency to be distracted – worrying about what they're going to do for fun that evening or whether or not we're going to finally get snow this season. Those are all non-physical limitations. The human body has a huge amount of potential but those limits tend to be much further past where we are willing to go."

"The discomfort though," Kaluna said. "There are all kinds of physical repercussions. That man. Reight. He's eventually going to die because of this."

"He knows that," Caspen replied. "He's not an idiot. I told you I don't make him do this. This is his. Believe it or not. This is all of theirs. And besides, discomfort is a necessary evil for anything worthwhile. Have you two not experienced a great deal of discomfort in the last year or so?"

Kaluna leaned against Sembado and stared at the frost covered ground while she quietly contemplated Caspen's response.

Chapter 24
The Cream Of The Crop

Sembado spent nearly the entire winter carefully orchestrating an improved understanding between Kaluna and Caspen. His most measured success came when he finally convinced Kaluna that their village would be run by their rules and that they need only borrow Caspen's principles with which they actually agreed.

Caspen, for his part, showed steadfast support for the progress and success of Sembado and Kaluna's future. As more tolerable temperatures arrived, Caspen began sending out the first waves of homesteaders. He spent several hours a day meeting with each group before they left and made a regular habit of retaining about one out of every hundred villagers. These special people, he told Sembado, were the most capable of the population and showed the most promise. Through various manipulations and propaganda, he carefully convinced each of these unique recruits to stay behind as their family and loved ones forged on into the wilderness.

By April, he had collected dozens of these chosen few and separated them into a new camp between the Circle and the hidden facilities to the north.

"They will be your very own villagers," he told Sembado and Kaluna one morning as they sipped coffee and oversaw the trainees' progress. "I have ensured that they are the most physically capable, intelligent, and willing to serve. Not one is over twenty-five years old. A few focused children to begin the next generation. These people will be able to serve you for the rest of your life."

"In what capacity?" Kaluna asked.

"That is up to you," Caspen replied. "But I would suggest we reveal a predetermined duty to each of them, here at my facilities. It would be much easier for you if they had their secret assignment in mind when you arrive at your destination."

"Train them with your people?" Sembado asked. "You aren't afraid of revealing too much?"

"No," Caspen said. "You two are easily the most independent thinkers in this entire facility and I've revealed everything to you. And look, you're still here. I've told you before: if you give people a special purpose, they will own it. They will keep it and nurture it and take pride in it. This group is especially thirsty. I am actually quite intrigued."

"When will we leave?" Kaluna asked.

"Again," Caspen replied, "That's mostly up to you. We will want to find a balance between the amount of supplies and building materials you take with you and the burden that creates for travel. Obviously, my kind of facility takes nearly a lifetime to develop and perfect, but I will be able to lend you enough of the electrical equipment to get a much better head start than I started with."

"How far are we going to go?" Sembado asked.

"The territory that I patrol and observe stretches for some distance," Caspen responded. "I never told you this but I've at least had the ability to watch you since you crossed the river. Now, I don't normally have drones out that way but my network can be quite extensive if needed. I would prefer our operations overlapped but only at a minimum."

"So how far is that?" Kaluna asked.

"Nearest I can tell," Caspen replied casually, "about five hundred miles in any direction."

"Five hundred miles," Sembado repeated with exasperation. "I had no idea!"

"Well, that's just to the edge of my operation," Caspen said sheepishly. He directed their conversation away from the curious students nearby. "You'll have to go a few hundred miles past that to really open up a territory of your own."

"A few *hundred* more?" Sembado said incredulously.

"Oh, don't be so dramatic," Caspen replied as they moved into a private grove away from the others. "With this crew, you're looking at three weeks, max. And that's to get a full thousand miles to the center of your own claim. You're probably going to settle much closer so that our circles of influence can at least overlap. You could be sleeping under your own roof a month after you leave here."

"Where does that put us?" Kaluna asked.

"Depends on which direction you head," Caspen replied. "Based on all the old maps I've seen, you would end up settling along some body of water. Either the Gulf to the southeast or one of the big rivers north of that. That's really an ideal location, compared to what I have to deal with here."

The generalized morning training drew to an end and Caspen had each of the elite recruits break off into smaller classes. As he had them led away to various parts of his facility, he granted Sembado and Kaluna a much needed reprieve from their taxing oversight.

They retreated to their cabin as the sun reached its summit in the blue sky overhead. Kaluna reached the bed first and excitedly crawled under a heavy sheet which remained piled on the bed from earlier in the morning. She curled into a fetal position, an unnecessary space savings for her small frame. Sembado plopped down on his side of the bed. He could barely get his shoes kicked off before falling backward against Kaluna's stomach.

"Ugh," she protested. "Your head weighs *so* much."

He laughed and shifted in bed, bringing his flowing red locks to rest on his pillow.

"That's because of all my brains," he joked.

"Yeah, right," Kaluna said. "You say that every time."

"Are you really ready to go another thousand miles?" he asked.

"Are you serious?" Kaluna replied. "We'll have horses this time. And if I'm being honest, I would *walk* twice that far if it meant never having to see Caspen again."

"Yikes," said Sembado. "That seems pretty harsh."

"I don't care," Kaluna responded. "I know you want to make peace, and I'm willing to do that for now, but I just don't trust him. I mean, a five hundred mile radius of drone coverage? Sembado, that's *ridiculous*."

"No, you're right about that," Sembado admitted. "I don't think the Complex could even boast that."

"Not without the internet," Kaluna added.

Sembado sprawled across the bed while Kaluna took her usual position, carefully tucked tightly against his ribs. Sembado closed his eyes with a soft sigh. Her soft skin slid effortlessly under his fingertips. His hand was down the neck of her shirt while he stroked her shoulder and upper arm under her sleeve. Kaluna turned her neck to rest her head between Sembado's bicep and clavicle. She kissed him lackadaisically, starting at the base of his neck and moving up his jaw to his chin. Sembado reactively craned his head toward her out of a tickling reflex. This created the fortunate circumstance of their lips being incredibly close to each other. They paused for a moment, gently pouting and breathing coffee on each other. It was fresh and sweet and smoky. Despite his obvious desire, Sembado could barely muster the motivation to lean forward another inch. Kaluna returned his effort tenfold and pushed her parted mouth passionately against his. They held each other in a stirring embrace for a moment before releasing to start all over. Kaluna kissed Sembado over and over. With each encounter, she grew more confident and shifted her body to a position of power. She climbed to her hands and knees so that her face hung over Sembado's. Her draping hair offered them a secret escape within the tight confines of its dark and shining walls. Sembado gathered the strength to wrap his hands around her torso and she slowly settled her chest against his as their searching mouths continued their erotic dance.

Their cabin door suddenly shuddered with a vicious pounding. Kaluna quickly threw herself off Sembado and bounced out of bed in one fluid motion. Sembado sat straight up in bed and firmly planted a pillow across his lap. A steady and muffled rattle accompanied the knocking noise

"What now?" she asked aloud, marching toward the door.

A second round of determined knocking answered her question. The soft rattling continued. She could barely unbolt the door before it was jerked open. The rattling noise immediately became distinguishable as rapid gunfire. A young woman stood panting in the doorway.

"Caspen called for you," she said. "The hill folk have attacked again."

"In the middle of the day?" Sembado asked.

"You hear 'em, don't cha?" the girl snapped. She ran off without waiting for a response.

"Grab my shoes," Kaluna called.

Sembado tried sliding out of bed with Kaluna's grace but tangled his feet in the sheets and tumbled over the edge. He landed in a heap but quickly located Kaluna's shoes. He whipped them across the room, one at a time, before fumbling with his own.

They ran out together and converged with the other citizens of the Circle at Caspen's cabin where a makeshift armory had been established after the last attack.

Sembado and Kaluna were each pitched a gun. Sembado first caught a compact submachine gun, which he quickly traded with Kaluna for a pump shotgun with a shortened barrel. They rallied with the others, horses brought about. Kaluna climbed atop one of the steeds. Sembado used his prosthetic to quickly hop up behind her. He landed with a heavy pop and the horse shot forward. Kaluna wedged her firearm firmly into a saddle holster while Sembado held his out to one side. His other arm was tucked tightly around Kaluna's slim waist.

They followed the others to the purported attack location. They were third in the cavalry line. Their leader was the young lady who had come and collected them from the cabin. Behind her was one of Sembado and Kaluna's neighbors. She led them toward the kinetic farms to the north before peeling off the main trail and heading east. The party's progress slowed to a quickened trot as their mounts struggled to effectively navigate the terrain at their increased clip. Movement to their left drew Sembado's attention but, before he could draw a bead with

257

his shotgun, he realized it was Caspen tearing in from the north.

Just as he appeared, a volley of arrows was released from somewhere ahead of their advance. The first bolt found purchase in the horse and rider just ahead of Sembado and Kaluna. The young lady at the front of the pack screamed loudly. The arrow had pinned her leg against the side of her horse. The horse flailed off course and came to a stop to their right. It bucked about wildly while a ghostly blue sphere grew from within its chest. Caspen quickly cut in front of Sembado and Kaluna on his way to save the young lady. He revealed a short, curved blade from his hip as he charged forward. In one clean swing, he broke the arrow just between the rider's leg and her horse's body. The girl fell from the horse and watched in anguish as half the horse's chest was devoured in moments.

Caspen quickly pulled his mount to a stop and circled around, driving it forward haphazardly.

"Forward!" he bellowed. "Move forward!"

Sembado hunkered down against Kaluna's back as she pushed their horse faster.

"There they are!" Kaluna yelled.

Sembado poked his head around hers just in time to see a group of camouflaged bodies scatter into the pine trees to their right. He held the shotgun at arm's length and pulled the trigger. The gun kicked up and nearly flew out of Sembado's grip. The loud blast startled the horse just off course but Kaluna corrected it. The pine trunk's bark exploded with the burst of buck shot. A dazzling exhibition of blue flashes followed. Sembado quickly decoupled his left arm from Kaluna's torso so that he could hold the powerful weapon with both hands. He instinctively squeezed the horse's haunches with his feet. His mighty prosthetic appeared to dig into the horse too much and it protested with a mid-stride jostle. Sembado had to concentrate with all his might to moderate the bionic leg's powerful grip. With the shotgun firmly in both hands, he pumped out the brightly colored shell and took aim at a large figure that lumbered between the trees on foot. The person had just dived behind another tree when Sembado blasted the trunk of the tree with a fresh round. A man appeared from behind the tree and let the blue spheres pop within inches of his face. His beady eyes flared behind the bushy black hair that covered his face. In one fluid motion, he drew back his arm and whipped it forward with a grunt. A shining hatchet streaked end over end straight at Sembado and Kaluna. Sembado quickly sprung up and planted his bionic foot on the horse's rump. He pushed off with all his strength. The powerful kick forced Kaluna and the horse forward and Sembado flew backwards. The hatchet darted through the space Sembado had just occupied and stuck into a nearby pine tree with a loud crack. Sembado pulled his legs under him and pushed them back as he continued to sail through the air. His outstretched bionic leg found the ground first and recoiled expertly to soften his landing.

He came to rest in a kneeling position, the shotgun gripped tightly in both hands. He pumped it again and moved forward into the trees. Caspen and the other stewards thundered by to his left. A deafening boom sounded ahead. A blue flash caught his attention; one of Caspen's riders fell from their mount. His eyes shot back to the right where a cloud of smoke hung in the air. There, he saw a woman duck behind a tree and upend a small container in the end of her long rifle's barrel. She stuffed two more in, tapping each one with a long brass rod. She caught sight of Sembado and rolled out of the way just before he sent a blast of blue spheres in her direction.

The woman ran ahead. The cumbersome weapon heaved from side to side as she went. Suddenly, she fell to one knee and shouldered the awkward weapon. Sembado saw a blur to the left. Caspen was charging at her on his horse. Before she could fire, he used his small cutlass to knock her barrel upward. He brought the blade down just as he passed, a spray of blood marking the spot where he sliced her right shoulder. The woman cried out and fell forward. She released the gun and fell on top of it. She rolled over and feebly attempted to raise the gun with just her left arm but Caspen had already circled back. He trampled the woman with his horse before quickly driving forward to his next victim. Sembado ran over and approached the woman's battered, bloody body. She looked up at him, fresh blood and dirt smeared across her brow and cheeks. He pulled her musket from her weakened grip and discharged it into the ground nearby.

He set the rifle back down next to her body. The woman reached up and grabbed his arm. Her dark brown eyes searched his. His inner turmoil and sadness twisted his emotional grimace as he slowly pulled his hand from her frail embrace. He could only break eye contact by closing his eyes. He left her behind as he moved forward into the trees.

***

The battle quickly drew to a close with Caspen and his war party successfully running down most of the attacking hill folk. The rest were driven back into the surrounding foothills. Sembado was able to avoid any additional encounters as the mounted counter offensive quickly moved the fighting out of sight. He halfheartedly patrolled the same quarter acre of trees until the others returned from beyond. To his relief, Kaluna was the first to make contact. Her grim expression matched the labored trot with which her horse plodded forward. Sembado touched Kaluna's bloody left arm as the horse sauntered up next to him.

"It's okay," Kaluna muttered, wiping the blood with her other sleeve. "It's not mine."

"That's okay?"

"Just shut up and get on," she replied.

The ride back to the Circle was a quiet one as the early evening shadows crawled to the east.

Chapter 25
Quite Indiscriminately

Sembado and Kaluna's emotionally exhausted withdrawal proved to be short lived. The only time they were allowed was the gap between their arrival back at the Circle and that of the rest of the war party. A simple but obligatory dinner was served and concluded with an assembly of Caspen's council inside his cabin.

Sembado and Kaluna arrived last and sat together nearest the door. The rest of the group sat in a misshapen circle around Caspen's main room. Caspen stood in the middle of the room and paced while he spoke. His elevated rhetoric reflected the rage that had not subsided. While the majority of the council appeared as drained as Sembado and Kaluna, Caspen's fuming energy was an uncomfortable highlight against an otherwise somber backdrop.

"We will begin planning a counter offensive immediately," Caspen stated as he marched back and forth. "I want to drive these savages out once and for all."

"I'm sorry, Caspen," a woman called from the other side of the room, "But don't you think we lost enough lives today?"

A few voices meagerly conferred with the protest. "Is this all because you think he's still alive?"

"Yeah, I do, Hena," Caspen growled as he spun around and confronted the woman. She averted eye contact as he imposed himself over her. "That's why we aren't going to send anyone back into those damn hills," he added, turning to address the group. "I propose sending in waves of drones until we can't see a single thing move."

"But all the animals," the woman named Hena replied. "That's unacceptable. We are still stewards, Caspen! You need to end this feud with Br…"

"Do *not* say his name," Caspen hissed in a guttural slur. The tension in the room reached an uncomfortable hum. Caspen breathed out slowly as his posture relaxed.

"Besides," he added calmly, "we have a solution now. I didn't want to tell any of you until the developments were complete but we have successfully adjusted our weapons to only target human DNA."

A hush fell through the room but was quickly replaced with elevated whispers.

"That's right," Caspen declared excitedly. "No more do we have to fear shooting these people and unnecessarily injuring their horses. No longer do we have to use modestly sized weapons for fear of taking out surrounding wildlife. We can now use larger weapons with more coverage and be confident in knowing that the only lives being lost belong to those filthy, murderous heretics!"

Hena's eyes brightened as understanding trickled through her uncertainty. Her excitement was shared by the group as the purified future Caspen described elevated their spirits and destroyed their non-violent misgivings.

As the rest of the room buzzed with enthusiasm, Kaluna and Sembado were careful not to reveal through their body language their cloister of doubt and disgust. They subtly took each other by the hand. The silent embrace was enough to confirm their shared resistance to Caspen's puritanical manifesto.

"Well," Caspen said over the din, "that's mostly it. We will be refining the details in the coming week or so. I will assign additional tasks as needed. Your confidence is assumed as this kind of information could lead the hill folk to any number of diabolical counter measures. So let's keep our lips sealed tight, huh, folks?"

The group solemnly acknowledged his request before rising to leave.

Sembado and Kaluna were the first to the door but Caspen called them back by name.

"Just for a moment, please," he said as the others trudged out into a cool, dry dusk.

Sembado stood with his back to the segment of wall immediately adjacent to the door while the other council members offered polite niceties as they shuffled by. Kaluna faced him, her back to Caspen and the rest of the room, and stared at a random point in space somewhere between Sembado's chest and chin. When the others had vacated the cabin, Caspen slowly walked over and shut the door. He paused for a minute before turning to Sembado and Kaluna. Their close proximity to the door forced

Caspen to awkwardly crane his neck backward as he addressed them. His personal space appeared to be as mutually violated as theirs.

"Uh, would you two like to have a seat?" he asked with an unexpectedly raised tone.

Sembado and Kaluna moved across to an open pair of chairs without a verbal response. They slowly sat down on the humbly cushioned seats as if they may catch fire at any moment. Caspen quickly walked to his personal chair which sat just across from them. He cocked it slightly to afford himself a direct vantage of their post. He looked at each of them thoughtfully but his hopeful expression melted to skepticism as he took in their hesitant and defensive body language. He looked down at his feet and sighed loudly.

"How long do we have to keep doing this?" he asked at his feet.

A ringing silence reverberated softly throughout the rustically appointed space. Sembado and Kaluna both kept their eyes fixed on their intertwined fingers.

"Here I've presented some of my most trusted advisors with a silver bullet in defeating the literal scourge of our every waking moment. And while they excitedly celebrate the possibilities of a peace-filled tomorrow, you two continue to sulk as if you remain lost in the desert. You do not need to smile, laugh, and dance for me but I beg you to show some kind of contentment in my leadership. At least in front of the others. It's discouraging for them. It's embarrassing for me. It makes no sense. They will look to you two before long and I need them to feel comfortable seeing you as a reasonable alternative to me."

"What do you mean?" Kaluna shot back, quickly snapping out of her morose stupor. "None of them are supposed to be coming with us."

Sembado had looked up in an attempt to catch Caspen's most immediate and natural facial response to Kaluna's charge. But Caspen, as usual, was able to execute the most benign response. His eyes and mouth betrayed nothing; an outside observer would have claimed Kaluna's accusation as meaningless.

"Our development of this specialized frequency means everything," Caspen replied flatly. "It is the end of this awful internal conflict that stewards have had to face regarding the orbs and their effects on non-human life."

"But it's not," Sembado replied. "We have other frequencies that can cancel that out. They can make it useless."

If Caspen had not leaned his head back to laugh so arrogantly, he would have seen Kaluna elbow Sembado emphatically in the ribs.

"Sembado, my friend," Caspen said with a light chortle, "we have frequencies that do things you couldn't imagine. The so-called authorities in the underwater facilities passed on a wealth of information that they hadn't even scratched the surface on. It's crazy, really."

Sembado and Kaluna exchanged looks of uneasy disbelief. Fortunately, Caspen regarded it as awestruck reverence.

"I know what you're thinking," he said with almost jovial excitement. "An orb frequency that wipes out humans? Why didn't they set this off sooner? I mean, even now we have all of these villagers going out into the world to live by our stewardly principles. Why? What's the point? All those extra people. They're just living to fulfill some ideological dead end. And then what? We're forcing them to live within their most disappointing potential. Why live at all? What does it really mean to steward at that point? To keep an eye on things? Make sure the forest creatures don't get out of line? Ha! Nature doesn't need people. It'd be better off without us! So then what? I want to keep living from day to day because that's one of my only instincts left but if you take this *special* purpose away from all these other *normal* people? Good luck. I don't think I'm anything *super* special but I've at least come to these conclusions. The rest of these idiots really believe that this is a life worth living. Just being another animal in the food chain. Just barely cohabitating with the wild and trying to leave the smallest footprint possible? Human beings weren't made for that! We are *stupidly* intelligent for a species that's just supposed to rub sticks together and stack some rocks on top of other rocks."

"But that's everything you promote," Kaluna responded desperately to the grim future Caspen painted with his caustic words.

"Yeah," Caspen responded with a snap. "Because I have to manage the goals and expectations of the rest of these morons."

The look of realization on Sembado and Kaluna's faces seemed to upset Caspen.

"Are you two serious?" he demanded. "You're too effing savvy and intelligent to not know what's going on here!"

Sembado's look of genuine confusion was enough to elicit Caspen's scathing explanation. He rubbed his hand forcefully against his forehead as he exhaled dramatically.

"I've told you two that our purpose for managing humans' impact on the environment should be practical and not emotional, right? It doesn't have to be a warm and happy satisfaction. It's so that we have a tomorrow to plan for. A future that we know we can exist in. So once you've reached that conclusion, then why on earth would you allow an extraneous amount of ignorant proletariats to take up your precious space?"

"The hill folk," Kaluna answered. "You want them gone because you think they're unnecessary competition?"

"No," Caspen replied firmly. "I think anyone who isn't part of my immediate operation is unnecessary competition. I cannot wrap my head around Mereth's goals. Forcing people to live a mediocre existence so that their children's children can live the same shitty struggle? What!? I just can't abide that. Is that *so* crazy?"

Sembado's hand was placed firmly over his mouth while Kaluna stared at Caspen with wide eyes and a gawking mouth.

"You two *will not* make me regret choosing you," Caspen stated as tears welled in his eyes. "I have done this too many times to feel defeat once again. You are about logic and order and realism and that's everything I've stated to you! We can wipe out all of the extraneous competition within my influence so that our footprint is reasonable and moderate. You know how these things work. I'm not talking about pain and suffering. This is quick and over. And then we can use some reasonable technology and expansion to build an advanced society that respects what the earth provides."

"But you're not that old," Kaluna interrupted suddenly. "Why do you need us? You have another twenty or thirty years of influence left in you. Why are you pushing so hard for an apprentice and replacement?"

"Because even this solution shows meaningless pursuit!" Caspen screamed unexpectedly.

Sembado jumped at the harsh response while Kaluna sneered in frigid disapproval.

"This has no end," Caspen stated with an equally cold yet more measured tone. "I can't dream beyond dream and wish for my most inner desires to come true."

He quickly stood and moved behind his chair. He paced the length of the room while he lectured Sembado and Kaluna, who sat in the tense volume of Caspen's address. He ran his hands through his hair as he considered his next words.

"I'm so done with this," he said quietly after a long pause. It was almost a defeated confession. "I've spent decades now ensuring my followers have so much meaning and purpose in their stupid, insignificant lives that I've neglected myself."

Another hush fell over the room as Caspen seemed to acknowledge the truth of his statement for the first time.

"After my wife died," he sighed with his eyes closed, "I lost that personal touch of encouragement. What am I gonna do? Care for these other random people like I did her? Like I was prepared to do for our little boy? I don't give a shit about these people. I only care about the meaning they bring to my life. And now that I know I can destroy their only existential threat in a matter of minutes, they don't need me anymore. So I don't need them. Or the artificial purpose they give me."

Caspen had slowed his nervous pacing to an emotional scuffle as he spilled out his inner demons to an astonished Sembado and Kaluna. He came to a complete stop, pushing his right thumb and forefinger into his tear-filled eyes.

"But that's why I need you," he said ever so quietly. "There are only so many outs for me here, and all the good ones involve you taking over for me."

"The good ones?" Sembado asked quietly.

"Yeah," Caspen replied even quieter. "The situations where I don't destroy every person I don't expressly need to keep living this silly farce of a lifestyle."

"Oh," Sembado said, genuinely taken aback. "So what are the alternatives?"

"I already told you," Caspen replied flatly. "You take over for me and bear the burden of this ridiculous, hopeful camp. Wiping out the other stewards, and the hill folk, for that matter, becomes your problem."

"So what happens to you?" Kaluna asked pointedly.

"There's a couple options," Caspen replied coolly. "I could move on. Literally. Just pack up a few supplies and start marching east. There's the real purpose. The only one we have left really. Survival. Struggle. Keep moving and trying and suffering day by day. At least then I know it would be for real and not just because I want to."

"And the alternative?" Kaluna pressed.

"Oh," Caspen acknowledged with disappointment. "I could kill myself. Probably by wiping out everyone else in my five hundred mile radius."

Kaluna's sweaty, clammy palm found Sembado's in seconds and quickly squeezed it to the point of pressured agony.

"So, I hate to put all that burden on you," Caspen said with a cold, emotionless tone, "but if you don't take this helm from my hands, that's the outcome you're left with."

While Sembado was utterly overwhelmed by Caspen's defeatism, Kaluna met it with passionate opposition.

"That's it?" Kaluna demanded. "That's all that you can give? You don't see any other future for yourself? Even if you kill off the hill folk and leave the other stewards to live, you have such a huge buffer before you really threaten the environment with the true impact that humans can pose. You couldn't even hope to affect the world in such a negative way in one lifetime."

"But that's it," Caspen replied with surprising serenity. "I can expect that. I *can*. With the recent developments in the orb technology and the possible advances in a generation or less...the natural world doesn't stand a chance. And believe it or not, I still care about that. I still care about the spirit of the stewards' creed. I would happily wish away my discoveries, understanding, and hope to all the following generations if it meant letting the flora and fauna being left to survive. Ha! I mean, that's the real arrogance of the stewards' plan. To think that the plants and animals actually *need* human intervention. Don't be ridiculous. At best, we complicate their success. But with our technology? *My* technology? I could start a new revolution in a decade. And it wouldn't be pretty. It certainly wouldn't bode well for the rest of earth's habitants. Not the four and six-legged ones, anyway. So please don't tempt me. That's the real issue here. I don't want the power. I mean, I do, but I know I can't handle the privilege. Who can? I guess that's why I chose you two. You just seem so friggin' idealistic. Like you would be able to resist the temptation of ultimate and absolute power that our technologies would lay at your hands."

Sembado wrapped his outstretched arm around Kaluna's shoulder as she leaned over her armchair into his awaiting embrace. Caspen's confession of a totalitarian, final solution had besieged her otherwise indomitable fortitude with grief, regret, and sorrow.

"What is another option?" Sembado pleaded.

"None," Caspen replied sourly. "Why on earth would you refuse a man who is literally telling you he is ready to *murder* every human being for a thousand miles?"

"One can hope," Sembado replied with a dry smirk.

"That right there is why you can't turn this down," Caspen responded. He nearly begged them to comply. "I don't know why you wouldn't. I'm promising to *literally* walk away. I'm leaving control of the most powerful land-based civilization in North America in your hands and you two are still blubbering about my tactics?"

"It's not that we don't appreciate the perspective that you're painting for us," Kaluna replied. "It's just *so much* responsibility. You have to understand that it would seem overwhelming."

"I do," Caspen replied. "I get it. It's a lot. But my love for keeping this world's heart beating is what drove me to ask this of you two. I'll say it again. I *still care* about stewarding the environment. I just don't think the stewards' view on our role is realistic. It's either way too optimistic about the power we hold over nature or it's way too restrictive on the potential we have to create meaningful change."

"I understand," Kaluna declared, standing to meet Caspen's eye level as best as she could. "What you've described is the best possible outcome for an informed population to play its part in the future of this world."

"Exactly!" Caspen said excitedly. "That's such a perfect way to put it!"

"Then I don't think we have a choice," Kaluna said, ignoring the spastic squeezes Sembado imparted on her hand. "We have to accept your offer."

Chapter 26
Supply Chain

Sembado stood in the doorway of his and Kaluna's cabin. Across the Circle, Caspen stood in his own doorway and looked on proudly as Sembado confined himself to his quarters. Caspen smiled happily while Sembado returned as benign a look as he could, closing his own front door.

"What the hell are you doing?" he demanded of Kaluna as soon as their confidence was secured. "Why on earth would you agree to that madman's demands?"

Kaluna went about her nightly routine as if she hadn't heard him.

"Kaluna, what were you thinking?" Sembado shouted.

"Would you keep your voice down?" she replied quietly. "You're going to make someone suspicious."

"Me?" Sembado hissed. "*I'm suspicious?* What the hell are you doing?"

"Are you serious?" Kaluna replied incredulously. "Do you really think I would move on that promise? Just because I agreed to it? After all we've been through, how can you still be so deekin' naïve?"

"Well how am I supposed to know when you're lying?" Sembado snapped. "This world would be a lot simpler if everyone just told the truth."

"Oh, calm down," Kaluna scolded as she crawled into bed. "I've already figured out what to do."

Sembado crossed his arms and blew out a quick, pointed sigh.

"Caspen's entire plan hinges on using his attack drones, right?" Kaluna continued, ignoring Sembado's defiant posture.

"Yeah," Sembado replied begrudgingly.

"Then all we have to do is take the electricity out of the equation," Kaluna replied with a matter-of-fact nod.

"What?" Sembado asked. "That's your plan? Yeah, that's easy. Let's just pull the plug and hope he doesn't notice."

"Don't be difficult," she replied. "It's not as complicated as you think. There are so many steps in the process: from producing that electricity to the drones executing their command. We only have to interrupt the chain in one spot."

"Have you thought of that too?" Sembado asked with genuine interest.

"I've thought of options but I don't have a preference yet," Kaluna replied.

Sembado moved to the bed and sat at Kaluna's feet.

"So what's your first idea?" Sembado asked.

"Well, look," she replied. "The first option is the easiest and most straightforward. I really don't think it will work, but it's worth a shot."

"And?" Sembado prodded.

"The generators," Kaluna responded. "The cyclists, I mean. If they don't push those pedals, then the drones can't do their thing."

"Yeah," Sembado replied skeptically. "Because any of them would agree to that."

"Well, I know they won't," Kaluna shot back. "But there may be a way for us to trick them or something. Hold off just long enough to figure something else out. That's the only real outcome of any of these possibilities...to delay Caspen's attack just enough to find a permanent solution."

"Well, what other solutions do you think we have?" Sembado asked.

"I think most of the others would involve some kind of actual sabotage," Kaluna replied. "Besides convincing the cyclists and kinetic farm attendants to take the day off, the rest of the operation is equipment and wiring. We could take that out but I guarantee they would have it repaired in a couple days. And that also assumes we wouldn't be caught on one of Caspen's damned cameras."

"Well, what about the folks down in the root cellar?" Sembado suggested. "They would be the ones carrying out the actual attack. Maybe we can convince them to hold off."

"Yeah, but that's just as dicey as going to the kinetic workers," Kaluna responded. "Plus, Caspen will probably be right there giving those computer techs the direct order when it happens."

"That's true," Sembado replied. He ran his fingers through his flaming hair. It was just starting to lay past his shoulders.

"I say we go for the kinetic workers first," Kaluna stated firmly. "If we are just asking questions about power and how they do what they do, then it doesn't seem as suspicious. Even if we were to ask them to stop producing power for a day, and Caspen found out, then he isn't necessarily on to us. But if we ask his drone pilots not to attack the hill folk, then it is a lot more blatant and direct."

"That's a good point," Sembado replied. "Well, I think that's the best place to start. We can always come up with a last minute disruption or interference but for now, let's go to the kinetic farm. At least we can ask some questions without having to commit. Our cover is already set, too: we're just getting to know our future followers."

***

The very next morning found Sembado and Kaluna hastily preparing for a morning walk through the woods. Caspen's posted look-outs greeted them kindly as they passed on warnings of hill folk sightings. Their jaunt was brisk and brief as they feigned a purposeful and productive march across the foggy fields to the towering structures of the kinetic power plants.

They reached the first building. It was the power house that Caspen had shared with them. The doors were propped open and large fans blew the inside's humid funk out into the open air. Sembado and Kaluna walked inside with as much official presence as they could muster. An unoccupied worker quickly scurried over to verify the need for their attendance.

"We're conducting the first of many performance reviews here," Sembado said firmly. He did not look at her face but instead observed the operation with a passable arrogance.

"Oh, I'm sorry," the woman replied. "We weren't expecting you."

"That's fine," Kaluna responded curtly. "That would kind of defeat the point of a surprise inspection though, wouldn't it?"

"I...uh...yes, ma'am, it would," the young lady said to Kaluna's feet. "Is there anything specifically I can answer for you?"

"Yes," Sembado replied. "I would like to know what your operation cycles are like. When are your peak hours and how well can you respond to an outage?"

"Umm, our generators' production rates vary," the young woman recited carefully. "But some are able to produce up to five hundred watts per hour. Now, most of our all-stars know it's less about max output and more about capturing the area under their work curves so the ones with the experience and endurance can push for four to six hours with full N.S.I. Accounting for the low voltage draw from the control system, most of our top producers can put out over a kilowatt before they're in need of recovery. Morgan has consistently put out two kilowatts for several months now. But that is *not* typical."

"That's a lot of good information," Sembado said encouragingly. "Can we review some of your technical terms? N.S.I. stands for what again?"

The young lady furrowed her eyebrows as she looked back and forth between Sembado and Kaluna.

"Umm...Nervous System Intervention," she said slowly.

"There's no need for that tone," Kaluna reprimanded as she glared down the young lady. "We're working very hard here to get up to speed on Caspen's processes and a little dignity for our lack of terminology seems the least you could do."

"I...I'm so sorry," the girl apologized.

Nervous goosebumps covered Sembado's body as he fought back all the decent tendencies in his nature that told him to console the poor young lady.

"So, how about those other stats?" Sembado asked the flustered young lady. "I also asked about peak hours and emergency response."

"Yes, of course," the young lady stammered. "Our production is as responsive as it needs to be. As soon as we get further message of an upturn in demand, we can pull in additional cyclists. Having said that, our typical peak hours are in the early morning and just after dawn. Any additional lighting loads tend to follow those trends. In case of an assault or defensive response like we've had with the hill folk, then we can bring additional bodies but that's also a case of directing the same amount of power to the priority locations. That's not our job though. We're supposed to specialize in producing the most power per pound and responding to demands as they happen."

"Power per pound," Kaluna echoed. "Can you explain that?"

"Yes, ma'am," the young woman replied obediently. "That is the amount of usable electricity for each pound of food our generators take in."

"That explanation seems a little incomplete," Sembado declared boldly.

"Uhh...I...I don't know what else to say," the young woman stuttered.

"Walk me through the process," Sembado said with a raised voice.

"Our generators are fed a very specific diet to target their nutritional needs," the girl said, tears welling in her eyes. "Some are fed a grower's diet to help them achieve gains while we are developing their initial muscle mass. Once their lean weight gain slows, we transition them to a maintenance and high energy program. At that point, we track the pounds of daily food intake and compare that to the amount of power they crank out. The generators' power per pound is their badge of honor. While we offer some incentives for their success, their internal pride is by far the most effective motivator we have. They are extremely competitive."

The tears of stress and confusion that welled in the girl's eyes had transformed to determined streams of honor as she described her swollen counterparts' camaraderie. Sembado exchanged a knowing glance with Kaluna. He used his eyes to beg her for the next move. Kaluna looked the young lady over before addressing her a final time.

"What's your name?" she asked the attendant.

"Molly," the young woman replied proudly.

"Molly, you've given us an excellent explanation," Kaluna stated officially. "It's very clear that you have a thorough understanding of your industry and craft and that you take pride in what you do."

The tears returned to Molly's eyes as she beamed with pride.

"You're welcome to return to your duties," Kaluna added. "As soon as you direct us to the nearest generators' quarters."

"Yes, of course," Molly replied. She walked them to the exterior door and pointed out an adjacent building. "That's the main barracks right there."

"Good work, Molly," Sembado replied. "Now get back to it, huh?"

Molly saluted with a fist over her heart and hurried back to her services. As she disappeared back inside, Sembado took a minute to breathe. A nervous smirk of bemused shame and disbelief slowly spread across his face.

"I know," Kaluna said quietly. "That was painful for me too."

"Well, don't lose confidence now," Sembado replied. "We're about to walk into the thick of it."

They finished collecting their wits and moved across the grass breezeway to the next large building Molly had indicated. They marched up to a pair of double doors and pulled one open. The space they walked into was as large as the generators' space but divided quite differently. This very large room was cluttered with rows and rows of stacked beds. Each stack was at least four high, with some areas towering even taller. Most of the berths were occupied, shambled curtains drawn around their occupants. The oddest element, to Sembado's observation, was the lack of ladders or stairs to the beds. His curiosity was sated when a cyclist on a fifth tier bunk opened their curtains and leapt down to the floor. The young woman's massive legs broke the fourteen foot fall effortlessly. More impressive was watching a young man ascend a similar height in a single bound. He did have to grab his bunk with outstretched arms and climb the rest of the way but Sembado felt the nagging sensation that these peoples' natural legs were nearly as capable as his bionic one.

As they moved in, they noticed that the rows were broken by larger common spaces. While most of the generators were moving to or from their bunks or sleeping, there were a handful of muscular specimens congregating in the commons. A small crowd squatted and watched as two of their cohorts lay on their backs and wrestled each other. They competed by each locking a single leg around the crook of the other's knee. They pushed and pulled and twisted their powerful limbs. Their audience cheered and laughed. The smaller of the two young men had just forced his opponent over. The onlookers exploded with raucous applause.

Beyond the miniature arena, a smaller auxiliary area was packed with banks of simple medical beds. Several of the beds were occupied by the powerful cyclists while three physical technicians scurried from bed to bed, adjusting treatments and applying topical relief. Electrotherapy was used to relieve tense muscle groups, salves and balms were applied liberally, and in some cases, the therapists laid hands to relieve specific pain and tension.

Sembado and Kaluna tried to appear as dominant as they had been in the power house but the hormonal force and grit that swirled around the bunk house was nearly palpable. It reached a peak and burst when the two young men that had been leg wrestling broke into a shoving match. They shouted insults as they pushed and prodded each other back and forth. They leaned into one another and dug their feet in as their conflict drew the attention of several others. Their crowd grew and encircled them as the shoving turned to serious blows. Powerful kicks were exchanged with sickening thuds. Sembado instinctively recoiled from the fight and attempted to shield Kaluna as the violence peaked.

Suddenly, on the far side of the crowd, bodies started to part and a harsher voice could be heard. A sound akin to a hoarse dog barking carried above the rancor. Sembado then saw the circle part and a massive body force its way into the fold. He recognized the aging man as the dominant veteran named Reight. He threw gawking onlookers aside and blasted his way between the two scuffling young men, giving each a powerful kick to the stomach. The young men yielded in retreat. Each held their abdomens tenderly as Reight's verbal onslaught continued.

"This ends now!" he shouted. His raspy voice sounded as if gravel were being turned through rough mechanical equipment.

"Ya'll think you're hot, huh?" the bulging brute admonished. Veins pumped out of his forehead, neck, and chest. He stomped his feet menacingly at the young instigators. "Either go push or get back to your effin' bunks!"

The wrestlers recoiled from Reight's threats. Each crawled to his feet and moved away. Reight continued to bark nearly incoherently as he scolded the surrounding cyclists. Each one turned and submitted away from the powerful alpha. It wasn't until the group had dispersed that Reight noticed Sembado and Kaluna staring at the commotion. He wasted no time waddling toward them. His reddened face tensed around his bulging eyes.

"What the hell do you want?" he yelled.

Sembado's attempt to confidently straighten his posture faltered in Reight's overbearing presence. Instead of a bristling and powerful pose, it appeared more like he was shivering. Too embarrassed, confused, and intimidated to recover, he continued to stumble through his idea of an assertive response.

"We're the one's askin' the questions," he said half-heartedly.

Reight's eyes flared. He appeared to be more annoyed with Sembado's wimpy tone than with the confrontational words it carried.

"What?" Reight barked. He cracked his neck and flexed his shoulders in a masterful version of Sembado's failed display.

"We are here to ask some questions about how you achieve your incredible output goals," Kaluna said firmly.

Reight only tilted his head back in response but it appeared as if Kaluna had successfully disarmed him.

"We are studying under Caspen and he has informed us that you are a true force of nature," she said, laying on the affirmations thicker as she went.

"Yes and no," Reight replied. He continued to regard Sembado dubiously while his eyes softened when focused on Kaluna.

"This *is* the pinnacle of the human form," he added, indicating his monstrous lower half. "But it was an achievement of both the human spirit as well as Caspen's ingenuity. I like to think that one is not as powerful without the other. This is why we respect each other like we do."

"Of course," Kaluna replied. "And how often would you say you push?"

"As much as I can," Reight replied. "At least five hours a day. I used to be able to pull two fours but my heart isn't what it used to be."

"Understandable, given the amount of power you must have produced over your lifetime," Kaluna offered with veneration.

Reight's only response was to display his calf and thigh muscles in a well choreographed flexing routine. He seemed to be even more awed than Sembado and Kaluna.

"What's the longest you've gone without pushing?" Sembado asked, showing exaggerated adoration for Reight's impressive demonstration.

"Why?" Reight snapped, immediately abandoning the flexing routine. "Did somebody ask?"

"What?" Sembado replied. "No, of course not. I'm just curious how long you could wait between sessions if you had to take a break."

"Hey, man," Reight replied, raising his raspy voice again. "Reight don't wait. Got it? If I wanna push, I'm gonna push. I don't clutch for nobody."

"Alright," Sembado replied. "I understand."

"Did Caspen tell you to ask me that?" Reight continued. "Is he thinking of putting me up? Because I can push harder and longer than any of these young bucks. You got that, Red?!"

"Yeah," Sembado stuttered, retreating pathetically.

Kaluna remained by his side as he slowly recoiled from Reight's fuming tantrum.

"This is so effin' typical!" Reight yelled. The distance Sembado offered did nothing to calm him down.

"All you brains do is sit and plot and scheme!" he yelled. "We're just in here doing your hard work for you. Giving our whole lives, just so that you can keep meddling and scheming. Is that it? Got other plans for old Reight, huh? You gonna make me go plow a field till I collapse?"

"No," Sembado shot back forcefully. "*We* want to delay the power generation. If we don't, Caspen is going to kill off thousands of innocent people."

Kaluna grabbed Sembado's arm and yanked wildly but the damage had already been done.

Chapter 27
The Caged Bird Is Singing Alright

"Caspen don't even know you're down here, does he?" Reight said through gritted teeth.

Sembado's stomach went ice cold before falling away to a depth unknown. Kaluna pinched and twisted his arm in an attempt to snap him out of his fearful stupor.

"We just need to talk this out with Caspen," Kaluna offered.

"Oh, you will," Reight spat. Reight called out to his cohorts as his face turned a deeper shade of crimson. He motioned for the reporting cyclist to go herald the developments. The man turned and quickly sprinted out the door. His powerful strides could be heard beating the dirt path beyond.

Kaluna started to inch toward the door but Reight snapped his fingers. The young female cyclist named Morgan dropped from an overhead bunk and landed between Sembado and Kaluna. Her firm grip dug into the skin of their arms.

They were held for several minutes while Reight continued to pace and bluster. Despite his outward anger, it was clear that he was actively suppressing even more inner rage.

Sembado stood silently in Morgan's vise-like grip and stared at the floor. Utter dejection consumed him as he felt Kaluna's eyes boring into the side of his head. He began choking on the internal self-loathing of his mistake. His spirit started to suffocate. He hung his head and sulked while the other cyclists' growing jeers did little to calm Reight's vibrating mass.

After an emotional eternity, thunderous hooves and voices could be heard from outside. The door blew open and Caspen marched in, flanked on either side by armed guards.

"Imagine my surprise," he hissed as he approached Sembado and Kaluna. "How dare you. I confided so much. *How dare you.*"

"Caspen, please," Sembado said with tear-filled eyes. "This is just a misunderstanding. We were just asking about operational ca…"

"Liar!" Reight screamed. Even Caspen flinched and retreated. Reight's gratuitous build bulged its reddened, veiny shell.

"Reight, please," Caspen said with considerable submission. "We can…Reight!"

The behemoth grabbed at his chest. His eyes flared and rolled. His lips curled around his firmly gritted teeth and he fell to one knee. He let go of his chest and released a blood curdling scream. His husky, gravelly voice masked the pain of the cry and transformed it into a guttural, wild growl.

The confrontation had already held the attention of many nearby cyclists but it wasn't until Reight cried out that the health aides took notice. The entire team converged. The first two were nearly bloodied by Reight's persistent thrashing.

Caspen backed away so that the health attendants could tend to their massive patient. He turned to Sembado and Kaluna with firmly pursed lips that were contorted into a harsh sneer.

"I've grown tired of the betrayal," he muttered. "How many lives do I have to save just to have them turn around and stab me in the back?"

"Caspen, you don't have to do this," Sembado pleaded.

"Oh, but I do," Caspen snapped. "There are no more chances. No more charity cases. You will pay for this. But not just you. You will die knowing the debt that hangs on your weak, visionless shoulders."

He turned his attention back to Reight's failing form as the nurses tried in vain to remedy the situation.

"I'm sick of staring at them," Caspen called over his shoulder. "Take them to the hold."

Morgan jerked Sembado and Kaluna away as Caspen fell to one knee and tried to comfort his prized achiever.

***

Morgan's eerie silence was a stark contrast to her brazen male counterparts. She quietly walked Sembado and Kaluna across the lawn toward the detention hold.

Sembado sulked along. His sense of defeat and Reight's gruesome fate weighed on him. Kaluna held his hand with a casual touch that told him it was a mere courtesy for his benefit alone.

"Morgan," Kaluna said softly.

The young woman did not look back. Her shoulders and backside rolled quietly atop her lumbering and powerful legs.

"Morgan, please," Kaluna repeated. "I'm sorry, but there's so much you don't understand."

"You're wrong," Morgan stated flatly. "Now isn't the time to speak."

She pushed them out into the murky overcast day that had taken over the fog. They walked toward a smaller building which they had not yet visited. It sat just at the edge of the clearing. The tall pines that stood immediately behind it looked like ominous giants in the midday murk. The front end of the structure was lined with a deep covered porch. The low-sloped roof continued out for nearly six feet. Morgan moseyed up to the front door and checked to see that Sembado and Kaluna were still close behind.

"You two keep your mouths shut," Morgan snapped.

She turned back to the door and pounded it firmly three times. Creaking footsteps preceded a call for identification.

"It's Morgan," the brutish young lady called. "Caspen has sent me with his two new recruits."

Several locks on the door clicked and rolled before the latch snapped and opened. A firelight inside highlighted the curves of the heavy-set old man. His figure was a series of bulges and folds. Shadows stretched out from under every feature, from his bushy white mustache down to the tunic that hung past his portly belly.

"Well, hello there," the old man said gruffly.

"Afternoon, Eben," Morgan replied. "I need to show these two the hold."

The old man furrowed his eyebrows with misunderstanding.

"These are Caspen's new overseers," she replied. "They are to be shown the facility."

"Oh, alright," the old man sighed. "There's no need to bark at me. You're the one who interrupted my nap."

"Yes, terribly sorry," Morgan quipped as she prodded Sembado and Kaluna inside.

The room inside was warm and inviting. A chair in the corner was situated with a plush cushion, footrest, and blanket. The matted padding confessed the years that the old man had been keeping watch. They followed old Eben as he shuffled through a series of smaller rooms that led toward the back of the building.

The old man tottered along. His age and weight played equal hell on his knees. He cooed and fussed with every step.

"How's ol' Reight doin'?" he asked over his shoulder.

Morgan gave Sembado and Kaluna a foreboding glare.

"Your brother's just fine," Morgan lied. "Doing a right bit better than you."

"Ah, bull," the old man retorted. "I bet his heart gives out before my knees do. You'd never catch me on one of those damned human hamster wheels. No offense."

He stopped at one final door. It looked different from the others in the building. It was secured with multiple locks.

"Don't have anyone in hold, ya know?" Eben grumbled as he finished the last lock and opened the door. A set of rickety stairs disappeared into the cellar below. "Yer gonna be showin' 'em empty cells."

Without warning, Morgan snatched the keys from Eben's hands and jumped behind him. He turned just in time to catch a very powerful kick to the chest. A muffled grumble trailed behind him as he flew through the open door. His aged body crumpled further as it ricocheted off the ceiling of the stairwell and tumbled loudly down the time-worn steps below. The old man rolled to a broken pile at the bottom of the stairs and remained motionless.

Sembado and Kaluna remained frozen as Morgan pushed the door shut and hastily fumbled the specific key and lock combo. She secured each and every bolt before turning to them.

"I will help get you out of here but you must promise to take me with you," she demanded. Her hand was extended in a sign of good faith.

Sembado's heart pounded in his chest. He remained glued to the wall.

"Yes," Kaluna replied, firmly returning the handshake. "What needs to be done?"

"The front of this building is very well monitored, but the back of it is slowly being consumed by the forest. If we can find a window that opens to the trees, I think we can sneak out unnoticed. By the time they break down that door and realize you're not there, we could be a couple miles out."

"But why are you doing this?" Sembado argued.

"There's no time to explain," Morgan scolded. "Just move."

She led the way through the gauntlet of side rooms until they found one with a dense forest view. They jimmied a window open and Kaluna was the first to slide out. She clung to the base of the window and dangled a moment before making the modest fall to the ground below. Sembado went next. His larger frame made for an awkward fit but his fall was cushioned by the favored use of his bionic prosthetic. He stood with Kaluna and peered from side to side for movement.

Morgan began crawling through the window but became wedged by her hips and thighs. Her upper body hung for a moment as she tried to wiggle from side to side. Kaluna rushed over and grabbed one arm, and motioned for Sembado to help. With their support, Morgan was able to pull her legs through and roll out of the window. Her feet made a loud crunch as they landed in the bed of pine needles that sprawled in every direction.

"This way," she said breathlessly.

They craned their necks all about as they trotted into the trees. As they began to lose sight of the clearing and the jailhouse, they abandoned their hunkered posture and increased their pace. Sembado soon had to rely on his powered leg's asymmetrical gallop just to keep up with Morgan's relentless gait. He shouted for her to stop when he realized that Kaluna had fallen behind and could not call for help due to her lack of breath. His prosthetic hummed happily while they determined their next course of action. Kaluna's pride succumbed to her fatigue, and she agreed to be carried by Morgan until her breath and strength returned. She climbed atop Morgan's back, and hooked her legs around front. After a few slight adjustments, Morgan was back to a full sprint. Her powerful legs beat the ground mercilessly. Sembado concentrated on nullifying the effects of his prosthetic's backfeed. The maddening tickle at the base of his head was steadily nurturing his subdued rage as he practically jumped along, eight feet at a time.

After nearly a half hour of sustained progress, Morgan slowed to a trot and called for a break. Sembado paced in quick circles as his leg cooled down. He clenched his fists and gritted his teeth through the pulses of directionless anger. Kaluna and Sembado kept watch while Morgan recovered.

"How...how are you not winded with those scrawny legs?" she asked Sembado breathlessly.

"This one does all the work," he replied, blasting an old tree branch in half with a powerful kick.

"Would you be quiet?" Kaluna snapped. "We can't be more than a few miles away. They could close that gap in minutes on horseback."

"If they knew which way to go," Sembado snapped angrily. "I'll keep it down, but don't be so paranoid."

"She has a point," Morgan added between gulps of fresh air.

"It's not him," Kaluna reasoned. "That deekin' leg blasts his brain with residual signals and can make him unreasonable and angry."

"That's awful," Morgan replied.

"Better than bein' stuck on one of those bikes," Sembado said.

"Not if they have you hooked up," Morgan argued. "Then you don't think or feel anything. Not until it's over. Then you deal with the pain and all."

"So why *did* you leave?" Sembado pressed. "Why did you help us?"

Morgan quietly reflected while she nearly finished catching her breath.

"I've been wanting to get away for months," she said quietly. "This opportunity seemed better than anything I could have planned."

"But why?" Kaluna asked.

"Why do you think?" Morgan replied indignantly. "Despite all their best efforts to keep us distracted and busy and focused, I never stopped wondering what was out there. I never fully let myself go. I mean, in the beginning, I went along with it because I didn't know any better. Especially with my dad being who he was. He was *so* important to that place. He was revered, even by Reight. Then he died and it was like no one cared. He was the first to go out like that. Caspen told everyone he had died doing what he loved and that made him even more of a hero and an inspiration. Then, when I started asking myself if that's what I truly wanted, I made excuses. I told myself if I could be their best, the best cyclist I could be, that would be enough to feel fulfilled. But it wasn't. It's taken me years to realize it. I don't want to be my father anymore. I lie awake at night, wondering what if. I...I thought of asking the others once but Reight...the others...that *is* life for them. They eat, sleep, and push. That's it. I...it just isn't enough for me. I couldn't believe what a stupid position you two put yourselves in, but I took advantage of it."

"Well, I'm glad you did," Kaluna laughed softly.

"Me too," Sembado confessed humbly.

"Well, that's enough for now," Kaluna stated. "If you're ready to go, I think we need to make some more distance between us and Caspen."

Just as she finished speaking, a deep rumble thundered in the distance. Sembado's prosthetic twitched. The sound gained a pitch and direction. The rapid cadence of galloping horse hooves was reverberating through the trees.

Morgan quickly gathered Kaluna on her back and followed Sembado as they hurried away in the opposite heading. They tore through the trees as fast as they could. Sembado edged away from the girls as his prosthetic made the minor but important terrain adjustments that Morgan's brute force could not. His prosthetic seared his stump as it pumped the powerful, deliberate motion. The sound of his heartbeat in his ear and Morgan's powerful feet beating the ground seemed to drown out everything else.

Suddenly, Sembado caught sight of a new motion out of the corner of his eye. The horseman seemed to be nearly silent as he rode up from their left side. As Sembado looked back to Morgan and Kaluna, he saw additional riders closing in from behind. He didn't see Caspen anywhere among them. He briefly looked to Kaluna. Her wide eyes seemed even more panicked than expected. She mouthed something to Sembado and pointed with her hand. He looked back ahead just in time to see a large pine tree quickly approach his face.

***

A large white circle floated in the center of Sembado's consciousness. A muffled ringing accompanied the ghostly orb. The tone of the ringing noise continued to sharpen until it was painful and engrossing. The white orb flexed and unfurled into a colorful and distorted enigma. It was a self-determined fractal of visible light. His eyes focused on the ends of the fractal's fronds as they defined themselves as intricate points and took on a green hue. They gathered in bunches and collaborated to form dense lines of brown and red. Sembado's eyes rolled into his head and back out. He blinked away the colorful illusion as the diffused sunlight above highlighted the needle-laden pine branches that intertwined overhead. The ringing in his ears persisted and a sharp pain suddenly engulfed his nose and right eye. The loud crunching of pine needles in his left ear shook him from his stupor.

He sat up and grabbed at his face, pulling his hand back when even the softest touch sent fire shooting through his head and neck. His prosthetic kicked and twitched beneath him. He reached out blindly, his hands groping through his distorted confusion. They were received by a soft and benevolent force. Fingers intertwined and pulled. He climbed to one knee, using Kaluna's hand as she silently steadied him to his feet.

It took Sembado nearly a minute to process the sight of a dozen horsemen ringed around him, Kaluna, and Morgan. He and Kaluna stood with their backs to the large tree with which he had just collided. Morgan stood in front of them with her feet planted firmly in a strong defensive stance.

"I said, you're coming with us," growled a man atop one of the horses. His face was unfamiliar through Sembado's hazy double vision.

"And I said, you can go to hell," Morgan said through gritted teeth. Her powerful legs flexed as she lowered her stance ever so slightly.

The horseman pointed to two of his followers and indicated for them to get down off their horses. The men complied after a brief hesitation. One of them dug through his saddlebag and produced a pair of old rusty shackles. The other unsheathed a long, rudimentary spear.

Morgan's posture tensed even further as the men slowly approached her. The spearman held his weapon with meager commitment. The other man held the shackles out at arm's length. His shaking hands rattled the chain that connected the two cuffs.

The men moved away from each other so that they approached Morgan from two different angles. She held her ground, carefully moving her head back and forth in order to keep both assailants in her sight.

"Stick out your arms," the shackleman commanded. He looked noticeably annoyed with himself when his voice cracked.

Morgan slowly raised her arms and brought them together. She hunched slightly as she presented her wrists to the man. He seemed more surprised than anyone that she had surrendered so easily. He approached her quickly, his eyes fixed on her forearms. Before he could react, Morgan sprung forward with a quick hop and planted both feet on the man's chest. He had already started moving backward from the momentum of her flight but his lungs didn't release an anemic grunt until Morgan pushed off simultaneously with her powerful legs. Bewilderment and duress spread across the man's face as he rocketed backwards, clipped the rear end of someone else's horse, and spun through the air like a rag doll. Morgan landed on her back but sprang to her feet in an instant. She turned to confront the spearman but stopped dead in her tracks. In the time it had taken her to dispatch the shackler, the spearman had subdued Sembado and Kaluna. He held them back against the tree with the jagged tip of his pole.

"We don't want any more violence," the leader of the riders called down from his mount.

"But we need to move out of here before Caspen and his goons show up. It's only a matter of time."

Morgan uncrossed her arms.

"You...aren't with him?" she asked defiantly.

"No," the man grinned darkly. "Not us *hill folk*."

Chapter 28
The Prodigal Son

The horsemen took a long and winding path across the northern edge of the wood. They assured Sembado, Kaluna, and Morgan that their route was avoiding Caspen's by nearly twenty miles.

"Why were you running from him?" the leader asked. His fresh face looked eerily familiar.

"Why should we tell you?" Morgan replied hotly. She trotted along on the ground because her legs could not straddle any of the horses. A tether of rope hung loosely around her neck.

"Whoa, there," the lead horseman called with a chuckle. "We're your best chance now. You'll need all the help you can get if he's after you. Trust me."

"We defied him," Kaluna replied from the back of the lead's horse. "And he didn't like that."

"No," the man replied. "He *really* doesn't."

"How would you know?" Morgan asked.

"Because I used to be one of his followers," the man replied. "My name is Brek."

"One of his followers?" Morgan scoffed indignantly. "You're his son! We've been told all about you!"

"What?" Sembado said through his aching face. "I thought his son died when he was a baby...with the mother?"

"No," Brek replied with a scowl. "And mom only died just before I ran off."

"When you killed her!" Morgan snapped.

"You don't know what you're talking about," Brek said dismissively.

"That's why you ran away," Morgan replied.

"I ran because my mother was dead and there was no reason for me to stay," Brek shot back. "His stupid equipment killed her. I was right there to see it. To see my mother writhe in pain, screaming for me, while her mind was blasted to oblivion by those awful machines. I tried desperately to turn it off. And turning off the system like I did *is* what killed her. I'm thankful it did. But I'm not thankful that I had to put my own mother out of her misery like that. So don't scold me with whatever twisted version of reality he's fed you. I have no appetite for it."

The riding party fell silent. Morgan lumbered along with her eyes trained on the trail.

"Why would he lie?" Sembado asked quietly.

"Are you serious?" Brek laughed. "Because he hates that I've embarrassed him and didn't want to play a part of his sick game. I was his prodigy. I was perfect to him. But I never agreed with his tactics and he nearly killed me for it. But I was able to escape into the woods. That was almost ten years ago."

"He was training us to do the same thing," Sembado replied. "He wanted us to be his replacements."

"I guess he had to find someone new after what we did to ol' Gordo, huh?" Brek said with a sinister grin.

"That was you?" Kaluna asked.

"Just puttin' the salty dog out of his misery," Brek replied. "He was about to take up my old man's mantle. He would have seen Caspen's *final solution* through to the end. He was a terrible man, Gordo. Almost as bad as my dad, except loyal."

"Well, he turned to us pretty quickly after that," Sembado replied.

"He would," Brek responded. "He always hated feeling alone. Like he needed someone to conspire with...probably made him sleep better at night knowing he wasn't pursuing his twisted fantasy alone."

"You mean with the advanced technology?" Sembado asked.

"Well, that part I understood," Brek replied. "I mean, I know he thought the stewards' principles were pointless by themselves. And I kind of agree. If the villagers are trying and failing, why not help them out where you can? I myself would prefer we live a simpler life than my dad has developed, but I still want to do it on *my* terms."

"So is that what you're doing now?" Sembado asked.

"No," Brek replied seriously. "We've been fighting to survive since I left my old man. The last decade has been one long pursuit. He's expanded his operation just to work on rooting me out."

"We were told that expansion was for the waves of new settlers coming through," said Morgan.

"Awfully convenient timing, huh?" Brek replied bitterly. "He started expanding those facilities long before he knew anyone was escaping from the ocean. I mean, think about it. If his job is to pass the settlers on, through to the east, then why would he need to expand his operation? He isn't permanently housing all those people, right? You think he's going to spend all those resources and have you people pedal those ridiculous machines just so he can send out more drones for spying?"

"No," Sembado replied quietly.

"What's that?" Brek called over his shoulder.

"He...he's using those drones for more than surveillance," Sembado confessed.

"You don't think I know that?" Brek laughed. His response elicited a light chuckle from the other riders. "If you think him using those drones to assassinate dissidents is crazy, then he hadn't showed you anything."

"What do you mean?" Kaluna asked.

"Those weapons are capable of anything," Brek replied. "Absolutely anything."

"You mean like healing and freezing people?" Sembado added knowingly.

"No," Brek responded dismissively. "I mean like targeting a single species *or* compound *or* element. I mean, they can decouple any range of molecular bonds you desire. All you have to know is the frequency and, for some bonds, crank up the power."

"But then you're only targeting one thing at a time, right?" Sembado said hopefully.

"Not when you can pulse through a list of frequencies in one attack," Brek said soberly.

Sembado swayed in his seat and it had nothing to do with the horse or the rough terrain. Brek seemed to be aware of the nauseating effect his insight had caused.

"Let's focus on the ride," Brek commanded firmly. "We're nearly there."

Even as he spoke, the terrain seemed to transform. The grade increased in a steady upward incline and large rocks and boulders began jutting from the pine needles that were piled on the forest floor. Through the breaks in the coniferous canopy, the high hills and distant mountain peaks were just visible. Shadows blurred into large patches of darkness as the sun fell behind them to the west. Brek and his riders chose a very particular course as they wound their way between the pine trunks.

"Don't you think we could be making some steadier progress if we rode in a straight line?" Kaluna said to the back of Brek's head.

"Only if we wanted to walk right over our mines and other traps," Brek replied. "We've been pretty successful in keeping Caspen out of this part of the forest for a couple years now. Before that, it was slaughters on a monthly basis. They would ride through and destroy anything their DNA trackers could hit."

"Then they've had that selective technology for some time?" Sembado asked.

307

"Oh yeah," Brek replied. "Did he tell you it was a new development?"

"Yes, actually," Kaluna chimed in.

"Typical," Brek said, shaking his head. "No, we've had that tech since I was a kid. You all probably didn't need it underwater because you weren't concerned about hitting an innocent species. We've put a lot of effort into protecting our wildlife. There's no reason the animals should suffer because man is beating themselves over the head with bigger, badder clubs."

"So why do you think he would say that?" asked Sembado.

"Because he has to ease your understanding into these new developments," Brek replied. "Also, he's a habitual liar and says whatever he thinks will get people to do what he wants."

"Man, you've really got it out for him," said Morgan. "He never seemed that bad to me."

"Manipulative is the first word *I* would use to describe him," Kaluna interjected. "If everything Brek is saying is true, it only reinforces all of the doubts and suspicions that Sembado and I have had about Caspen."

"Hey, we're coming up on our establishment here," Brek interrupted. "Let's keep your relationship with Caspen quiet for now. My people really don't trust him and I think they would pass that suspicion on to you."

"Well, what about me?" Morgan asked. "It's pretty obvious what *I* am."

"Let me do the talking," Brek replied.

Morgan's sour scowl revealed her dissatisfaction with his response.

"Get that rope off her neck," Brek commanded to her keeper. "That's only going to make her more of a spectacle."

The man holding Morgan's tether helped her remove the rough, jute cable over her head. She rubbed the area around her neck where the spiny fiber had irritated her skin. The inflamed ring of flesh was an ironic contradiction to the freedom she had just been awarded.

Brek led the team toward a thick hedge of overgrowth and shrubbery. He guided his horse expertly through a small passage that was nearly invisible from their approach. The caravan slowly moved through the opening in the brush in a single file procession. The secret throughway emptied right at the foot of the rocky formations beyond. Piles of fallen rock had accumulated at the base of the hills. The mountains became increasingly steep and devoid of vegetation as they rose. Sembado could see movement in the crags and holes just ahead: a small horde of children were igniting the lanterns and torches that lined the paths into the mountain base. Just above in the rocks, the mouth of a great cavern was highlighted by a combination of the fire light, sun's dying rays, and its orange and purple sunset.

The travelers were spotted by one of the children and the excitement of their return quickly spread through the system of shallow caves. Men, women, and mostly children poured out from hidden reveals to merrily great the riding company.

"These are the dangerous hill folk," Brek declared sarcastically. "About eight out of ten of the adults are Caspen's exiles. The others are recovered wanderers."

Sembado looked around excitedly at the hill folks' modest habitat. Their simple but effective gadgets and accommodations warmly reminded him of Kaluna's people and their ingenious solutions to life's basic worries. He turned to tell her so but was struck by the sight of the tears streaming down her face. Her uncharacteristic emotion was a stark transition from her guarded candor just moments before.

"What is it?" Sembado implored. "What's the matter?"

Brek eased on the reigns, unsure if Sembado was addressing him. He shuffled and contorted in his saddle to gain a better view of Kaluna's distress.

"What's going on?" he asked pointedly.

"I can't do this," Kaluna blubbered. She wiped her tears away angrily.

"Can't do what?" Brek demanded, signaling for the travelling party to hold back.

"This," Kaluna repeated with wavering anxiety as she motioned to Brek's villagers ahead. "I can't get introduced to one more group of happy children who don't know they're being brainwashed. I can't let them soften me up just in time to realize that their parents are some new flavor of psychopath. I can't and I won't!"

"Alright, alright," Brek said impatiently. "Calm down already. I don't think it serves to your point but most of these kids aren't ours."

Kaluna aggressively wiped her nose and eyes with her sleeve. She looked from Brek to the children and back.

"Whatta ya mean?" she asked through a truncated sniffle.

"They're mostly orphans, thanks to Caspen," he replied. "None of the rest of us have any interest in having our own. Not while we're running for our lives every other week. He's out to eradicate us, I tell you. I know that for a fact! Besides, we've already got our hands full with this lot. So look, I get it. I know where you're coming from. *Literally*. We're just bringing you in for the night, right? I didn't say you and me had to be pals. But we're both trying to steer clear of Caspen, right?"

Kaluna wiped her face one last time and looked dejectedly at the hill folk as they streamed down the edge of the hills in energetic, single file lines. She finally nodded her head in agreement and Brek called the party onward.

The awaiting hill folk greeted Brek and the other horsemen lovingly. Many of the children took great joy and interest in Morgan's appearance. At least one had noticed Sembado's bionic leg as well. Brek was able to deftly defuse any suspicion among his people as he casually introduced Sembado and Kaluna as additional escapees from Caspen's camp. The nature of Morgan's grotesque form was familiar to a handful of Brek's villagers. They whispered the explanation for her physique loudly to their ignorant friends and family.

The travelers were ushered under an overhanging rock outcropping that made their gathering undetectable from above. Brek was greeted by a short, squat blonde woman who pulled him in for a loving embrace and a kiss.

"Kiera, this is Sembado, Kaluna, and Morgan," he said to the blonde woman.

"I'm Kiera," the woman said before Brek could finish. "I hate when he introduces me like that. It's just so damn formal. Ya'll doin' okay after that journey? You look hungry."

She scurried away on her stout legs. It wasn't until she turned to go collect some food items that they noticed the bulky crossbow that hung off her back by a strapped harness.

"She's an excellent shot," Brek said with a proud grin. He hurried off to help his wife prepare a quick meal for his riding party.

Their late dinner consisted of a collection of dried fruit as well as the breast of some kind of wild bird. Sembado and Kaluna ate a large portion but Morgan continued well after they were finished. A smoky goat shank was thrown on a spit so that she could take in her normal level of protein.

They ate late into the night and were eventually shown sleeping quarters by torch light. Animal hides had been stretched over piles of pine needles in order to fashion a usable mattress. The effect was comforting but the heavy

312

smell of sap was overwhelming. Nonetheless, Sembado found himself in a deep sleep within minutes of lying down.

Chapter 29
You Can Only Serve One Master

Asking around the next morning allowed Sembado, Kaluna, and Morgan to divine Brek's location: he was busy training a group on long weapon tactics at the bottom of the nearest gulch. The surrounding trees nearly blocked out the direct sun and offered excellent concealment from air attacks. Brek curtailed his lesson when he saw Sembado and the others. The students were paired up and made to spar while Brek walked Sembado, Kaluna, and Morgan down the worn path that traced the bottom of the valley. They walked along quietly, the interspersed sun beams offering a regular dose of warm light as it broke through the high canopy. The clacking of the students' wooden weapons slowly died as they worked their way further and further from the sparing area and the main camp.

"I realize that I dumped a lot of new and terrifying information on you last night," Brek said. "It can sound farfetched and suspicious, but there are things you need to see that will either make you more confident in what I have planned or they might just scare the crap out of you."

Sembado followed closely behind Brek. Kaluna and Morgan whispered quietly at the rear. They walked on foot to a point where the path on the valley's bottom twisted and turned out of sight behind a large rock feature. Brek eagerly motioned for them to make the last turn.

As they rounded the last curve, Sembado, Kaluna, and Morgan's mouths all slowly fell open in utter disbelief. The rocky slope of the mountain's foot had been somehow dissolved. Large spherical voids peppered the rock face. Each divot was about two to three feet in diameter. It looked as if some huge rock golem had slowly eaten away at the surface. The extent of the damage seemed localized but the depth of the consumption was quite noticeable. It was as if the giant pockmarks in the middle of the erosion had been made deeper and deeper. Sembado slowly shuffled up the nearest cavity and ran his hands along the cool inner surface. It was completely smooth, as if the rock inside had been polished by a giant, energetic jeweler.

"What...what is it?" Sembado asked as he ran his hands over the undulating pock marks.

"One of Caspen's attacks," Brek replied. His response elicited turned heads from all three of his visitors.

"I told you he can target any molecular bond with those things," Brek added firmly. "Each one of those voids is a drone attack. They come down, do their thing, and then fly off. Our best luck is when they don't have enough juice for their return flight."

"But rocks?" Sembado asked sadly. "Why on earth would he waste all that time and energy on rocks?"

"Don't you see the shape there?" Brek asked expectantly. "He's trying to punch into the mountain. He's trying to eat away until he can break into our caves."

"That's insane," Kaluna scoffed.

"That's how a lunatic would try and break it," Sembado added with a dismayed snicker.

"No arguments there," Brek replied with a sickened chuckle. "You should know that by now."

"Plants, birds, rocks, humans," Morgan stammered quietly. "What else can he devour? What else can those things do?"

"So, that's another reason I wanted to discuss things with just you three," Brek responded. "The programming potential for my father's drones goes well beyond the feature of the orbs. They can be hotwired to self-destruct, to explode, to burst into flames, etcetera."

Morgan's face became pale and distraught. She leaned against the rocky wall to her right and swallowed back tears.

"What's wrong?" Kaluna asked.

"This," Morgan muttered. "I've helped in all of this. I've helped kill countless animals and destroy the environment. And...how many people?"

"Well," Brek measured his words carefully as he spoke. "Caspen has killed hundreds but you didn't have a hand in every one of those."

Morgan broke down into a full blown sob.

"And you were just pedaling a generator," Sembado added emphatically. "There's no way you could have known what he was doing with that electricity. Did he ever actually *tell* you?"

Morgan shook her head through her weeping.

"Then that's all the more reason for you to help me execute my plan," Brek said encouragingly.

"Which is what, exactly?" Kaluna asked. "You want to try and program them to kill themselves?"

"Not exactly," Brek replied, placing a hand on Morgan's shoulder. "We can also turn each and every one of those disgusting drones into a small, guided EMP."

"A what?" Sembado asked.

"An EMP," Brek replied. "It means all of those flying dervishes would blast the surrounding electrical equipment, including themselves, with a pulse of energy, which would fry their internal circuits."

"So you want to hack the drone controls?" Kaluna asked.

"Not just the drone controls," Brek replied. "I also want to use the attack to destroy my father's camp and any chance of renewal or rebuilding along with it."

"How would you do that?" Sembado asked.

"Well, like Kaluna said, we would have to hack the drones so that we could pilot them back to his so-called *root cellar*. We would also target the kinetic facility. These energy pulses would render those exercise cycles useless."

"So what's keeping you from doing it?" Sembado asked defiantly.

"We're afraid of the consequences," Brek replied. "We're literally talking about sending everyone back to the way it was before any kind of technology."

"How?" Kaluna asked. "If you're only piloting those drones close enough to affect your targets?"

"It's not that simple," Brek replied. "If we send out the signal that we've developed, it would direct any of the orbs within its range to detonate at the commanded frequency. That means the orbs built into the drones but also any that have been weaponized in bullets, my wife's crossbow bolts. *Everything.* And with the tower we want to use, we don't know how far the signal will reach. One of Caspen's escaped scientists thinks it could repeat to other towers that are still operational to the west. We would *literally* be wiping out any modern technology within the signal's range."

"Yeah," Sembado said skeptically, "but isn't that how we're supposed to be living? How *you* think we're supposed to be living?"

"Not as long as Caspen and his network of followers survive," Brek said bitterly. "And I have to at least try and steal what technology I can in order to keep up."

"He wants to kill everyone," Sembado said to Brek forebodingly.

"I know that," Brek said dryly. "He's been killing my people off one by one for years. That's why I'm showing you this."

"No," Sembado added firmly. "He wants to kill all the other stewards, the ones who are competing for his land

and resources – that network of followers. He thinks they're unnecessary dead weight and he's going to kill them all as soon as you're outta the way."

Brek sat quietly and scratched his chin.

"All the more reason to take down his system," he said defiantly. "He has done enough damage and he needs to be wrangled in. If anything, fighting for all those other innocent people will just encourage my folks even more that this plan is the right thing to do."

"And then what?" Kaluna asked. "Then we can all follow you until you lose it? I told you I was done with this. Just because these kids aren't yours doesn't mean you can't indoctrinate them into following your own twisted version of righteousness."

"Oh, would you stop?" Brek snapped. "I don't wanna lead anyone. I certainly don't wanna lead you three. You're all a big pain in the ass, no matter who you're following. I don't want your loyalty. I don't want anything from you. Not because I'm a good guy, but because it's easier for me if I don't owe you anything."

Kaluna pursed her lips and crossed her arms. Sembado sighed deeply.

"Look, I'm not asking for your commitment," Brek said impatiently. "Have I asked for your commitment? No. But if what you say is true, then it doesn't matter where you go. Caspen *will* track you down and he *will* kill you. So you might as well give this your best shot."

Chapter 30
All Or Nothing

The next couple days were a tense holding pattern as the team of unlikely allies simultaneously waited for Caspen's indiscriminate attack to commence at any moment and prepared for their own operation.

Sembado, Kaluna, and Morgan fell in line with Brek's villagers and did their best to help prepare for both offensive and defensive measures. The villagers' attitudes varied between passionate idealism and nihilistic acceptance. Sembado struggled to say the right thing as he encountered such violent extremes in the reception of his small talk. He had resigned to socializing with Kaluna and Morgan alone until an energetic young man approached the station where they were loading and preparing a pile of weapons.

"Hey there!" the youthful recruit said excitedly. "I'm Arloch. I was the very first orphan here in Brek's village. That's kind of my thing."

Sembado and the others greeted young Arloch warmly, and he settled in to help load magazines.

"So what do you think of Brek's plan?" Sembado asked Arloch. "It seems like the best course of action to me."

A somber appearance fell over Arloch's youthful face. He made an exaggeratedly pensive face before he replied.

"I think death is awful," he concluded with a sage nod. "No matter who the target is. But in some cases, like this, it's a necessary evil."

Sembado exchanged a bewildered look with Kaluna and Morgan.

"I agree," Kaluna lied. "These operations are rife with danger. But how many casualties do you really expect?"

"Well, we're shooting for most of Caspen's Circle, right?" Arloch asked with an expectant chuckle. "I mean, if we can discharge all their weapons at once, that's bound to turn up some pretty impressive results."

"Truly," Kaluna replied. "And what do you think about the magnetic pulse plan instead?"

"Well, that's just a back-up, isn't it?" Arloch asked. "In case we can't get the other one to work?"

Arloch's energetic sharing had drawn attention from the adults. Brek himself was wading through the supply party to address the young man.

"Arloch, my good man," Brek said with a friendly tone, "would you be so kind as to help the others there prep those traps? You have such a knack for those."

"Yes, sir," Arloch replied enthusiastically.

Brek stood quietly in Arloch's place, his eyes fixed on his feet.

"You could have just been honest about your intentions," Kaluna hissed, careful not to draw more attention. "What good does it do leaving us in the dark?"

"You lot are so freakin' idealistic," Brek replied quietly. "I couldn't risk your influence spreading in my people. They have to stay focused."

"But this isn't the only way," Sembado replied. "*This* should be the last resort, not the other way around! And if you're worried about being able to control the effects of the EMP, what makes you think releasing those damn death spheres all over the place is going to be any better?"

"Because I can get my people away from them," Brek responded. "We can abandon our weapons and tools temporarily until the operation is over. At least then, they'll be dead, we won't, and we'll also still have our technology operational. How is that not better for us?"

"Because then you have to live with being a slightly more noble version of your father," Kaluna said angrily.

The elevated energy of the disagreement was starting to attract the other villagers' attention.

"No," Brek replied. "I don't accept that. Not even close. Every one of those people deserves what's coming to them. They have knowingly perpetrated the laws of nature for their own sick, twisted success."

"Not my people," Morgan stated firmly. "I had no idea what my purpose was or what it helped achieve. I acknowledge that most of those people are dedicated to their death, but does that make them guilty?"

"Most of them are clear of the influence of this, aren't they?" Brek asked.

"I don't know," Morgan answered angrily.

"None of us do," Kaluna said. "There's no way of knowing where those deekin' things are lurking. Who has one in their pocket or holster. I may agree with you that Caspen and his close associates deserve this, but he has them just as convinced that you do too. How does that *not* make you the same?"

Brek clenched his fists until they popped and contorted his face in poorly subdued anger. He threw his hands through his hair and sighed heavily out of his nose.

"I can't expect you three to understand exactly where I'm coming from," he said quietly as he looked out into the dense forest. "There are so many years here. So much pain and betrayal. Maybe it'd be easier for you to sit this out instead of help."

"Brek, I don't think *you* understand," Sembado said purposefully, looking the bitter young man straight in the eye. "We're the ones that have been through this next step. Kaluna and I helped orchestrate and negotiate an entire revolution in our underwater home. *We* don't think *you* understand. We've learned incredible lessons about patience and balance and compromise. We've even learned when and where you can't always accommodate those things. But right here? Right here is a perfect example. You *literally* have an opportunity to make a choice. And I'm sorry, but this one is clearly between right and wrong. You can either level the playing field and force everyone to live the life they've promised to live or you can kill off your competition and start living the life that you've criticized them for living. I don't know how this is even a decision for you."

Brek stared at his hands which softly curled on the table in front of him. He gritted his teeth behind his taught lips. He spastically reached up with one hand to pick and brush away some tickling debris from his overgrown whiskers.

"It's so easy for you, isn't it?" he said, slamming his hand back down on the table. "It has to be so easy to make these noble stands for justice or you wouldn't be doing them every chance you've got. Did you do this to my old man?"

"Yes, we did," Kaluna replied defensively.

"And how did *he* respond?" Brek asked.

"You know how," Sembado answered. "He threatened to kill us if we betrayed or abandoned him."

Brek growled and threw up his hands.

"It'd be so much easier to operate like that," he said. "Doing whatever I wanted and not having to accommodate anyone."

"Is that it?" Morgan muttered quietly. "Is that your real problem with him? That you don't even care about the way he does business? You're just jealous that it's him and not you?"

Brek glared at Morgan while his arms slowly crossed in front of his chest.

"Then say I'm wrong," Morgan said firmly.

"I don't have to say anything," Brek snapped. "I'm the one making the decisions here. You three *were* supposed to be prisoners."

Sembado and Kaluna scoffed at Brek's emotional outburst. They slowly drew nearer to each other.

"And you probably still should be," he added to Morgan. "So don't act so entitled to share your opinion when you should be considering yourself lucky you're allowed to speak at all!"

Morgan's aggravated appearance melted away to reveal an even stonier façade. She slowly stood up. Her muscles tensed as she carefully restrained herself from reacting. She slowly looked over to Sembado and Kaluna and then re-fixed her sparkling eyes on Brek.

"I've only just escaped a lifetime of having my actions literally controlled by your father," Morgan stated with cold and calculated articulation. "So you'll have to pardon me when I say I'll be damned if another man from *your* family tells me what to think or say."

She turned without further comment, and disappeared up the hill to their cavern retreat.

"You need to make a choice," Sembado said warily. "And I realize it is yours to make."

"Are you really sure either will even work?" Kaluna asked. "I mean, before you decide – do you really have the facts straight?"

"What do you mean?" Brek asked.

"Well, the orbs on those drones aren't that big," Kaluna responded. "The ones in the bullets either. If you do decide to go with the EMP option, is it really going to reach as far and wide as you hope?"

"Well, from what we know, yes," Brek replied. "There seems to be a tie between the frequency and the amount of power required to run it. More specifically, consider the frequency that ate away at those rocks I showed you. Besides having the correct frequency to disengage the various compounds that make up that mountain, a very high level of energy was needed. That same amount of energy, applied to a less intensive frequency, would produce a much more wide-spread result. I do have to admit that the EMP-type frequency that the typical drone-sized capsule could emit would be quite effective. A much wider sphere of influence than the attack orbs, for sure."

"Then why not just go that route?" Sembado asked. "There's another perfectly compelling reason to use that form of attack instead."

"There's more to it than that," Brek replied. "There would be an additional step with that plan."

"Why?" Sembado asked. "What step?"

"Well, with the attack orbs, we would simply be targeting Caspen and his lackeys. If we went with the magnetic field option, then we would want the effect to be felt as far and wide as possible and really wipe out as many electronic components as we could."

"That's fair," Kaluna agreed. "So what's the problem with that?"

"There's a communications tower involved," Brek replied. "Someone would have to climb it to help send out the signal. With enough power, we would be able to light up the other towers in the old network and spread the disabling frequency across the whole west coast."

"So we'll climb the tower," Kaluna said expectantly. "That doesn't sound like much of a problem to me."

"It is when Caspen's expecting that," Brek replied solemnly. "And could be sending his fleet of drones after you while you're trying to climb."

"We'll figure something out," Kaluna answered. "You shouldn't go to your awful back-up plan just because you're afraid to climb a comm tower."

"I'm not afraid," Brek said hotly. "But I need to be down here protecting my people."

"Yeah, sure," Kaluna replied sarcastically. "They'd be real lost without you."

"Well, no one else had volunteered," said Brek. "So what was I supposed to do with no one to carry out that plan?"

Kaluna grabbed Sembado's hand under the table and gave it a firm squeeze.

"We'll do it," she said.

"That's not what I'm asking of you," Brek replied.

"I don't care," Kaluna responded. "We'll take Morgan and climb the damn tower, if that's the only thing keeping you from moving ahead here."

Brek sighed and looked down at his fidgeting fingers.

"Talk it over with your people then," Kaluna said with an impatient sigh. She pushed her seat away from the table and stood up. "We'll be waiting for your answer."

She turned and walked away without giving Brek or Sembado a chance to respond. She disappeared up the path that Morgan had just taken. Brek crossed his arms and huffed out a dramatic groan.

"Try and talk some sense into her, would ya?" he said to Sembado.

"Go talk sense into yourself," Sembado responded hotly. "I'm on her side. If you're too much of a coward to do the right thing, then get the hell out of the way and let us take care of it."

His prosthetic shot him up too quickly and he knocked over his seat. He stood it back up and stomped away, leaving Brek to explain the awkward exchange to the others.

Sembado caught up with Kaluna before she returned to their humble guest quarters.

"I stood up for you," Sembado said quietly. "For once in my life, I didn't apologize."

"We need to get as packed and prepared as possible," Kaluna responded, reaching for his hand as they walked. "And thank you."

They shared the silent embrace the remainder of the hike. They returned to find Morgan restlessly shuffling and straightening the scarce amenities in their shared space. She tried to act as if she didn't notice their return but her honest nature got the better of her.

"What did he say?" she asked.

"He hasn't decided," Sembado replied.

"But we're going to prepare to leave anyway," Kaluna added. "I volunteered us to go to this comm tower."

"Fine with me," Morgan said. "I'm getting sick of sitting around and talking."

"We'll need some kind of range weapon to keep the drones at bay," said Sembado. "A gun would be preferable."

"How far away is it?" Morgan asked.

"He never told us," Sembado replied. "I thought you might know."

"I've never seen anything like that," Morgan replied. "I haven't left Caspen's camp since I was a little girl."

"We'll need some kind of copy of the frequency as well," Kaluna said.

"We'll get it," Sembado stated firmly.

***

They spent the remainder of the day collecting a small cache of weapons and ammunition. Brek's villagers seemed all too eager to help them locate an extra backpack which they discretely filled with a variety of meager provisions. Soon, the sun was falling in the western sky and fire was stoked under the communal overhang.

Sembado, Kaluna, and Morgan made a point of sitting against the far wall of the open cave, away from Brek and the others. Sembado sat cross-legged and quietly picked at his boiled cactus. A small commotion across the fire drew his attention upward. Brek's wife, Kiera, was fervently scolding him. The crackling fire and noisy din of the rocky surroundings drowned out her words but her venomous body language and demeanor were not lost on Sembado. Kiera pushed and prodded her husband until he stood and then pointed right at Sembado and wagged her finger back and forth. One final shove moved Brek into a defeated shuffle as he circumvented the fire and its attendees in order to approach Sembado and his companions. Brek stopped about four feet short of their small semi-circle and took a knee. He did not speak right away, the awkward silence was intermittently broken by the crunching of food or the pop of the fire.

"We want you to go to the tower," he said quietly. He closed his eyes and squished his forehead in little circles with his fingertips. "I've been told that you've already collected some weapons and rations. Please let us know if you need more or if there's anything else you don't have. What you've offered to do is a very selfless and appreciated gesture."

"Did she have you write that down?" Morgan said.

Brek looked up with a bemused smirk.

"Very funny," he said. "I think you should leave as early as possible."

"As soon as it is light enough to see," Sembado replied.

Chapter 31
The High, High Road

Sembado's eyes were open for several moments before he realized he was awake. He stared into the blackness of the chamber. The warmth of Kaluna's body was pressed tight against his chest. He could feel her hands curled up in front of her. She breathed slow, humid breath on his clavicles. He carefully shifted his weight to move off a stubborn pine needle that pushed up through his bedding. Morgan could be heard grunting in her sleep. Sembado's eyes concentrated in the darkness. As they adjusted, he could just make out the opening to their chamber.

He carefully slid out from next to Kaluna and piled another fur in his place. As he stood, the popping of his feet and knees sounded like feeble gunshots in the pre-dawn silence. He shuffled toward the chamber doorway and out into the common space beyond. He stepped out into the cool night air and took in the beauty of the darkened landscape. The stars and moon cast brilliantly black shadows under the pine forest below. The crisp and silent air seemed to be full of possibilities. Sembado slowly surveyed the wooded features. The movement of some small, lumbering animal caught his attention. He watched from his concealed perch while the animal sniffed and clawed at fallen logs as it traveled along the tree line. Sembado stood and observed as the bright white glow from the heavens above was slowly transformed to a warmer white. The sunrise was obscured by the mountains above him but the ambient glow turned the bluish white moonlight toward a yellowish hue. Sembado sat down on a nearby boulder and took in the exhibition of morning light.

"What are you doing?" Kaluna asked from the mouth of the common space.

"Couldn't sleep," Sembado replied. "Watching the sun come up."

"That means first light," Kaluna responded before turning and walking back to their chamber.

Sembado sat a little longer but soon other bodies were stirring and there was plenty that he could be doing to aid in their speedy departure.

Brek appeared at the lighting of the first fire and carried out a few pieces of fruit for Sembado and the others. They sat and ate the juicy morsels while Brek explained when and where they would collect three horses. He also described the accommodating chariot-like cart that his people had assembled for Morgan so that she did not have to go on foot. Brek disappeared as they finished eating but returned shortly after with a large scroll of paper in hand. He unfurled it to reveal a large, hand-drawn map of nearly the entire region.

"We're right here," said Brek, pointing to a line of triangles. "Caspen's Circle is here, with his main camp just to the north here. The communication tower is over here. It's just off the map but you will see it by the time you get that far."

"And the frequency?" Kaluna asked.

"Ah," Brek said excitedly. He pulled a small, simple container from his jacket. "This is the hard drive. This was smuggled to us and is not in very good condition. This contains the command language to execute the EMP wave. The control module and interface are about halfway up the tower frame. You will need to get up there with this in hand. It should pair automatically and pull enough residual power from the tower to pass the signal. The tower should have some minimal solar generation. The send and receive functions are purely reactionary, though, so if you can get this out to other towers, they will pass it along automatically."

"How far of a ride is it?" asked Sembado.

"You should be there by late afternoon," Brek replied. "*If* everything goes according to plan. And you'll travel a pretty well-worn game path so the journey should be as expedient as you make it."

"Well, let's get started," Morgan said.

"Indeed," Brek agreed, "we're wasting daylight."

The team was led down to the bottom of the slope where the three horses were being held. Morgan's chariot was strapped onto a larger stallion. The large wooden wheels had been fashioned with metal banding and a simple yet effective suspension system.

They took stock of their weapons and ammunition one last time before mounting their steeds and bidding Brek and his followers goodbye.

"I sure hope you succeed," one of the women said.

"Either way," Sembado smirked darkly, "you should know as soon as we do."

He urged his horse forward with a firm flick of his heels. Kaluna followed right behind him. Morgan's chariot kicked up a trail of dust at the rear. They found a steady riding pace for the morning and charged forward to their fate.

***

Several hours of riding found the sun well above the mountain peaks to their left. They continued south at their considerable rate while the game trail they followed veered right and then left.

They broke their steady pace around noon when they came across a small stream with which to water the horses. Sembado and Kaluna's stomped to a breathless stop while Morgan circled in her mounted chariot. Her large, powerful horse seemed less winded than the others. She stepped off the wooden platform and led her horse to the creek, stretching her legs as she went. She explained to Sembado and Kaluna that, despite the wheeled cart being equipped with leather strapped suspension, the riding stance still required firm, continuous leg work. She seemed to welcome the return of self-inflicted physical anguish. They ate through a small portion of their food supplies while the horses recovered from the morning's grueling demands.

Once the horses were rested, they led them by hand across the small creek. Kaluna had to lead the chariot horse by the reigns while Morgan and Sembado wrestled the stout, wooden cart across the stream for nearly a half hour. Their efforts could have earned another break but Kaluna, with the others' approval, insisted that they continue to make time.

As the sun began moving to the west, it created short shadows off the tree line. Sembado led the others to ride in the shade while the afternoon temperatures picked up. Their path was a continuously revealed surprise as they rode along a large sweeping curve of trees. But soon the trees began to thin and the steady slope of the mountain ridge to the left began to break and heave into smaller undulating formations. The path continued over hill and dale with more and more of the towering pine trees being replaced by their shorter cousins, shrubs, and cacti.

Then Sembado saw it, rising up beyond the foothills to the southwest: the apex of the communication tower. He pointed and shouted. Kaluna and Morgan each responded with a spirited yelp. The tower seemed to grow out of the ground as they drove their horses closer and closer. The distance was deceiving. Even after the entire height of the tower was within view, they rode for several more hours. Their stomachs growled and the sun hung low as they travelled within a hundred yards of the tower's base. They agreed to stop short and rest, servicing the horses as best they could while they saw to their own needs as well.

They gnawed on sundried rabbit meat while they watched the surrounding sky. Brek's prediction of his father's tactics hung on all of their hearts and minds.

"Fink it'll worg?" Morgan asked through a mouth stuffed with the sinewy jerky.

"I sure hope so," Sembado said, stretching out his arms and legs.

"What will you two do if it does?" asked Morgan.

"Finally settle down and live a decent life," Sembado said with a shrug.

"I hate to admit that I was getting really comfortable in the cabin Caspen had given us," Kaluna added.

"What about you?" Sembado asked Morgan.

"I really don't know," she replied. "I haven't had a minute to think for myself since we escaped. Or really before that, either."

"Well, we don't want followers or villagers or citizens," Kaluna said between mouthfuls of jerky. "But we could use some honest, hardworking neighbors."

"That sounds really nice," Morgan replied. "Let's get through this first though, huh?"

Kaluna nodded agreeably.

They finished their provisions and began their final approach. Sembado craned his neck back so he could take in the whole height of the structure. Its old metal tendons were rusted and broken in places. The nearest of the six guy wires was broken and lay limp across the landscape.

They sauntered their horses alongside the severed cable. Sembado struggled to fathom how the tiny, thread-like wires that held the tower erect and balanced could be the same as the massive braided steel rope that snaked along the ground. They approached the broken end. The minor wires that made up the woven assembly were a frayed bouquet of sharp, wavy metal. Somewhere up above, the other half of the cable dangled in the wind. They moved on to the base of the tower which was planted in a substantial mass of concrete and steel. The tower's main vertical elements were arrayed in a hexagon. Each of the large steel pipes was connected to every other pipe in a complicated but uniform web which stretched nearly 100 feet across.

Sembado and Kaluna jumped down from their horses while Morgan slowly circled in her chariot.

"I could climb as well," she called from her cart. "But I think I would serve more of a purpose patrolling down here."

Sembado and Kaluna concurred, and a redistribution of weapons left Morgan with a selection of two long guns and a hatchet. Kaluna carried Brek's hard drive loaded with the EMP frequency in her small backpack. She stuffed a small handgun in the back of her pants while Sembado tossed the sling of a modified shotgun over his shoulder.

The tower's outer shell of brace work included two ladders, one on either side of the symmetrical layout. Sembado and Kaluna each picked a ladder and began the ascent quite unceremoniously. Morgan watched from below while slowly circling in her horse-drawn vehicle.

The climb was arduous. Barely fifteen minutes had passed when Sembado was already soliciting Kaluna's permission for rest, shouting across the distance that separated them. The small, round bars created uncomfortable pressure points on their hands and feet. Sembado found himself fighting the urge to already rely on his bionic limb for the majority of the work.

When Sembado paused for their third break, he made the mistake of looking down. It was not the height that caused his discomfort but the seemingly little progress. Morgan was becoming smaller, but a quick glance upward revealed just how far they still had to go. The peak of the tower disappeared in the distortion and vanishing point. Even their destination, which was supposed to be halfway up, could barely be seen.

They were about a third of the way up the height of the tower when Sembado heard the first buzzing noise. He called out to Kaluna but she had already spotted the drone as it approached Sembado from behind. He tried to access the shotgun that hung across his back but the sharp hum was closing in too quickly. In a desperate flurry, Sembado swung off the ladder by one hand and brought up his bionic leg just in time to kick the impending quadcopter. He closed his eyes and turned his face away as the drone's weapon quickly blew out a hissing blue orb. The ghostly sphere's shell reached just to the prosthetic's calf and retracted harmlessly but the blast of energy did send aggravating signals back up to Sembado's brain. The drone hovered in place for just a second longer before Sembado brought his powered leg back and booted the drone off course. It swerved and swirled through the air. The curved trajectory sent the little machine straight into one of the structural tubes.

"Keep your eyes peeled," Sembado called. "That one was close. Is that gun ready to go?"

"Yes," Kaluna cried out against the wind.

Their aching arms and legs were pushed past the point of strain and discomfort as they actually increased their rate upward. The platform for the controls was in sight but the drone attacks were increasing in frequency. Sembado had mastered his kicking technique, although the pulses of energy to his prosthetic were making him increasingly angry. He yelled at Kaluna to hurry and catch up, but his prosthetic powered him faster and faster in the climb.

The drones were now approaching in packs of two and three. Sembado was able to spin the shotgun's sling around just in time to blast two at once. Kaluna shot the third with her pistol. She was at least thirty feet below Sembado's progress but the diameter of the tower was shrinking with every step.

He continued to hop forward on the prosthetic leg, clearing three rungs at a time. He slid his hands along the ladder as he jumped, careful not to let the considerable wind carry him away. After nearly ten minutes without a new drone attack, he realized that the increased speed in both maintained winds and gusts were probably to credit for the decreased drone assault.

Those little quadcopters bob and sway even in calm conditions. I bet Caspen is livid watching us climb too high for his stupid toys.

The control platform was now just twenty feet up. Sembado looked down and across to where Kaluna had been for the last half hour. She was nowhere to be seen. Sembado frantically craned his head around the obscuring framework until he spotted her tiny body, desperately clinging to the ladder nearly one hundred feet down. He stood and watched as she slowly placed one foot above the other. She used the crook of her elbow to feebly grasp the rungs while she paused. She made slow progress but was within shouting distance, or at least she would have been if the wind wasn't howling between the framed tubes. Sembado watched in frustration as she paused again. She was close enough that he could see her legs seizing when she slowly lifted them to the next step.

"You're almost there," Sembado called as she reached the step to be level with him.

"Go up to the platform!" Kaluna shouted over the whistling breeze. She wore a pained grimace on her face. "I'll be there in just a minute."

Sembado hesitated momentarily before following her direction. His biomechanical limb propelled him up quickly. The platform was just overhead. The five remaining guy wires connected to the tower just below it. He took one more breath and pushed himself up onto the steel deck. His arms and natural leg shook uncontrollably. His prosthetic glowed an uncomfortable heat against his amputated stump. But none of that pain compared to the horror and surprise of seeing the sinister grin curled across Caspen's face as he waited patiently at the control station platform.

Chapter 32
Man Achieves Flight

"It figures he'd send you in his place," Caspen said, distractedly pushing buttons.

Sembado ignored him and focused on pulling his body completely up onto the platform. His shoulders burned from the repetitive motion. The arch of his normal foot was raw. He slumped onto his side and breathed heavily. He discarded the shotgun to one side. His prosthetic pulsed waves of heat through his leg that transformed to fury by the time they reached his brain. Somewhere below the depths of his consciousness, a tenacious force awoke. It drove its will through his pain and anguish like a javelin, spearing his muddied perception of reality with a single message: Get to her. He huffed out a labored grunt as he pushed his weight onto his hands and knees. The subconscious instincts of his id pushed him across the metal platform. It did not recognize the forty feet that had to be traveled. It simply pushed in one direction. Sembado's knuckles and knees chaffed in moments as he made his way to the other ladder. The pain in his body slowly melted away as he concentrated on the image in his brain. It was a single set of delicate, brown fingers that were curled over the top of the platform. The knuckles were tensed and bloodless. Sembado's body swayed as his animalistic shuffle accelerated forward. He closed the last ten feet in a moment. He collapsed onto his chest as he reached the edge, the top of Kaluna's ladder.

Sembado's arms and face hung over the edge. Kaluna was frozen in place on the last few rungs. Her arms and legs had refused to move any further. She looked up with a deep sadness in her eyes while the wind whipped her hair against her face. Strands of her dark mane had stuck and lodged in her mouth but she could not afford the luxury of removing it. Sembado reached down and grabbed each of her wrists. In an awkward and painful shuffle, he dragged his bionic leg under his body. He gritted through the heat and pain of pushing up and lifting both his and Kaluna's body weight onto the platform. He staggered backward and they landed in a heap of joint cramps and muscle spasms.

Caspen only regarded them curiously.

"Why on Earth would you both come?" he asked indignantly. "Is it a compliment that you think it would take two people to sabotage my life's work?"

Sembado stared straight up at the bits of sky that showed through the woven frame of the communication tower as it stretched into oblivion above. Kaluna was sprawled across him but made tiny little movements to pull herself to one side so that she could lie in the crook of one arm. Each adjustment was a labored endeavor accompanied by a breathless whimper.

"Well, that's what you get for trying to climb a thousand feet so quickly," Caspen jeered. "I gave myself six hours to climb this damn tower. Thought I would be seeing my son one last time, but instead, it's just you two. Surprisingly, an even *bigger* disappointment."

The wind whipped and whistled through the complex assembly of geometric shapes that made up the tower's skeleton. Sembado tilted his head to one side to better see and hear Caspen. He had turned back to the control module and was feverishly pushing buttons and making adjustments. The controls sat in the center of the tower with a small canopy built over it. He suddenly whipped around and made direct eye contact with Sembado.

"Did he really think I'd stay away?" Caspen asked with a troubled expression. "Like I wouldn't make time to come up here, confront him myself? I mean, didn't you tell him the awful things I had said? Didn't he realize that I would need to get up here to set off my attack? That if I wanted to, I could set fire to the world from up here and he and I could watch until it burned out?"

"Probably because he isn't interested in helping you kill thousands of innocent people," Sembado replied.

"What?" Caspen barked, moving quickly across the platform. He loomed over Sembado and Kaluna with contempt twisted across his face. "What did you say?"

"He doesn't want to help you kill people," Sembado repeated.

"Bullshit!" Caspen snapped. "If you believed any of his benevolent nonsense, then you're even dumber than I thought. Brek is the one who discovered the human DNA frequency. *He* made more advances toward my goals than anyone else. I bet you he didn't share that part!"

Sembado carefully repositioned Kaluna so that he could sit up and not be subjected to Caspen's disdain. He pulled his knees to his chest and crossed his arms over them.

"Probably because he regrets it," said Sembado.

"Oh, and that magically absolves him, huh?" Caspen said incredulously. "Lucky guy. Why didn't I think of regretting what I've done? Is that all it takes to get in you idiots' good graces? Feel bad? Did he say he was sorry too?"

"He told us what really happened to your wife," said Sembado.

"That he took her from me?" Caspen replied with angry confusion. "Confessing he killed his mother makes him admirable to you?"

"Why do you lie about everything?" Sembado shouted. "He saved her from the pain of your malfunctioning equipment. You're not angry with him. You're angry with yourself! You just want to kill him off to erase that truth!"

"The truth is whatever people want you to tell them," Caspen replied. "He would get so hung up on that."

"What other option does he have?" Sembado argued. "Completely drown in his bitterness, like you?"

His bionic leg popped under his chin; it wanted to stand up.

"You don't understand anything," Caspen said. "You're just some dumb brat with good intentions and no direction. Don't act like you've accomplished a fraction of what I have. What my son has, for that matter. You've cared for stuff. That's it. Good job."

He sarcastically applauded Sembado, stepping closer as he clapped in his face. Sembado's leg buzzed again and he quickly stood up to move away from Caspen's taunting.

"You're going to avoid me?" Caspen asked bitterly. "Up here? You're going to try and walk away? Forget what I said. You're not a noble idiot. You're just an idiot."

Sembado looked at the control panel and all the flashing messages and scrolling text.

"Who's the idiot?" Sembado asked, turning to face Caspen from across the platform. "You're the one who was waiting up here just for a chance to get the best of some guy who doesn't want to be your son."

The color momentarily ran out of Caspen's face before being replaced by crimson outrage. His eyes flashed wide and his nostrils flared. He clenched his fists at his sides. One of them brushed the grip of a holstered pistol.

"You should stick to your passive uselessness," Caspen hissed. "It's a much better fit for you. I'd tell you to leave the piss and vinegar to her but she doesn't seem to be doing any better."

Sembado's prosthetic buzzed the base of his brain with a near-constant onslaught of interference. He slowly moved between Kaluna and Caspen while gritting his teeth in a silent reply.

"I don't understand," Sembado said quietly.

"I know you don't," Caspen replied quickly. "That's what I've been trying to tell you."

"No, dammit," Sembado snapped. "I don't understand why you came up here. If you knew someone was coming, me or Brek or whoever. Why would you come up here just to have us stop you?"

"Or have me stop you," Caspen said. "One of us is always going to try and stop the other. The part you don't understand is that I don't have any expectation of getting down from here alive."

Sembado froze in his tracks while trying to simultaneously process what Caspen said and where Kaluna lay relative to him.

"I've damn near spelled it out for you," Caspen said bitterly. "I will let the world burn. I will let everyone die. Why? Because if I don't do it now, then no one ever will and it will all end up where it was. One big, smoky, cesspool for tomorrow's children to wade around in."

"But that doesn't make any sense," Sembado reasoned. "Why would you be concerned about the next generation but be okay killing off the people who will become their parents?"

"Oh, you mistake me," Caspen laughed. "I don't want there to be *any* generations after. After a lifetime of painful and dedicated pursuit, that is the answer stewardship has offered. We aren't necessary. Absolutely not. Every human could die off and the world would keep moving. It would probably improve."

"But what's wrong with people just choosing to live a simple life?" Sembado asked.

"You're such a naïve fool," Caspen said as he more purposefully brushed his pistol's grip with an open hand. "I've already told you. People get bored. They get curious. They ask questions and wonder. Those are supposed to be some of the best differences between us and animals, but you know what? I think they're awful. What a sick joke! We were doomed from the get-go. Here's a world that can only support the first half of you becoming the most dominant species on Earth. Oh, but don't try too hard. Don't get too advanced. Because then you'll be forced to kill off everyone you've ever known just so that you can sit and sulk while trying to eke out a life like a fucking caveman!"

Sembado tensed at Caspen's pointed and agitated behaviors. The gap between them was closing, with the control panel just behind Caspen and Kaluna directly behind Sembado.

"I just don't believe..." Sembado started to say.

"You don't have to believe anything," Caspen bellowed. "I'm not asking you to believe. It's not imaginary. These are the facts, dammit! Human beings are an invasive species! That's it. And when you take away our ability to invade, then we sit and wonder. And without distraction, humans *devour* each other."

Sembado had recoiled from Caspen's outburst. He stood back near Kaluna with his fists clenched and his prosthetic poised for action.

"And what was your big idea?" Caspen asked angrily. "You were just going to stroll up a thousand foot tower and pull the plug on this whole thing? You want to pop off Brek's little electromagnetic waterfall?"

"It's the only non-violent way," Sembado responded.

"Don't be an idiot. It's the only way he can drop my defenses long enough to come and take over my camp," Caspen said.

"But there wouldn't be anything left," Sembado replied.

"My God, Sembado," Caspen said. "There's food! There's weapons! There's plenty!"

"I don't think it's going to go down like that," Sembado said. "He has his own food."

"Well, great," Caspen replied. "And what is your big plan, huh? You were gonna come all the way up here to kill the electronics? How do you expect to climb down without that contraption functioning? Or get around and survive your bullshit lifestyle after this? Hope some other poor bastard who's half-starved is going to throw you some scraps?"

Caspen's comment hit Sembado right in the gut. The possibility of losing his powered prosthetic had never once entered the calculations of his decision. His stomach burned at the imagined struggle and anguish that the future would hold for him. He pictured Kaluna helping him through a dense and overgrown forest. The image of him struggling to cross even a modest creek was anxiety-inducing.

349

"We'll take our chances," Kaluna said softly.

Sembado turned around just in time to see her climb to her feet.

"What did you say?" Caspen called accusingly.

"She said we'll take our chances!" Sembado shouted, squaring his body off between Kaluna and Caspen. Kaluna stood just behind him but off to one side. She placed her hands on her hips and tried to conceal the pain that pulsed throughout her body.

"Yeah," Caspen said shaking his head. "That would require you to do a lot of work at that control station that I'm not really open to you doing."

"I think you underestimate how many people's asses I've kicked with this thing," Sembado said hotly as he wiggled his bionic foot. "I have no problem kicking just one more. Consider it a last hoorah."

"I was waiting for this," Caspen said, slowly pulling the pistol from his pants. "So let's not make it any harder than it has to be."

Sembado instinctively spread his arms out in a vain attempt to guard Kaluna with his body.

"No, no," Caspen said, pointing the pistol dramatically. "Hands straight up. You know how."

Sembado gritted his teeth and glared contemptuously as he slowly raised his hands above his head.

"And you," Caspen added to Kaluna. "Come on out. No need to hide."

Kaluna did come out from behind Sembado but she was holding her pistol as well. She gripped it with both hands as she slowly side-stepped out from behind her partner.

Sembado remained frozen. He moved only his eyes. They darted back and forth between Kaluna and Caspen.

Caspen responded by quickly cupping the bottom of his gun with his previously free hand. A menacing light flashed in his eyes as a psychotic grin spread across his face.

"I really do think he's an idiot," he said to Kaluna. "But you...I can't figure out if you're incredibly clever or equally as stupid."

A gunshot cried through the wind without warning. A blue bubble popped and was gone. With it went most of Caspen's fingers. His gun landed on the deck before he could respond. He looked from his charred and blistered knuckle stumps to Kaluna and back.

"Neither," said Kaluna. "I'm just sick of hearing you talk."

Caspen then looked down at the handgun that lay between his feet. A loathsome glance to Sembado briefly preceded Caspen's violent kick at the firearm. Sure enough, the gun slid across the deck and tumbled down into the great beyond. He recoiled toward the control panel, cradling his disfigured hands against his chest as he moved. With a combination of fury and dread painted on his contorted face, he turned and started punching buttons on the console. He cried out each time one of his tender amputations struck a button or switch.

Sembado's heart raced as his stomach crawled up his throat. Kaluna motioned for him to move forward while she maintained Caspen in her sights.

Sembado moved forward slowly. His limbs shook as his racing heart overwhelmed his body with adrenaline and sent his bionic leg into another agitating feedback loop.

"There's nothing left for you to do," Sembado said with an elevated tone. "You have lost."

Caspen refused to acknowledge him and instead continued furiously beating on the control boards.

"I said it's over!" Sembado yelled angrily.

"Is it?" Caspen asked as he whipped around. Any fear or apprehension had drained from his face and was replaced dually with more insane menace.

Sembado slowly backed away. He did not understand Caspen's implication. He stopped when he and Kaluna were side by side. Her pistol was still trained directly on Caspen's chest. She grimaced slightly as she squeezed the trigger. Sembado closed his eyes in response, but a soft click was all he heard. He opened his eyes to see Caspen grinning psychotically from across the platform. His eyes followed Caspen's gaze to where Kaluna was fumbling with the handgun. She had just confirmed that it was out of ammo.

She asked Sembado a question as she fumbled with the magazine release but the buzzing of the wind had overwhelmed her words.

The buzzing?

Sembado turned just in time to catch sight of several new drones flying in from their right. They veered and teetered in the wind as they fought to converge on the tower. The first one clipped the handrail of the ladder and flipped end-over-end. It rolled across the tower's deck and detonated. But instead of a quick blue flash, this drone's orb ate a three foot circle out of the steel grating that made up the deck. The material was quickly devoured in a shower of molten sparks. The drone plummeted lifelessly through the large hole it had just created. Sembado looked up to see Caspen grinning maniacally.

Kaluna cried out a warning and Sembado joined her in jumping backward just in time to avoid another steel-eating drone attack. The damage was inflicted to both the deck and the tube steel that supported that portion. A loud pop sounded and vibrations could be felt emanating through the structure.

Drone after drone whizzed in from the surrounding sky. Sembado was careful not to try and kick any away. His leg was comprised of many composites but he did not want to take any chances.

"We have to get to the console and cancel the attack!" Kaluna yelled over the wind and commotion.

Sembado looked across the platform and realized that the attacks were not striking randomly. Caspen was using the drones to purposefully isolate Sembado and Kaluna from the rest of the control deck. Even over the wind and drone noise, Sembado could hear Caspen laughing diabolically as he continued to mash buttons on the control panel.

"I'll have to jump across," Sembado said into Kaluna's ear. "Give me the hard drive."

Kaluna dug the small electronic brick out of her pocket and forced it into Sembado's hands. He stepped up to the gap in the platform that had been created by the drones. The decking bent and flexed where it was no longer supported. He reactively backed up just before dodging another drone strike. He and Kaluna retreated further toward the platform edge.

"We're running out of room," Sembado observed. "I have to stop this now."

"I'll have him in my sights," Kaluna replied. "I love you."

Sembado paused for just a moment, kissed her firmly on the mouth, and returned her sentiment before running forward and using his prosthetic to heave himself over the ever-growing gap. He hit the platform and rolled forward. A drone devoured the grating on which he had just landed. He quickly clamored to his feet. Caspen had turned and had his back against the console with his arms outstretched to block it.

"You're too late," he said bitterly. "What's done cannot be undone."

Sembado stepped forward with a determined rage. After all of the struggling of failing to manage his prosthetic's feedback, he was finally ready to harness it. And yet, the anger was too deep. It was carnal and basic, not elevated and chaotic like he hoped it would be. He simply approached Caspen and grabbed him by the shirt with both hands. But Caspen's disfigured fingers did not outweigh the fact that he was a healthy, middle-aged man. He cuffed Sembado's hands away with lighting speed and agonizing power. Before Sembado could react, Caspen was raining down with a fury of blows to his head and shoulders. Sembado reactively covered his head while he was soundly pummeled. His prosthetic hummed in response to the mayday signal his brain was sending its way. Just as Caspen was about to deliver another powerful blow, Sembado reached out with his prosthetic and kicked him hard in the shin. The sickening crunch was nearly audible over the surrounding pandemonium.

Caspen doubled over as he howled out a string of obscenities. The reprieve was just long enough to allow Sembado to gain his composure and land another deft kick to the chest. It sent Caspen sprawling on his back. He clawed at his chest with his fingerless paws as he struggled to catch his breath.

"Hurry!" Kaluna screamed.

Sembado looked up to see her standing on an ever-shrinking steel island which threatened to collapse at any moment. He ran to the control board and produced the hard drive from his pocket. He mounted it in the docking receptacle and waited for an on-screen prompt. He pushed through a number of commands before a processing indicator drove through a series of automated scripts. Warnings flashed all across the control page. A small map was automatically enlarged and showed multiple uplinks being activated between Sembado's location and the other neighboring towers.

"I think we did it," he said excitedly. He turned to see how Kaluna was fairing just in time to observe another drone arrival. It rocketed directly toward Kaluna, who was able to duck out of the way. The drone skipped across the minimal remaining deck and popped a transparent shell that drove across the platform. It hit Sembado without warning and his prosthetic collapsed underneath him. Searing pain and emotional mayhem erupted through Sembado's body and mind. He writhed on the ground as the echoing pulses of overwhelming discomfort washed across his conscience like cruel waves on a defenseless beach. And as soon as it started, it was over. Sembado opened his eyes and sat up. He crawled up on his natural knee. The connection to his prosthetic was lost. He used his arms to pull himself up onto the control panel. The screens, buttons, and keyboards were dark and lifeless. He turned to share a triumphant smile with Kaluna but she was regarding him with concern. A shadow in the corner of his eye warned him just before Caspen slashed across his chest with a dagger. Sembado jumped back and stumbled. His prosthetic was incredibly cumbersome without power. He hobbled backward as Caspen moved forward, brandishing the knife flagrantly. He had to hold it with both hands to maintain his grip. He attempted another sloppy swipe but Sembado was able to dodge the blade and grab ahold of Caspen's wrists. They struggled back and forth, all the while Sembado tried prying Caspen's stumpy knuckles off the short hilt. Caspen tried returning Sembado's shin-kicking technique but landed the blow on Sembado's disengaged prosthetic with a loud crunch. He dropped the knife as he limped backward in pain. Sembado reached down, grabbed the knife, and whipped it out into the wind. He picked himself up as squarely as possible and started to limp toward Caspen. He balanced on his prosthetic with every other stride so that his pace increased as Caspen retreated in a cowering shuffle. Sembado drove Caspen to the edge of the platform.

"Your mistakes will be the undoing of man," Caspen snarled. But, before he could say another word, Sembado acted. Harnessing the momentum of his asymmetrical limp, he popped up on his lifeless prosthetic and kicked Caspen with all the might his natural leg could muster. It was such a powerful kick that Caspen flipped over backward as he cleared the edge of the platform. His blood-curdling scream trailed off into the wind's blowing fury as he plummeted to a mangled death. The force of the kick made Sembado land hard on his back. His head struck the metal decking with a deep thud. All went black.

Chapter 33
The Exhale

The wind fluttered Sembado's fiery locks as his eyes slowly opened. His body was lurching over and over again. He hung in an uncomfortable position as his torso and legs were tossed to and fro. He opened his eyes to a disorienting vision: he teetered above the ground from hundreds of feet up. He panicked and jerked around for just a moment before a firm pressure tightened across his waist.

"Keep still, would ya?" Morgan demanded. "It's hard enough crawling down these stupid steps.

Sembado stretched his neck from side to side. Part of his view included his left leg. The bare stump stuck out over Morgan's front. It barely missed the ladder rungs as she slowly descended. He looked down past Morgan's massive lower body. Kaluna was slowly crawling down below them. She had Sembado's prosthetic slung over her shoulder.

"How long have I been out?" Sembado asked loudly. The high altitude wind was as powerful as ever.

"An hour or two," Morgan replied. "I started climbing as soon as I saw the flashes and commotion. I was about a third of the way up when Caspen's body came down. I ain't never seen anything pop apart like that. When I got up there, Kaluna had already removed your leg and was trying to drag you to the ladder. But those holes in the decking were too far for her. And I gotta say, you're a lot heavier than you look."

"I can try and move down myself," Sembado protested. "It'll be easier than the climb up."

"It is easier," Morgan replied. "But there ain't no way I'm gonna be able to get you off my shoulder without one of us falling off. We're halfway down. Just take it easy."

The climb down was slow but steady and Morgan had Sembado laid back against the tower's foundation in less than thirty minutes. She stretched her legs as she left to collect their horses. Kaluna hobbled over to Sembado. The descent had wreaked fresh havoc on her arms and legs. She plopped down against him and closed her eyes.

"You did it," she said quietly, cherishing the relative silence from the lack of wind.

"We did it," Sembado replied. "It's over."

"No," Kaluna replied softly. "It's only just begun."

Epilogue

One Year Later

Chapter 34
The Storm Front

The thunderhead crawled high into the sky. It reached its austere, anvil shoulders across the heavens. Sembado had seen one like this before. It was last year, just before the harvest. He leaned against the grassy exterior of the hovel he and Kaluna shared with Morgan and marveled at the coincident elegance and power of the clouds' formations. The wind kicked up. The front would be bringing in a blast of fresh, cool air. A couple chickens ran past him in search of a calmer environment. Sembado would evict them from the sod hut later.

The ability of the howling breeze to bring him back to that fateful day on the tower was unsettling. He let out a deep sigh and pushed off the wall and onto his cane. The sturdy Osage branch had been trimmed of all but a few thorns. He had them left in place as a reminder of nature's fury. His wooden prosthetic was fine enough but the last week's humidity had played hell with its articulation. The whole thing seemed to be swollen and stiff. In a few days, the cool, dry weather would shrink it back and things would be back to the way they were.

He looked out fondly as Kaluna followed Morgan through their field. Morgan was happily dragging a make-shift plow through the small plot of soil. Kaluna followed behind with a sack of seeds hanging from her front. Little Ella followed close behind. She was the last of Brek's orphans to be claimed and Kaluna insisted on bringing her along. Sembado was not surprised at the warmth and love with which Kaluna had showered the little girl. It was the silly antics and playfulness that continued to catch him off guard. Kaluna was never not teaching her new charge a way to sharpen or skin or dig. But every lesson was taught with humor and grace and fun. Sembado stood in place, leaning on his cane, and watched his female companions find splendor in each other's company.

Behind them, the storm expanded its darkening mass in the western sky. Kansas had proved to be much more abusive than he had hoped but surviving their first winter had provided a limitless confidence. This storm would come, and it would bring a reckoning. But it, like so many others, would pass. The storms always passed.

In the distance, Sembado could see their neighbors collecting their belongings to guard them from being blown away. They had settled in a loose network of other stewards. Most were Caspen's old followers. None of them seemed any more enthusiastic on a central authority than Sembado and Kaluna were. A general agreement had been reached on help, sharing, and outreach.

This summer and fall would bring a new log cabin for Sembado and the girls. He and Morgan had already scoped out a nearby copse of trees. Their neighbors had agreed to lend help with the understanding that Morgan would be available for plowing as needed.

Sembado smiled to himself as he thought back to just a couple years before when he hadn't even heard of the Elephants' guild, let alone the Spring or the Stewards. The contrast between the easy nature of that life and the lack of meaning it held continued to amaze Sembado each time he considered it. Virtual reality in the 4D arena had given way to a revolution and revolution had bowed to compromise. But compromise was not always possible with a zealot. Somewhere in the middle of truth, peace, and humility, he and Kaluna had found their calling. It was life and survival and dignity. Fighting for today and hoping for tomorrow. They had finally secured a life worth living.